CONSPIRACY THEORY

RICH RESTUCCI

SEVERED PRESS
HOBART TASMANIA

CONSPIRACY THEORY

ISBN: 978-1-925493-01-6

For my parents, Richard and Barbara. They put up with my crap for years and never once quit on me. They still haven't...

I'm always relieved when someone is delivering
a eulogy and I realize I'm listening to it.
George Carlin

FOREWORD
BY JAMES SCHANNEP

Second chances. That's what this foreword is about, because that's what this book is about. Hell, it's what this whole damn genre is about. Oh? What's that? You're a wage-slave, in debt up to your ears, and no one in your life really, truly respects you? Well, all that can change in an instant once you're a zombie slaying badass. The point is, zombie apocalypse = second chances.

This is actually my second chance at writing this foreword. Rich Restucci was kind enough to ask me to write a foreword to the first Chaos Theory, but I took too long trying to impress you, Dear Reader. To live up to the high standard of writing set forth by this author we love so much (and I know you love his writing, because here you are reading the second book!). Well, turns out, Mr. Restucci gives second chances too. So here goes.

If all zombie stories are about second chances, what makes this one even more second-chancey? For starters, our hero is the ultimate anti-hero. He's a prison inmate serving hard time, and even if society doesn't know it, we know deep down he's a good guy. We want to see his redemption. As if that weren't enough, our protagonist then recovers from a bite-wound and gets (wait for it) a second chance.

Someone with immunity to the zombie plague is basically unheard of in zombie fiction. It's practically against the rules. Verboten. Yet anyone with a working knowledge of immunology can tell you—if it's a virus—there's at least a small percentage of the population who will fare better than others. Someone will conquer said virus and become immune. A man who gets a second chance.

It's sheer genius, really. A plot so seemingly obvious, yet one ripe for the telling. The kind of idea that makes other zombie authors slap their foreheads and say, "Why didn't I think of that?"

Allow me to tell you why, Dear Reader. Because Rich Restucci has the goods. He doesn't need a second chance. To make matters worse (better, for readers) is the genius behind his marriage of the shambling undead with the sprinting infected. And he gives us both—in the same story!

So hats off to you, Rich Restucci, you magnificent bastard. And to all you readers out there, I hope you enjoy your second chance with these characters as much as I did. Without any further ado, here it is, a second helping of *Chaos Theory*.

James Schannep is the author of the Click Your Poison™ series of interactive books. INFECTED asks, "Will YOU survive the Zombie Apocalypse?" Learn more at jamesschannep.com.

THE END OF THE BEGINNING

The floor is always cold. Every time I step foot off this hospital bed, my feet tell me how cold that damn floor is. The tiles are freezing and they won't even give me socks. Slippers are out of the question. I mean WTF? What harm could socks or slippers do? My effing tootsies are cold. All I have to wear is a blue hospital Johnny, not that I'm a fashion king, but my ass is hanging out.

My room, which is basically a cell, is twelve paces by nine paces not including the bathroom. White walls with a drop ceiling with nothing but steel and concrete above (I checked). Concrete floor painted dull gray. Several instruments are in here with me, most to monitor me, but I don't have to stay hooked up to them. There are six cameras in here and two in the bathroom, but the worst thing is the window. There's a giant glass window set in aluminum tube that separates me from the corridor. There are always two guards in chairs right outside my steel door. Why would they have a steel door but a giant glass window you ask? Because that shit is bulletproof. Says so in the lower right corner of the window in yellow. I wonder if a tank round would go through this baby.

I feel like a fish in a hospital fish tank. There's always somebody dressed in blue scrubs staring through the window with a clipboard. Usually two somebodies or more. They never talk to the guards, and the guards never talk to them, or me. Ever.

There is a door on my bathroom, but the cameras have shattered any illusions of privacy. I can't even drop a deuce without an audience. I rubbed one out on my fifth day here, and within seconds of blissful completion, the hiss of my steel hermetic door sounded, and there was a nurse in here with those two armed guards demanding my tissue. I know right? Eew.

I have no exterior windows, but I feel like I'm underground. I don't know why I feel this way, maybe it's because something above ground would be easily spotted, and there's no way this place isn't a secret.

Plausible deniability.

Everything is for my protection. Me. I'm a bit of a celebrity around here. I'm *important*, as all the doctors and guys in suits say. I'm immune. A little more than a year ago, something really fucked up happened. Nobody knows how or why, but the dead started not staying dead. Now that in itself is a bitch to wrap your head around, I know, but what's way worse, is that these dead folks come back hungry. They don't want pizza or spinach dip, they want you. They want to eat you, and nobody bothered to tell them that food is all about the presentation. They eat people alive.

They're slow and stupid, but they have numbers on their side, and humans are now on the second rung of the old food chain. They supposedly outnumber us thousands to one. I should mention that these things, these former humans, these *infected*, are damned hard to kill too. Only messing up their brains will stop them. Shooting, stabbing, or crushing their noggins puts them down for good. Burning them so much their brains cook, or electrocuting them works too, but shoot it in the chest? Poison? Drowning? Nope, they could give a shit about bodily trauma. I've seen them with the lower halves of their bodies curiously absent, crawling after the living with important pieces of them trailing behind or missing altogether.

They spread their infection via bites and scratches. Once you're infected, you're screwed. You might not die, but that's just as bad. The people who don't die turn into Runners.

Picture a hundred and seventy pound feral cannibal, as crazy as a shit-house rat, but with no conception of fear and a wicked tolerance to pain. They run into bullets just like their undead cousins. When they die, they come right back as a pus-bag. Slower, but way more durable.

I should also mention that these things are *everywhere*. Can't chuck a dead cat without hitting one. Or sixty. In ones or twos they're not too bad, unless they're close, but in swarms and hordes your day can go to shit quickly.

But there's no way you can't know about the infected. No way you're reading this and don't know. This is why I'm here. I've been bitten, but fought off the infection. To the best of my and the doctors in this place's knowledge, I'm the only one on earth that didn't get infected via contact with infected fluids. The only one. Me. One in six billion give or take.

Montana. I'm in Montana somewhere. I haven't been outside since I was brought here, but I've heard people talking when they thought I wasn't paying attention. Or they just don't give a shit. They don't care because I'm never leaving this facility again.

Initially, it was harder on me. They treated me like Kobe beef: very important, but ultimately I would die for a better purpose. They stuck me with needles a hundred times a day, and took every single fluid type you can think of. They shoved needles in my spine and in my head too, and they were decidedly not so nice about it. They even took some of my eye juice, and that sucked. It's called aqueous humor, but that shit wasn't funny.

I was strapped down to my hospital bed for weeks, a bed pan under me to evacuate into. Finally, I asked to be let up and when they said no, I thrashed and fought every time they came near me. Even strapped down, it was way harder to steal my juices. They couldn't sedate me because it fucks with their tests, so I was becoming a danger to myself, and I'm important remember. When one of those needles went through my vein and I bled internally, they let me up. After that, it went better for all of us.

I cooperated. For a while.

I asked for stuff to read and then a pen and notebook to write in, and they gave me some books. Then they gave me this flexi-pen and a notebook too. Somebody checks it every day, but I told them if they try to redact anything, I would go back to fighting them. The psych doc told me it was good to keep a journal of what was happening. There are undoubtedly dozens of those concerning me right now. Still no socks. Fuckers.

I'm going to save humanity. I've had doctors, nurses and even a general tell me so. Not those guards though. They won't speak to me no matter what. I've tried joking with them and they won't smile. I flip them off or flash them a fruit basket through the glass, and they don't even acknowledge I'm there. Dicks. I call them Jose and Hose B. These guys barely speak to each other, and they rotate out every twelve hours with Neil and Bob.

You should probably know that I was brought here by force *for the greater good*. Under duress, I had to leave my friends behind. I have a shit ton of buddies on an oil rig, the Atlantis, in the Gulf of Mexico. All of them survivors of this horrible plague. All of them I had met within the last year, and all of them are family. My best friend is a fantastic specimen of a man. As I wrote in another journal, he's a cross between Stephen Hawking and the Hulk. Near seven feet of solid muscle, this guy is also a bona fide genius. Like next level smart. But he's mute. Sometimes that's a good thing. Then there's Kat. She's the toughest teenager in the world, I shit you not. A great kid, who I think of as my little sister. She has a boyfriend now, a soldier named Alvarez who would give his life for her. There are several others, especially a woman whose company I enjoyed, but I will leave out their names for their safety.

I'm leaving them out because the son of a bitch who stole me comes here and reads this notebook every other day or so. He already knows Ship and Kat. You hear that Lynch? You're a low-flying prick who should have his dick bitten off by one of the infected. Actually, they would have to find it first, you sack-less shitbird. I bet it looks like a dick, only smaller.

Redact this asshole: (I'm flipping you off, Lynch).

Guy is badass, but certifiable. Yeah, nutty as a fruitcake. Thinks that I'm going to save everybody, and will kill anyone and everyone who's even moderately close to in his way. Bastard was going to shoot my best friend for kicks. Well, he did shoot him once, but it's hard to keep a good Ship down.

Actually, now that I think of it, everybody thinks I'm going to save everybody. Problem is, with the thousands, and I do mean thousands, of tests these doctors have performed on me, they've come up with bupkis. Goose-egg, donut, nada, niente, nothing. There is no difference between my fluids and anybody else's fluids. The doctors have no idea why I didn't die from being bitten when absolutely everyone else gets infected. I have no special antibodies, no difference in metabolism, my cerebrospinal fluid is normal, and so is my eye juice.

I was never abducted by aliens. They asked.

I didn't have any clue how long I had been imprisoned until the doctor that came in this morning said that in four months of tests there was nothing to show for it. Four months. Is that all? I thought it was a year at least, but I was hoping for only a month. Four months I've been away from my friends. Four months I haven't been able to help them.

The doc that was here today has replaced my last one. He had no name tag, but I call him dick. I purposely didn't capitalize that, because it's not a name if you catch my drift. At least the last one spoke to me like I was a human being instead of spam. Dick, (I had to capitalize it there, it was the first word of the sentence), has been around for a couple weeks. Aldous was my last doc and I liked him. Dick is a dick. He's a dick for many reasons, but the dickiest is because two hours after he gave me a shot yesterday, I started getting sick. The injection site around the shot turned the same color as my bites had turned after being bitten, and then those awful black lines showed up. I got horribly sick, but only for about twelve hours, then I felt better. A bunch of assholes had watched me through the night via the fish window, and I could see Jose and Hose B exchanging money on several occasions. Fuckers were betting on how long it would take for me to die. Doctor dick came in this morning and was all shocked. He thought I should be dead too. He came in with a few other doctors and the guards and they strapped me down and took all kinds of fluids again. I don't know if you've figured out what they did to me, but put your helmet on kids because I'm about to drop all kinds of knowledge.

The bastards infected me. They shot me up with goo from an infected. Saliva, blood, whatever. Sons of bitches. I could have died from an infection. Not the plague, but any kind of infection. I mean they shot me up with some dead guy's *stuff*. The very thought of it gives me the willies. I mean ick.

It took a minute to believe they did it to me if that makes you feel any better, but I knew for certain when I got sick and looked at the catheter area of my forearm. It was all kinds of messed up. I knew but I didn't want to believe. Then I remembered where I was.

But I got them back. I made those fuckers pay. Doc dick reached up to shine his pen-light in my eye and he got too close. I was strapped down, but not my head. Yup, I growled and bit him. I whipped my head forward and clamped down on the meat of his left hand. There must have been a moment of disbelief for that asshole, but only just. His look of surprise turned to one of pain, fear, and horror all at the same time.

It was epic.

He started shrieking, and everybody looked at me. Then it was pande-friggin-monium. Three doctors, two nurses, two military guys in suits and ties, and Hose B, all tripping over each other like fat kids running for cake. They were bolting for the door. Doctor dick grabbed his wrist, and I have no illusions that he would have just sat there and let me eat him. I spit him out, and he yanked his mitt away and quickly inspected it. Oh there was just a little blood, but that was enough. Jose was the only one who kept his shit together, and I almost feel bad for the bastard in spite of myself.

He didn't look the least bit scared as he yelled at me to *say something* or he was going to blow my head off. I hawked up a wad and spit the thing a good three feet right into his face. "How about fuck you?"

He wiped his face and looked at the pink loogie smear. Dawning came over him and then he did look scared. "You bastard," he said. "You just killed me." It was the second and last thing he ever said to me.

"Oh relax," I said, "you can't get…"

He raised his M4 and aimed down the sight at my head.

The sound of gunfire was super loud in the small room, but hey, this wasn't my first rodeo with that. Last time this happened, I did get shot in the head. Well, grazed but still.

What didn't compute was why Jose jerked to his right and crumpled to the floor. My ears ringing, I looked at the blue instrument box on one of my medical thingies. It was popping and fizzing and smoke was coming out of a hole in the side. It was also dripping with Jose. Lynch stepped into the room and looked at me shaking his head, wisps of white smoke coming from the barrel of his M9.

He told Hose B, who was outside the room staring in through the fish window to get the F back in the room. Doc dick was standing there trying to rationalize himself out of his own doom.

Been there, but I didn't feel bad for this prick. I couldn't infect anyone anyway, they had proved that. I'm not a carrier, I just come down with symptoms and my body tells the plague to fuck off.

But this asshole was terrified.

Lynch pointed at the doc and said, "Isolate him." Hose B nodded and took the doc out, still holding his paw. The spook smiled at me, shook his head again, and said one word, "Epic." Then he laughed and sauntered out.

At least we agreed on something.

And right now you're thinking; *Only a graze? Pussy.* Well fuck you, try it.

Damn I gotta pee.

SHORT BUT SWEET.

You would think, what with my melt-down, The Powers That Be would have me permanently strapped to that hospital bed as I had been initially. Nope. My little tantrum worked wonders. I've been out of my hospital prison room too. Two armed guards and an armed Lynch escort me everywhere, but I've gotten to see some of this facility.

It's big.

I was on a hospital floor, and as I suspected, we're underground. There are no exterior windows anywhere, so I asked about it, and Lynch told me we were seventy feet below the surface of Baldy Mountain, forty-five miles south of Havre Montana. I guess nobody cares if I know anymore, or at least Lynch doesn't care. I don't think he really cares about much. Except me.

There are six levels below the surface, and my room is on level three. Yeah, I still have to reside in my room, and the tests haven't stopped. But I get to play basketball. Yup. There's a full exercise facility inside this facility. Weights, a pool, tennis court, and a mini b-ball court, perfect for two on two. I've been eating up the competition. Far be it for me to brag, but I've been going HAM on these military pricks. Generally, my partner is Lynch, and he's fucking good. Better than me and I'm good. Well, in comparison. I held my own against the big boys in the big house. White men *can* jump. Oh, if you didn't read my first journal, I'm an ex-con. I didn't mention it before, because it's not overly important.

I've also been playing backgammon, chess, checkers, and some game where I move stones back and forth across this wooden board. Again, I usually play with Lynch, and he beats me at everything every time. Bastard isn't just a living weapon with lightning fast reflexes and a snippy attitude, he's damn smart. He doesn't read my journal anymore, so I can give the prick a compliment without his head getting all big.

I've been exploring the facility, which everyone calls Area 8, and as I've said, it's big. Two hundred and eight steps from my room to the elevators, and there are more rooms past mine. The gym is on level three with the hospital. Levels one and two are administration, with offices, barracks, cafeteria, and storage. Level three has a few offices, and tons of medical equipment in addition to the workout stuff. There's also a small firing range and training areas. They have all kinds of guns, and this is just what's for the range. Absolutely *everyone* is armed, and there's supposed to be an armory someplace on this level, but I don't know where it is. I got to pop off a bunch of rounds to keep me frosty. I like the M16s they have here, and they also have HK416s. The Brass (important people like Generals, and doctors from USAMRIID) all have personal guards with FNP90s, which are these little submachine guns, and I got to shoot one of those too. I prefer my old M4 to all of them.

Level four is laboratories and weapons storage, with some kind of satellite-tracking facility. I haven't been up to the surface, Lynch says I can't, I could get a hang nail or something.

My explorations are accompanied, but the only place I haven't been allowed to go other than the surface is Level Six. You need special clearance for that, and Lynch won't tell me what's down there. Level Six has its own elevator. That makes me nervous, I don't know why. There are no guards on the bank of six elevators that ferry people up and down to all the other floors, but the lift down to six has its own guard shack. Not just guards, but a small structure that you have to pass through just to get to the lift.

There are three hundred people down here, and Lynch says that the facility in the mountain above is just as big. He also told me that other than the occasional stray zombie, there hasn't been an attack on the base since the beginning of all of this. Most of these people, other than the soldiers, haven't even seen any infected. They've been closed off down here for a year.

They know their families are dead, the country is dead, and the world is dead. They got to watch it in high definition during the first few weeks of the plague. I've spoken to some of them, and they're mostly friendly, but standoffish. I played a game of chess with a lab guy named Frank at three this morning. He kicked my ass too.

I can't roam freely, and there's still a pair of guards outside my room, but I can come and go as I please as long as the gun-toting guards or Lynch come with. Hose B hasn't come back as one of my door guards, but I did see him working on the Universal at the gym. He gave me death eyes.

I haven't seen doctor dick since I bit him though. Lynch said he's fine. They watched him for a while, ran some tests, and then let him out of quarantine. I hope they took his spinal fluid and eye juice too. Prick.

Yeah, so that's that. You've got the general layout of the facility, and my role here as guinea pig. You've figured out that Lynch is not my favorite person, even though he did save my life from a freaked-out Jose. You know my friends are all far away. That pretty much sums it up. I did get some shoes too. A pair of combat boots, and a pair of cross trainers.

I know what you're thinking: "Where are my damn zombies? This is a zombie story right? Not a stupid tale of some guy getting experimented on? I did not pick up this tattered and yellowed (and probably blood-spattered) journal to read about a government stooge with his lab rat reject. I want the living dead."

Well, you've got them incoming. There will be zombies a plenty in the next chapter, I'm just too tired from running and dodging and shooting and being thirsty to write anymore. Besides, backstory is vital. It is critical, need-to-know information in order for you to make a rational, informed decision on whether or not to chuck this notebook in the fire to keep you warm.

Don't. Not yet. Unless you're *really* cold.

Oh, and I got socks.

ZOMBIES, ZOMBIES EVERYWHERE, AND NOT A DROP TO DRINK

I want a beer. Most times when I'm really thirsty, I want a soft drink or water, but damn a beer sounds good. Not one of those Yuppie micro brews, or foreign heavy beer. I want a mass-produced, ice cold, fizzy, American brew.

But water would do.

I'm hoping the fact that I'm thirsty and have no access to liquid has dawned on you. *How,* you are obviously demanding, *how is it possible that you are thirsty, when you currently reside in a facility designed to withstand a nuclear holocaust, stocked with food and drink a-plenty? You even told us there was a gym for Christ's sake!"*

Let me tell you how fast everything can go to shit: *Seconds.*

I was in the gym you were just thinking about, playing a game of two on two. Lynch was on the other team, and I was finally, *finally* beating him. I was with Tim, he was some type of satellite technician who never, ever took off his ID badge, even when he was playing hoops. Lynch was with some Air Force Chief Master Sergeant named Brick. I don't know if that was his first or last name, everybody called him Chief Brick. Game was to twenty one, (gotta win by two), and we were up nineteen to eight. Nineteen to eight, and I was on fire. Couldn't miss.

So Lynch calls a time out for a piss break and goes to the can. I'm sitting there bullshitting with Tim and Brick, my guard, (I called this one Stoic, after that Viking King in How to Train Your Dragon), not talking at all. My guards never talked to me, they were probably ordered not to. So I grab a towel and I'm guzzling some of my Gatorade when these two guys walk into the gym from the open door behind the tiny bleachers sixty feet away. We all turned to look, not even breaking our conversation. It was just two guys, walking toward us. Stoic just turned back and looked at us, not giving them a second thought. None of us did.

Brick had been talking about Larry Bird vs. Magic Johnson, and how that was possibly the best rivalry in all of pro hoops. I disagreed and said that the Bird/Dr. J. games were better. Tim says, "Yeah, but Kareem had that sky hook," and he proceeds to do one. The ball goes *thump* and sticks between the rim and the backboard. Stuck. Brick and I start giving Tim shit, I even caught Stoic with a half-smile.

So we're standing under the ball, looking up at it, me telling Tim that he jammed it so he should jump for it, when we hear a scuffle. The three of us turned around to see the two guys that had come in tearing into Stoic, who never even fired a round. His Adam's apple was gone, a gaping hole into his throat spurting and gushing his life away. One of the things is making this awful crunching sound as it crushes Stoic's larynx cartilage between its molars like a fist full of Fritos. Stoic never made a sound, but the tearing and ripping of his flesh giving way will haunt me forever and I've seen some shit. I could see he was trying to scream, but there was nothing left of his throat to make anything other than gurgling noises and coughing sounds as his lungs tried to expel the blood that was undoubtedly flooding them.

Tim didn't move, the shock of the moment overcoming him, but Brick and I moved to the bench to get weapons. I grabbed Tim's M9, and Brick grabbed his. Two shots rang out before I could even raise my weapon, and in my head I was praising Brick for gunning down the two stiffs who had fallen to the ground. Perfect head shots. Brick, however, was looking at me, his weapon pointed somewhere in the vicinity of the basketball court.

"We're in it now," Lynch said, the smoke from his M9 wafting into my nostrils. As my nasal passages were assaulted by the stench of newly fired pistol, my auditory senses came under attack from that same alarm klaxon that you've heard in every B movie ever made that had an alarm klaxon. And that shit didn't stop for nine hours.

I looked at the door that the screams were now coming through, "What the fuck does that mean?"

"The alarm means a perimeter breach," Brick said checking his M9 magazine. "The screams are an indication of a more imminent danger."

Lynch nodded. "Or the alarm could mean an escape."

"An escape?"

He looked at me. "What are you a parrot? Yeah, an escape."

Tim and Brick looked at each other, then at Lynch. "You mean a prisoner escape?"

"Well, kinda. There are almost two hundred infected caged on Level Six." He said it like we were all morons for not figuring that out."

Boom. There it was. Shockingly, the people in charge thought they were intelligent and could contain hundreds of carriers of the worst plague in human history *inside* a secure facility. Not three days ago I had asked about infected attacks on this structure, and had been told those attacks had been nonexistent. Which means there were no infected in the vicinity. Which means they had to import the fuckers here and stick them downstairs.

"You knew! You fucking knew those things were here and didn't do shit about it?"

"Of course I knew. I thought it was stupid same as you, but what could I do? Dude, I'm not a soldier, I'm not a lab guy. I do what needs to be done. I get called in when nobody else can do the job. You and me? We just happened on each other back in Tennessee, and I knew how important you were immediately. The instant I found out you survived a bite, no one else on earth mattered, and I wouldn't have just died, but killed to protect you. I don't give a shit if I'm an asshole. I always do the job, and that's why I'm so awesome. Now let's book." Book. He had used *book* like I would. Sanctimonious dickweed. He moved toward Stoic's non-moving form, while looking at the door that the screams were coming from.

This guy. I had a weapon, and I was half tempted to shoot him in the back of the head. Two things kept me from doing it: Number one; he was the best guy to save my ass in this particular predicament. Number two; the second I raised the weapon, he would use his Jedi-ninja powers to spin and shoot the gun out of my hand, probably blowing off my trigger finger in the process just to teach me a lesson. We both knew he wouldn't kill me, but my fingers are important to me, and as I didn't want to be lunch, I followed him.

Still in his shorts and a tank top, Lynch pulled a combat knife from who knows where (I still wonder if it smelled like poo) and plunged it into Stoic's open eye. For shits and giggles, he stabbed up under the dead man's chin as well, burying the knife to the hilt. Lynch retrieved Stoic's HK416 and checked the magazine.

We all looked through the aluminum bleachers toward the far door at a woman in a lab coat who came into the room screaming. She was running full out, and we saw why in the next moment. Two Runners slammed into the open doorway rocking the door, and with no hesitation sprinted after the still screaming, hysterical woman. She ran straight at us, her eyes growing wide and throwing her hands up, "Don't!"

I had no idea what the hell she was talking about until I saw Lynch aiming the assault rifle at her. Two shots in rapid succession and the woman jerked, her hands coming to her chest.

She stopped, but she didn't fall. She moved her hands up and down her body as confused as I was. She turned and looked at the two Runners, one with a hole in her head, and the other struggling to breathe with a portion of his right lung splayed out on the concrete behind him. He looked at us, eyes full of rage and not a little sadness. That look made me think back to the first time I was bitten, when I thought about swallowing a bullet. What if these things are still you, but something has taken over and you're trapped inside looking out while your body commits the most heinous acts possible?

The thing tried to stand and growl, but only succeeded in gurgling and blowing a blood bubble from his right nostril. It still scratched and clawed its way in our direction, its life's blood pumping from the high chest wound in thick crimson torrents.

"You," Lynch said pointing to the woman, "come here now. Keep your weapons on her," he told Brick and I. She came to us heaving, wringing her hands and crying slightly.

The spook grabbed his black bag from the bottom bleacher and pulled a suppressed Sig P226. He slung the HK416 and then pulled another suppressed Sig. He handed one to me and told me to give

Tim his M9 back, which I did. "Watch her," he said and sprinted to the open door. He took a quick peek out the door and closed it hastily. It was a steel door with a window laced with chicken wire. It had a push bar on this side, and was not unlike any gym door you've ever seen.

I asked the woman her name and through the tears she said it was Sara. Her lab coat was spattered with blood and I asked her if she had been bitten or scratched. Suddenly very aware of the infected blood on her, she peeled that coat off with lightning speed. She looked herself over, and then looked at me, terrified.

"I need to check," I told her, and she nodded. "I'm sorry, but you have to take your shirt off." She did, and I told her to lift her arms up and checked her for bites. She was wearing white pants, and there was no blood on them other than on her left knee. She rolled her pant leg up and I could see she wasn't bitten.

"She OK?" demanded Lynch as he returned.

"At least for now. I didn't see any bites or scratches."

"We'll check more later. I hate to be cliché, but let's move. They'll be in here in a few minutes." Fists on the door he just closed accentuated his statement. He thumbed toward the door, "See?" The window was packed with faces, all of them looking at us like we were tasty morsels just out of reach.

Which was kind of true. The out of reach part. I'm not going to speak on the tasty thing.

We moved to the double doors on the side of the gym that empties into the hospital wing. Lynch stopped us at the doors, then looked Sara up and down like she was a new tool. "Hang on," he opened his black bag again, fishing in it for a quick moment. "Do not fire unless you absolutely have to. This isn't suppressed, and you will call every dead bastard down on us if you shoot." He handed an M9 to Sara. "Then there's the fact that I don't want to be shot."

"I... I don't," she stammered.

He raised his eyebrows. "You want me to take it back?"

"No," she said quickly.

"Only if they get past us then. Last resort."

She nodded, and he opened the door, sweeping left and right. That damned alarm was *loud*. WAH! WAH! WAH! The hospital wing didn't have the alarm piped through as loudly, but it was still there. There were also panicked people everywhere. The long corridor was filled with doctors, patients, and some military looking for something to shoot. It wasn't chaos, but it was getting there, and I had seen this before.

So had Lynch. He shook his head and sighed, "Everybody shut the fuck up!" It was like he flipped a switch. If it weren't for that damned klaxon, you could have heard a pin drop. All the folks in the corridor looked at him. "We need to fortify this wing pronto. There are infected at the far door in the gym. It will not hold forever."

He started giving orders, and people started following them like he was the President. There were maybe forty people here, and half of them pushed every single piece of furniture toward the double doors, which one of the soldiers had secured with a serious electrical cable. The problem was that this was also a push-bar door, and the bar was on the other side. The door couldn't be locked other than in the open position either.

He had the other half of his little army start stockpiling all the food and water they could, but he kept the five of us together, and he said in a low voice pointing at me, "This man lives. I don't give a shit about anything else, but he lives, is that understood?" Tim and Brick looked at each other, but all of them nodded and I felt like a dick.

"We need to lock down the eastern elevators." Lynch grabbed two guys in scrubs. "Come with us." The seven of us ran down the corridor, and I looked into some of the other rooms as we did. Many of the people in the beds would not be able to run. We reached another door, and this lead to the section of the hospital where my room was. It was locked and the guard let us through. We ran down the corridor again, but it was shorter, only three rooms on each side. I must have been a high roller, because all the other rooms were still empty. They all had those windows and hermetic doors too. We got to the end of the hall, and another guard let us through, staying on the hospital side of the door.

We were in a small elevator lobby, corridors going to the left and right and hooking around corners. Lynch checked one corner and Brick and I checked the other. There was nothing we could see.

The spook looked at the stainless steel doors to the lift. "We need to use this elevator to get to the surface."

One of the guys in scrubs looked incredulous. "What about all the people in the hospital area? Why are they gathering food and water if we're leaving?"

Lynch was looking at the illuminated floor indicators above the elevator doors. The white light had been stuck on five, but it blinked out. "Back up," he said and raised the HK416. We lifted our weapons too. "Solid firing line, nobody in front of anybody else, Sara, you fire if you have to." The two guys without guns (which was weird, because everybody carried a weapon down here, even the guy who pushed the mop), backed up so they were on the side of us. The light over level four came and went, and Lynch knocked on the window to the door back into the hospital wing. The guard looked through the window, and Lynch told him to open the door. He did.

"Aim your weapons three feet in front of the door. Do not fire at the first thing that moves. Take a moment and make sure you're firing at infected before you pull the trigger."

How the hell was he so calm when I was consistently soiling my shorts?

The circular light behind the 3 above the door popped on and there was a *ding!* The stainless steel doors slid to the sides, and we were witness to a nightmare. The back of the elevator was coated in arterial spray, which stuck out in stark contrast to the shiny steel. Three forms, two in lab coats and the third a mottled-black, rotting monstrosity, were kneeling over another prone form also in a lab coat. The pus bags were shoving choice bits of the hapless victim into their greedy maws, and there wasn't much left. They were really pigging out. I watched as one had to yank twice to pull away something purple and when the thing hefted it to its mouth and bit into it, it squirted all over his pal to the right.

It had been a while since I had seen this shit. Apparently I wasn't the only one, because both Sara and the louder of the two orderlies gagged.

In slow motion, all three attackers lifted their heads and swiveled them in our direction. The two in lab coats had been savaged, and were missing important parts of them, but the rotten one was so far gone I couldn't tell if it had been male or female.

"That's what we're fighting, people. No quarter asked and none given." Lynch fired his weapon three times before any of us could recover from the overwhelming feelings of pity and disgust. All three zombies crumpled. Perfect head shots again. The doors tried to close, but one of the slain undead had fallen into the door path and the steel panels kept bouncing off his corpse and re-opening. The spook stepped forward and shot the one they had been feeding on. He stepped into the elevator and did something, the doors remaining open. Then he looked up. "I need a boost."

I didn't have a holster on me, so I passed my Sig to Tim and moved to help. I stepped into the elevator, the stink from the rotten one so bad I almost gagged. Almost.

Lynch looked at me as I bent down and reverse-steepled my fingers for him. "Don't get any blood on you."

Don't get any blood on me? Was he fucking serious? There wasn't a square inch of this metal box not dripping or puddled with gore. The undead did not believe in napkins. Not being able to keep my mouth shut; "I can't get infected," I told him.

"I can. If you're covered in that shit and bump against one of us, our infection risk goes up."

"But you're standing in it!"

"Am I?"

I looked down. So I was wrong. There was a square inch of the floor not covered in infected zombie goo, and this prick was perched on it. How he consistently pulled this kind of shit off was beyond me. He was smug about it too. It's the little things.

He reached up and pushed the emergency escape hatch which I had thought was bullshit and elevators didn't have. They do. At least this one did, and it opened up, which I thought was kind of dumb. How the hell were you supposed to get up there if you were alone and there was an emergency? He stood on my ten fingers and I helped him peer into the shaft above the car. He was getting heavy when he popped back down and said, "This'll work."

"What'll work?"

"We're taking the stairs."

I looked up through the hole in the roof of the elevator car. I didn't see any stairs.

We moved out to the rest of the group, preparing to discuss what to do, when gunshots and screams came through the open doorway. We all looked back the way we had come, into the hospital area, and we could see through the window in the far door that the living and dead were fighting hand to hand. The guard tried to run back to help, and Lynch grabbed him by the arm, "There's only death back there."

The guard shook loose and ran back past my room toward the far door. Lynch shook his head and double tapped the poor bastard in the back with his Sig. The guard fell forward and Lynch ran up to him and shot him in the head. He picked up the guard's HK416 and ammo belt. He stooped and picked up a pistol as well, reloading as he returned to us. Brick had his weapon pointed at Lynch's chest. "Why did you do that?"

Lynch didn't even look up. "He was gonna open the door," he said, like Brick had asked a stupid question. He passed me the rifle and the ammo belt, and gave one of the orderly guys the dead guard's pistol. I tried to give the last guy the Sig that the spook had given me, and Lynch looked at me like I was mentally challenged. "Don't do that."

Slaps on the window sixty feet away had us looking at the door out of my wing. The dead were pressed against it, and some of them had been folks we had been talking to not twenty minutes before. Several were Runners, and they were beating the shit out of the window.

"Shouldn't he have a gun?"

"There will be plenty laying around on the floors above, trust me. In the meantime, you keep those, and shoot anything that gets past me, living or dead."

"Living?"

"Yeah, if somebody gets past me, then I'm dead. I want you to shoot that guy. I want you to shoot him if he's the President. How many times I gotta say it? You have to live. Not to mention, if he just killed me, I don't like him."

The far window spider-webbed, and then a chunk of it busted in. It was that safety glass that had the chicken wire inside it, so it cut the crap out of the Runner that was ripping at it. I know they have a tolerance to pain, but I think the bottom line is that they want to tear into us so badly that they just don't give a shit. This particular Runner, a woman in what used to be a white lab coat, pulled on the glass so hard I saw her pinky finger shear almost off. She looked at her lacerated hands, little finger hanging by threads of flesh, then roared at the ceiling and propelled herself at the glass. I don't know if it was her rage, or the fact that she and the others were all working together on the window, but that shit caved right in, and she climbed through, dripping and pissed.

Lynch shut this door and we ran to the elevator. I didn't see it, but I heard that Runner slam into the door behind us. This would be the last door between them and us.

You know, hindsight is twenty-twenty. In retrospect, I probably should have told you that the two orderlies were wearing red shirts. They weren't really, and the Star Trek reference not-withstanding, I didn't tell you their names, or overly describe them, so you can guess what happened to them.

The orderly with the gun pointed it in our particular direction and said he was going back. Lynch didn't even turn around. "Go then."

"Don't go," I yelled at him. "There's nothing down here for you, everybody's dead!"

He shook his head, "You don't know that!" He backed up until he was near the corner of the junction, and ran off back down the hallway parallel to the one in my wing. Shocker incoming: We never saw him again.

"You first," Lynch said to Brick. "Anything up there gets one in the noggin."

Brick nodded, and the spook ten-fingered him up. "Still clear!"

"Why don't we just use the elevator?" demanded Sara.

Prick actually rolled his eyes. "Cuz it could open on one of the floors above us, and I don't know what's up there."

He pointed at me. "You're next." I went, and it was dusty and greasy up there, with little lighting from the emergency lights that seemed to go up forever, but there were no infected. Sara came next followed by Tim. His ID badge fell off and he totally panicked. "I need that!" Lynch scooped it up, wiping it on a white portion of one of the zombie lab coats.

We heard the glass give way on the door twenty feet down the corridor, and we knew that they were coming. Lynch jumped and Tim and I caught his hands, hauling him up. The screaming from the Runners got louder quickly, and the unarmed orderly turned, pissed himself, and leapt toward us with that desperate, terrified look that you've seen countless times since the beginning of the plague. Tim and I caught him, and Lynch pitched in a hand, but nine-fingers came shrieking into that blood-stained car and grabbed the orderly's midsection. Bitch didn't bite him though. She looked right at me and started climbing up the guy like a spider. She wanted the whole buffet. I couldn't tell who was screaming louder, the infected or the guy she was using as a ladder. Lynch let the guy go, and fired off a shot into the thing's face. She let go instantly, and fell back into the car, but the moment she had jumped on the orderly, he had gained a hundred and twenty pounds. Lynch had taken his hands off of the poor kid to shoot the Runner, and Tim and I couldn't handle the extra weight. He slipped from my grasp, falling back into the car and slipping on the rotten thing below, going on his ass in the goo. The elevator filled with infected and they swarmed him, biting and tearing. He gave me a short, helpless *Oh shit!* look, and then he was covered by them. The only ones looking up at us were the ones that couldn't reach him.

Lynch shut the hatch and sighed.

Over the din of the feeding below us, I heard Tim whisper, "Nobody should go out like that."

Lynch exploded, "Are you fucking kidding me? I'm tired of babysitting you assholes! Man the fuck up! *We're all going to go out like that*, and the quicker you get it into your damn heads, the quicker you'll be of use!" He stood, the rest of us looking at him like his face was made of something scary. "I hope that badge was worth it." He located a ladder and started to climb.

We followed.

We climbed. We stopped at the next floor, a big yellow 2 on this side of the doors. There was a small foldable catwalk that lead three feet from the ladder to the doors. Lynch folded it down and closed the distance, his fist up in the universal *be quiet* signal. We heard running and some screaming, and he shook his head and we began climbing again.

It had only been maybe fifty feet, but it was wearing on me, and I wasn't the only one. Sara was huffing, and so was Tim. We got to the big yellow 1, and Lynch repeated the thing with the catwalk. We didn't hear anything, and apparently neither did he, because he pulled his knife and pried the doors open.

The elevator lobby was empty. No blood. No bodies. No people or zombies. I didn't know if that was good or bad at the time, but hey, no zombies is no zombies, so I was opting for good.

Lynch climbed out first, scanning the area in a crouch. The rest of our little party followed him, never making a sound. We were there, just standing, waiting for someone to make a decision, when an orderly, and three guys in riot gear, two with M4s and one with a FNP90 rounded the far corner and aimed right at us. Why was there an orderly up here?

Brick hit the floor, the rest of us stood like morons until Lynch went all ninja and I was on my ass with him protecting me.

One of the soldiers lowered his weapon. "Friendlies." The others did the same and they came to us quickly. "Chief Master Sergeant," one of them said. These guys apparently weren't soldiers, but Air Force. Or at least they knew Brick.

They helped us up. "Wilkes, report," Brick said.

"Chief Master Sergeant," the kid on the left began, "this level is not secure. Hostiles are everywhere. Our orders are to make our way to the PX, eliminating hostiles as we move. There's a group of friendlies in the PX, but they've been cut off, and are low on ammo. We're carrying a thousand rounds of five-fifty-six, and twelve hundred five-point-seven," he indicated the MOLLE packs they were carrying, "and we're going to distribute when we get to the PX."

"Give me two five-fifty-six mags," Brick said.

"I'll take a full MOLLE," Lynch chimed, and I jumped on the band wagon and told the boys I could carry a pouch too.

The guys looked at each other for a moment, and then Brick said, "*Now* Airman First Class." They gave him two magazines, but didn't give shit to me or the spook.

I was perplexed. "What the fuck?"

"Not giving rounds to a civvie," Mr. First Class told me.

Lynch stared him down. "I'm *not* a civvie. I vouch for him. Give them to us or I take them."

The kid swallowed hard, obviously very aware of who Lynch was, and in the midst of his indecision, everything, once again, went to hell.

Airman First Class Wilkes stood stock still, but the kid with the P90 began to bring it up, and that was enough for Lynch. He moved like a cat, his left foot kicking out and impacting the Achilles of the kid slightly. The spook spun backwards and used the back of his right leg to drop the kid onto the floor. Lynch had barely moved, and made it look like a dance. The kid was hanging, back down, no doubt wondering what the hell just happened. Lynch was holding the P90 by the top, suspending the Air Force stooge by the weapon sling. *With one hand*. He looked sideways at the other kid with the M4, and said with venom: "Don't."

As all this was happening, the infected had found us, and a group of them rounded the same corner that the three Air Force kids had a minute prior. They also came from the other direction, boxing us in.

Well shit. And WAH! WAH! WAH! Because that effing alarm was still going on.

These were all pus bags, mostly fresh too, no Runners.

Lynch pulled the kid off the floor, and everybody started shooting. My ears were gone quickly, lost to the din of gunfire. I could no longer hear the moans of the dead over the ringing in my melon. The Air Force guys, including Brick, were doing well, dropping many infected. Lynch was efficient and didn't miss, and I did more than my fair share. Tim's pistol was empty in five seconds, and he didn't score a single head shot. Sara had her hands over her ears, as did the orderly, except his mouth was open and it looked like he was yelling.

But I couldn't hear a damn thing.

Lynch was yelling something, and then grabbed the kid with the P90, the kid looked as terrified as I felt, and spun the weapon toward the spook. In true virtuoso fashion, Lynch grabbed the weapon and pointed it at the ceiling, where two rounds impacted before the kid took his finger off the trigger. Lynch grabbed a MOLLE pouch full of ammo and yanked a clip…oh shit, sorry Ship, a *magazine*, performing the best tactical magazine switch I had seen to date. Lynch forcibly spun the kid back around, and we continued to fire.

I ran dry, Brick ran dry, and we reached for more mags. Then I think courage ran out. The only thing that we didn't seem to run out of was infected. Where the hell did they all come from? An hour ago there weren't any, how did everyone get infected so fast? How did they all turn so fast? I wonder if zombie porn stars are still hot? Damn I'm thirsty! I was just playing basketball, I need a drink. OW! That brass it hot!

That's the shit that rips through your mind when you're terrified and firing at the living dead and alarms are sounding.

So you keep shooting.

I pulled a hot bullet casing from my neck line where it had deposited itself and decided to keep on keeping on. With bullets.

The infected gained ten feet and we kept firing. They got closer, stepping over or on their pals, and we kept firing. Airman First Class Wilkes ran dry, but it was terrible timing because at that very moment they were in amongst us and we had to go hand to hand. His M4 was pushed to the side and three of the things grabbed him. Many of these ones were fresh, but a couple were nasty. The smell was overpowering, and Sara and Tim began to gag. Lynch was still firing his HK, but I had run out of ammo and couldn't reach the MOLLE pack on the floor. I was grabbed from behind, and started to panic a little when I realized it was the spook just chucking me to the side, out of harm's immediate way.

Wilkes was engulfed, and went down screaming and trying to re-load. I couldn't hear him very well, but I could see he had his mouth open like he was screaming. The kid with the P90 switched to full auto and just slammed rounds into anything in front of him. To his credit, he put his game face on and started smashing skulls with his rifle when he ran out of ammo in three seconds. He knew he didn't have time to slap in a fresh mag. He didn't get the chance to scream when they pulled him into the crowd.

The third kid pulled his knife as there was no time now for any of us to reload. He did this awesome stab move up under the chin of the first one to latch on to him, and then stuck another in the forehead. The knife slid off and got another one in the eye, but neither of them was done, and they tore into the poor kid. Brick tried to rescue him and got a bite on his forearm for it before he could pull back.

Not that there was any place to pull back to. It was game time. The only person without a weapon was the orderly, and he saved my ass. He yelled something that sounded like "Fuck this," and ran full on bull-rush into the crowd behind us.

He fought like a cornered lion. Not only did he make it through, but the pack that wasn't chewing on the Air Force kids was turning to make grabs at the orderly. Lynch noticed this, grabbed my wrist in his iron grip, and dragged me through the crowd, who mostly had their backs to us. Brick went back for a paralyzed Sara, but the paralysis left her and she put her gun in her mouth just as he reached her. Brick skidded to a stop and turned around running, not waiting for the gunshot, but we lost him as they closed in behind us. I hope he made it, but I doubt it. He was bitten regardless and so condemned. I couldn't hear anything, so I don't know if Sara actually checked out on her own, or if she was part of the banquet. I guess either way she got eaten.

We fought through the crowd, and it was way easier than I thought it would be. The things had all turned around to snack on the guy in blue scrubs, but he looked like Barry Sanders (yeah, I know I'm dating myself) and just juked past them. The orderly made it through and turned around to yell as us. He got a good look at what was shambling after him, us in the middle of them, and doubtless lost his shit. When he was plowing through them, they were kind an obstacle, but when he turned around, he knew exactly what he had just done. I would have had a woody, and thought myself awesome, fist pumping the air, this guy screamed and ran away down the hall.

The path in front of us closed, and I ran into the back of a dead soldier in desert camo. I had no choice but to fire, and that almost killed us both. The weapon was suppressed, but if you've ever heard a suppressed weapon fire, it isn't like the movies. There's no *pfffttt* like you think, it still sounds like a gunshot, just muffled. They all turned and looked at us. Lynch shot three of the things with his Sig, and pushed me through. He had shot them all in under a second it seemed, again, perfect head shots. Two others grabbed him and he fired but one grabbed his arm, and his shot went wide. The fucker missed. I had never seen that before, and it was life changing.

Not that it mattered. The pistol slide stayed in the open position, and he dropped it immediately, coming away with his big ass knife in his paw. He dispatched the one latched on to him with the knife, and did this spin-Judo thing, breaking the arm of another one. He propelled himself backward and was on his feet running with me quickly.

The two of us sprinted down the hall after the orderly, but we never saw where he went. The corridor was maybe two hundred feet, and through a set of big doors I saw the motor pool area. It was full of infected, feeding on the fallen. There were dozens, maybe a hundred or more, and we had just been through a couple of packs of fifty. I have no idea where they all came from or how everybody got dead and then undead so quickly. It didn't make sense, but we couldn't go through the motor pool even though the giant doors to the outside world were a mere hundred feet across that cavernous room.

The dead were halfway down the hallway, and Lynch said, "In here," and opened a door with a frosted glass window. No way they weren't going to bust through that in two seconds. He pushed a desk against a wall, and then jumped up on it. He grabbed my HK, and I let him. He had lost his to the zombies someplace. He used the polymer butt of the rifle to smack into a big vent above the desk. Once, twice, three, and on the fourth time it kind of pushed in. Then he pulled it and it came loose. "In," was all he said. He passed me the HK, and the MOLLE pack of ammo minus the two mags we had used.

The vent was dusty, but huge, easily big enough to move down on all fours. I turned to look back but didn't see Lynch. "Come on! They'll be through that door in ten seconds!"

He was standing on the desk, and he looked in at me. And the guy smiled. "Can't," he said and passed me a knife. He held up his arm, and I could see a very small, semi-circular bite mark just above his elbow that was barely bleeding.

The first slap of a bloody palm impacted the glass on the door and Lynch looked sad. Then he smiled briefly and was all business. "Live," was all he said, and he jumped off the desk. I heard it slide across the room, and then the glass broke and the moans and cries got louder. I heard the desk sliding and I knew it was time to go.

I have absolutely no doubts that Lynch destroyed at least ten of those things with his bare hands before they overran him. The moans and cries of the dead filtered through the duct work, but I never heard Lynch scream.

I crawled down the vent in total darkness, fully expecting a dead hand to grasp my ankle, but that shit never happened. I went over a couple of grates that looked down, and didn't see anything below except for floor, but I was so terrified I just kept going. I got to a T junction, and light came from the right. I went that way and came to a grate. End of the line unless I turned around. I looked through the grate and saw a room with a bunch of computer screens. There was a guy in a pair of blue shorts and a yellow T-shirt sitting in a wheeled office chair bawling like a baby.

It was Tim. I had totally forgotten about him.

I called out to him and think he pissed himself at my disembodied voice. He looked around frantically, raising his weapon, which I knew to be empty. "Up here," I whisper-yelled and he did that same head search, coming up empty. I was able to turn around in the vent, and kicked at the grate, which went clattering into the room. He cried harder when he saw my sneakers dangling out of the vent, and I passed him my HK416. He helped me down, and then he hugged me.

"I thought I was the only one," he said between sobs.

I hugged him back, and asked him where we were.

He looked at the screens, then back at me. "Sat-com relay station. Secure for now."

I looked up at the vent I just climbed through. "Yeah, about that..."

He raised his eyebrows and looked at the vent.

"The other end of that aluminum death-tunnel has a couple dozen infected slipping around in what's left of Lynch."

"Didn't like him much. He scared me."

"Guy was certi-fucking-fiable, but he did have his merits. Did I ever tell you he shot my friend?"

"I'm sorry."

I looked at him. "Nah, he was wearing Kevlar, and to the best of my knowledge is sitting on the deck of an oil platform catching some rays with a margarita and the rest of my friends."

"Sounds good actually." Tim was visually calmed. "Can we block that vent?"

"I dunno, but we should sure as shit try. Do we have any food in here?"

"No. There's a cafeteria down the corridor."

I looked at him and we both chuckled. It may as well have been on the moon.

The door to this set of rooms was simply not to be fucked with. Steel, no windows of any kind, it was more a hatch from a nuclear silo than a door. There was no other way into the room save that damn vent. I looked at Tim's badge, neatly clipped to his T-shirt. Going back for that badge had saved our lives, even if it had meant the death of someone else.

But we were shit out of luck on supplies. I had four mags of five-fifty-six, but there was no ammo for Tim's weapon.

It was then I realized how thirsty I was.

JUST A PEEK

The world I knew was gone. I had known it for some time. Every major city on the planet is lifeless. Every big town, every small town. Of course there must be survivors. A farmstead, or some folks in the hills. People who were either not in populated areas, or somehow escaped them as or before the plague struck may have survived. There is no doubt that humans are no longer the dominant life form on the planet. I know this.

Yet when Tim showed me recordings of satellite footage from cities around the world, I cried like a school girl with a skinned knee. It was awful. It was horrible. It was *humbling*. I felt so small. Insignificant.

The way I felt right then was probably the total opposite of the truth. The very fact that I am human and alive is a testament to how important I am. How important we all are. Lynch had been right, but he had been wrong; we *all* need to live.

Tim was NSA. He wasn't a trained killer like Lynch; he was a geek who loved computers and basketball and painting fantasy miniatures. I don't know what that last one is, but Tim liked it. I guess the NSA had need of nerds too. He had been given permission to access certain satellites of questionable integrity, and had been looking all over the globe at whatever either he or the upper echelon had deemed necessary.

Initially, he had an army of folks with him in both this room and a more secure location in the mountain above us. He had monitored troop movements until all the troops were dead, and subsequently the movements of hordes and swarms of infected, reporting positions to whoever needed to know.

Tim had shown me how to use the satellite software. He wouldn't give me his password, citing treason, but he sat and watched me as I pulled up satellite images from last week. The resolution was unbelievable. I could make out the license plate of an overturned tanker truck road train south of Darwin Australia. WRX 110.

I switched the feed photos, jumping around the planet just picking file names that were cities with dates. Both video and high-definition stills. Hamburg, Germany was crawling with undead. They were packed into the streets, undulating like wheat in a breeze. Delhi was the same, as was Moscow. London was partially destroyed, the Thames full of half-sunk and burned-out boats and vehicles. Kyoto had roving bands of undead searching for flesh. This to me said that there were still living people in that city. San Francisco was the same. Mexico City was burned mostly to the ground, infected shambling everywhere. Beijing was just gone. There were very few large structures, most were rubble, and everything metal looked melted. Nothing moved, not a bird, not a zombie, not even the breeze looked to be stirring in Beijing.

I had to do it. I had to look. I was from Boston, and I had to know…

It was a mistake.

The fires had long since died out, but you could see they had raged unchecked. The Hancock Tower, a Boston icon of blue glass, was dotted with shattered windows, smoke stains and burn marks on the sides. The Zakim Bridge, a modern marvel, was twisted, bent, and black, its many support cables dangling. The burned-out hulks of cars strewn about on what was left of the bridge proper. The structure was likely destroyed to halt the spread of infection north from the city. I had used this very bridge in my escape from Boston with a bunch of prisoners and guards and their families. I used the software to check out Fenway Park, home of the Red Sox. It had been turned into a makeshift tent city. A tent city that was now home to thousands of infected, stumbling around bloody tents and hastily erected barricades, all pus bags. Boston, like all the other cities I had looked at, was dead.

I had suspected that everyone I had known was dead. This pretty much confirmed it, and even if by some miracle some of my old friends from the neighborhood had survived, I would never find them. Never see them again. I wish them the best.

"Sorry man," Tim breathed from over my shoulder. "I was from a suburb of D.C. D.C. is gone too. I got to watch all of these cities fall. I have all of that footage too. It…it was one of my tasks to catalogue it. I… I haven't seen a living person in months in any of the cities."

The alarm klaxon stopped right then, and I looked at the clock, 0137. That time stuck in my craw for some reason. I thought about it for a moment and had an epiphany. "Tim! How do we move the satellite so we can get a pic of someplace we want to see?"

He looked at me like I had three heads. "Move Sentinel Three? We can't move the bird, it's geosynchronous."

He had lost me with the sentinel thing, but I wanted to sound smart and cool. "Oh, that means in a fixed position right?"

He raised an eyebrow. He looked *exactly* like Ship when we used to talk about something he thought I should know about. Prick even started to roll his eyes before he caught my menacing glare. I nipped that geek superiority shit right in the damn bud with a look.

"Uhh…no, that's geostationary. All our com-sats are geostationary. The spy sat I can access, Sentinel Three, has an orbital period of one sidereal day. It matches the earth's sidereal day, just under twenty four hours." I must have looked all kinds of dumb because he continued, "The bird moves with the earth. If I had the access codes, I could adjust its rotation or orbit slightly, but that would be it. I can access the feeds, but can't control the satellite. Basically, we have to wait until it passes over a portion of the planet's surface we want to look at, and then we have twenty-seven minutes to take photos or video before it's out of position again."

"When will it be over twenty-seven degrees, eleven-forty-three north by ninety-oh-one, thirty-seven west?"

"Let me sit." He took over, and muttering to himself, began some calculations, "Ninety zero one… About zero four forty six. Little over three hours. Why, what's there?"

"Atlantis."

He was dumbfounded. "Wait…what?"

"Yeah, my friends are on the drilling rig Atlantis in the Gulf of Mexico." I had another epiphany. "What about here?"

He didn't get me, and this time I rolled my eyes. "When will the spy thingie be over *us*? Can we see what's up outside?"

He swallowed hard. "Moron! I can't believe I didn't think of that!"

He did some more calculations. "Shit, we missed it. It would have been a relay from Sentinel Two, but it passed over us fifty-seven minutes ago."

"How many satellites are there?"

He hesitated, obviously not wanting to divulge that info.

"Dude, you already let me use the software, and I know about the Sentinels, your treason is complete there, Obi Wan. Besides, who's gonna throw you in prison? Everybody's dead."

Tim never did tell me how many satellites. We spent the next half hour shoving whatever would fit into the vent, and we were as quiet as we could be. I couldn't hear any infected or sounds of any type through the vent, but you never know. We had it blocked up for maybe six feet, but anybody who really wanted in was getting in, and that was downright unsettling. I sat in a chair and fell asleep.

I was dreaming about zombies in a Taco Bell when Tim gently shook me awake. "It's time," he told me, and I had no idea what he meant. "Sentinel Three will be in position in three minutes."

I hadn't been asleep long, and woke up pissy about it, but also thankful as the dream had been going badly. What kind of self-respecting Taco Bell has no tacos? I rolled the chair over next to Tim, and we pulled up the feed I wanted. There were different zoom levels, and I was way, way out to start with. Tim used his computer mouse to blow up an area on the map, the center of which was the coordinates I had given him.

There she was, in all her glory. My home. Atlantis. We were seeing her from a few miles up, through some small clouds. I asked if Tim would zoom and he did. The clouds moved, and I could see more than just a little dot in the Gulf. He zoomed again, and I could see a huge dot in the Gulf. I could make out individual objects, one of which was unfamiliar. A boat anchored off the southern edge of the rig. Must have been a long anchor chain, because that was some deep water. Tim zoomed in again, and I could see guards walking on the deck of Atlantis. I could also see that they were talking, and one of them clapped another on the back. I couldn't tell who they were, as I could only see the tops of their heads, and one was wearing a hat. It was an old style, tiger stripe boonie hat that you would have seen on a Green Beret in Vietnam. I didn't know who it was.

I wanted to see more, but Tim said unless they looked up, we wouldn't be able to ID them. He had to zoom out a little, and when he did I got a better look at the boat I had seen. It wasn't a boat, it was a ship. It was gray, and from the angle we were at I could see it was a destroyer. I couldn't read her designation, but there were people all over it. It was before five in the morning, and she was bustling. These people were alive too, I could tell from their movements and what they were doing. The good thing was that they didn't seem to want to invade Atlantis...unless they already had.

Tim zoomed back to the deck of my home, and we watched as people moved about her. One person came out rubbing their eyes. The person stretched a huge stretch, complete with a yawn that could have swallowed a football. I know it was a big yawn because this person was looking straight up with their head back. A sharp intake of breath from me had Tim asking if I was OK. I pointed to the screen. "That's Kat!"

Tim smiled. "Good!"

An exceptionally manly tear may have been shed right then, I will neither confirm nor deny. The two guards I had focused on earlier moved toward Kat and they had a conversation. The one in the hat leaned in and gave Kat a smooch, and I knew immediately, it had to be Alvarez. I smiled even broader, and the smile must have been as contagious as the plague, because Tim was right there with me, teeth bared.

Where was Ship? No, Dear Reader, not the destroyer, my bestest pal and legendary smarty pants. My buddy Ship. He was an early riser, but I couldn't catch his massive frame on the monitor anywhere. I stared at Kat for a bit, and the angle of the feed started to change slowly. The change picked up speed, and soon I could barely see what was going on. A minute later and the feed went black.

"Sentinel is moving off, sorry."

"Yeah, I figured as much. Thanks man, I..." I looked past him and noticed something odd. Two of the last things we had shoved in the vent were a couple of sweat shirts that had been left behind in this room during the chaos. They were on the floor. I stood and went to move them back into the vent. Hey, anything that muffled our sound, and stood between us and Lynch's dinner party was a good thing. There was no chance they could reach that vent anyway. It was a foot over my head.

I picked up the sweatshirts and moved to put them back. We had shoved a small, wheeled stool into the vent too, and as I put the shirts back on the ductwork, I noticed that the wheels were closer to us than before. Then the whole thing moved toward me half an inch and there was a thump from the vent.

Fuck.

I was hoping for rats when I asked Tim for a flashlight. Maybe someone else had gotten in the vent from another direction? Maybe that someone was a morally casual, bikini-clad Playboy Playmate who owned a liquor store.

Tim gave me a little pen-light and I shined that shit into the vent. Behind some of the crap we had stuck in there; a few computer monitors, some paperwork, a seven-tier file holder, a clock and two phones, I saw a few pairs of dead eyes staring back at me.

Did I mention fuck? Cuz fuck.

That was when the moaning started.

ESCAPE

There were more than just a couple of eyes looking back at me. The damn vent was full of them. How the hell had they gotten in there? Zombie pole vaulters? Zombie ninjas or acrobats? I grabbed the end of the wheeled chair and pushed the pile of crap further down the shaft. Having seen me though, the infected were going ape shit, and fought back.

I calmly asked Tim for the vent grate, screws and a screwdriver. He complied, but the grate was bent, and we were only able to get three screws in it. Really, all it would do was slow them down some, but some might be enough.

I checked my HK416 and ammo pouch. Four full mags in the MOLLE and one in the weapon. Tim's M9 was out of ammo, so I passed him my Sig, with one extra mag and three loose rounds. That was all the .40 cal ammo we had. He looked at the weapon and swallowed.

Then he looked at me scared. He swallowed again. "What's happening?"

"Well Tim, old sock." I let the charging handle on my rifle slide back into place with a satisfying noise. "We're leaving."

"But…"

"Tim! Are you thirsty buddy? Hungry yet? Did you not see the infected in the vent shaft? We stay, and we're dead from thirst in a few days. That's *if* those pus fuckers don't get in here and tear us to pieces, and let's face it, that grate wouldn't stop a pissed-off hedgehog let alone a bunch of infected dead people." I put on the MOLLE ammo pack, and looked at him. "Time to man up, pal. We were never staying here anyway."

He nodded, wide-eyed, too terrified to say anything. I must admit, had I had a damn thing to drink in the past day, I just might have soiled my skivvies.

"Which way to that motor pool place we saw yesterday?"

I had forgotten Tim hadn't been with Lynch and I when we had seen the trucks, but it was probably better this way because the place had been crawling with infected.

He thought for a second. "Out, left, twenty meters, right, and a quick left."

We moved to the door, and I put my ear right up against it, reciting what he had just said to myself. I couldn't hear shit, but that didn't surprise me, this particular door may have actually stopped the Hulk in his tracks. It was a sliding door too, and when I put my hand on the handle, I heard Tim breathe, *"Oh shit..."* I had to agree. Hopefully the entire corridor wouldn't be filled with dead cannibals. "Aim for the head. Take your time. *Squeeze* the trigger, don't jerk it. Don't miss. Above all, stay quiet."

Listen to me. I sound just like Lynch.

I had the door open and was in the gray painted concrete hall in half a second. One of the lights was flickering, casting momentary shadows on the walls and down the corridor. There was Blood. Lots of blood. A corpse on the floor that was trying to move was slightly behind us, but it was so far consumed that it would never walk. One pus bag was sitting on the floor, its back to the wall. It turned and looked at us, standing immediately. Tim raised his gun, and I put my hand on his, pushing down slightly and nodding in the negative. The thing began to advance, and I pulled the big ass knife Lynch had given me from where I had fastened it on to the MOLLE pack. The thing closed on us, reaching. It growled that growl that they growl, and I moved toward it.

It was relatively fresh, in woodland camo with horrible wounds on its neck and face, and positively *dripping* with gore. Bloody eyes focused on me, it came rather quickly, but it wasn't a Runner. It got to within three feet of me and hissed, turning into a cheetah and speeding up exponentially as it lunged. I was ready though and sidestepped. It missed and I stabbed it through the eye. Ceasing all sounds and forward movement, the thing dropped immediately.

"Holy shit that was awesome," Tim whispered.

I scanned the rest of the hallway, and only Tim and I and Mr. Eaten were present and moving. I put my finger to my lips, shushing him. He got it and nodded. I stooped to check out the dead man. He had two magazines for a Beretta, but no weapon. He also had handcuffs, pepper spray, and a folding baton. I took them all as fast as I could, and gave the mags to Tim, demanding my Sig back. Tim loaded his M9 and we moved on.

We got to the first turn, and I held up my fist, having seen this countless times from all the military guys I had been hanging with (and every war movie ever made). We stopped and I took a quick glance down the intersecting corridors.

Empty.

Was it scarier to be surrounded by the things or not know where they were? I was pretty sure the hall to the left was where Lynch had bought it, which means that room was potentially full of pus bags. I mean, they did get into the vent somehow. We had to go right anyway. Oh, and I'm going with surrounded is more terrifying. I don't want to get surrounded, and if they aren't in sight that has to be better, because they aren't trying to eat me. Not being eaten is way less scary than being eaten: Fact.

Another fact: the moment you think you're in the clear is when you should be the most alert.

We went right, and just as Tim had said, there was a quick left. I could see the motor pool through a huge window. As I mentioned sometime before, it was a huge, hangar-like structure made of concrete, maybe sixty feet high, and a two hundred feet across. It was not as devoid of the living dead as I would have liked though. Fifteen, maybe eighteen of them were just doing what they do when there's nothing living around. Kind of swaying like stoned, lighter-wielding hippies at a Grateful Dead concert. Others were sitting down on the floor, and still others were wandering aimlessly. Two of them caught my attention quickly though.

One had been an older man, perhaps in his late fifties. He was wearing all kinds of those little bar and medal thingies on his torn and bloody uniform. It was the colonel that had picked me up from Atlantis. He was in his dress best, and he was shaking and looking at his fingers, which were constantly flexing into claws. A Runner for sure. The other was a female dressed in tattered and filthy street clothes. This one looked every which way. She would grab one of the shamblers and scream at it, then look under a truck and move on to another shambler, repeating the screaming thing. She put her hands in her hair and pulled, screaming at the ceiling and shaking her head. Her hands came away with some of her brown hair, and that seemed to piss her off even more. She launched herself at the nearest pus bag and began scratching and tearing at it.

At first it couldn't care less, but then she raked her broken nails across its left eye, and it pushed her away. She took the hint and did the hair pulling thing again.

I studied the place and ducked back before any of them could see me.

It was right then, watching her totally out of control, that I consigned myself to staying alive as Lynch had demanded. This poor woman and the colonel in the room with her were infected. They were not evil, the thing that had invaded their brains was. Whatever this thing is, virus, bacteria, voodoo magic, or a pissed-off god, I was going to beat it. I was going to stop this damn plague, and save humanity. I suddenly felt a deep and mourning sorrow for the two poor souls in front of me.

Don't get me wrong they still had to effing die. They were in my way. Can't save the planet if I'm dead, right?

Eight vehicles were in the big room. One was a tractor trailer; it looked like a cattle truck. Three Humvees, two had fifty cals in their turrets. One staff vehicle, a sedan. One green Chevy Blazer. The last one was an MRAP, and it was my baby. That is what I was going to steal. I had learned how to drive these in Mississippi at Keesler AFB. An MRAP is like a beefed-up, six-wheel truck, although this one only had four. MRAP stands for Mine Resistant something, I don't remember. It was less than a tank but more than a truck, and unless the living dead had suddenly procured anti-tank weapons, they weren't getting us once we were inside. We weren't dying today.

Unless they got us before we got in.

Or if there was a platoon of them already in it.

Or if it was out of gas.

The driver's side door was ever so slightly ajar, and the only thing between it and the extremely open giant doors at the end of the tunnel was the Blazer. Oh, and a bunch of zombies. Can't forget the zombies. Critical importance here.

I looked at Tim. "We're taking the MRAP. We open the door and you shoot the colonel." I peeked through the big window again and pointed. "I don't care if you use all your ammo, he's a Runner, and you don't have to pop his dome, just get him to not run at us. Legs or center mass, anything to stop him. I'm going to take the woman and anything else that gets in our way. We solid?"

He nodded, and I realized I was about to step into yet another shit storm. Staying here was not an option though, and I heard movement down the hall behind us. Couldn't see anything around the corner, but I had no illusions about what was back there.

I opened the door to the motor pool and stepped out on to a concrete landing. Six steps down and we were on the floor. We had progressed five feet from the landing when the first one spotted us. It was sitting and leaning against the tire of one of the Hummers. It didn't growl, it just stood up and started moving our way. That was enough for some of the ones near it, and they looked in our direction. *They* all friggin moaned, and it was on.

I fired the HK at the woman on full auto, a quick burst, but it was insanely loud. I didn't score a head shot, but I stitched three holes across her back and she fell forward. I moved the barrel of the weapon to my forward position and shot a pus bag that had turned to face us. I heard Tim's M9 bark twice, and we started running for the MRAP. I didn't look back. Several other dead bastards got put down on the way to the truck as well. Just before we got to it, a bloated, rotting thing started crawling out from underneath our vehicle, and I blasted it before it could get out. I heard Tim's pistol fire again, and we were at the truck.

"Get in! Crawl over and I'll cover, I'm driving! For fuck's sake, check the back!"

He swung the door open and stepped up, climbing in. Firing twice more at two that got close, I dropped the 416 so that it hung on the single point sling, and hauled myself into the cab, slamming the door and engaging the lock. I quickly checked the back. It was empty and the door was locked. The top turret hatch was closed too.

Two seconds later, the first thump of dead hands slapped against the side of our new toy. Many more thumps and slaps followed. One industrious pus bag pulled itself up onto the second step and looked at me, trying to bite through the steel-louvered, bullet-proof glass. OK, bullet resistant, but zombie-proof for sure.

I put my middle finger against the window, "Fuck you, douche-canoe." I looked at Tim and we both smiled. Then my smile turned into a frown. He caught it immediately and looked scared, "Keys," I whispered, "I don't have the keys!"

I'm not going to tell you he shit himself, but there may have been some leakage. I grinned evilly, pushing the start button. "Don't need keys chief."

His mouth formed a giant O, and his eyebrows shot to the sky. "You dick!"

The MRAP came to life with a throaty diesel growl, and I chucked her into first gear. With thirty thousand pounds of mass, the Blazer in front of us was an afterthought, and I nosed it out of the way, backing up and moving around it. I drove slowly, anything dead in front of me quickly being smooshed into strawberry (in some cases blackberry) jam, and in moments we were out in the sunlight.

Course, the dead bastard that had climbed up the side of the truck was still hanging on, wrecking the view of the mountains to the side.

Pricks just never let me enjoy anything.

The MRAP rolled forward, thumping a few of the things that were outside in the sun. Some of them flew off to the side, others crunched beneath the vehicle's massive tires as we drove out the mouth of the mountain.

Six more cattle trucks were outside, one on its side, empty with the top broken open, two others had their back doors open and were also empty. Three were full. They did not have cows in them.

Dead arms reached through the slots in the trailers. We could hear the moans over the growl of the MRAP. The vehicle had its own air filtration system, so we couldn't smell them, but the smell must have been atrocious out here in the sun as they were. Dozens of them were wandering the fields in front of the facility.

I had seen this type of stupidity before. It was on a container ship in the Gulf of Mexico. It had been a total cluster-fuck there as well as here. Our provisional government must have decided, in their infinite wisdom, that study of the creatures was of the utmost importance. While I tended to agree, I didn't think that bringing a thousand of the things into what was probably the most secure facility on the continent was a well thought out strategy. Even one of those things inside could have ended it all.

As it turns out, they had procured more than one.

We drove by some military vehicles, badass types like tanks and Bradleys and LAVs and stuff. All just sitting there, surrounded by zombies who wanted nothing more than to eat me. I knew that prior to inviting a thousand or so undead to the area, there hadn't been that many around, which cemented my position on our government: idiots.

They had a great thing going here, and this could have been a base to help take back the country someday. I'm just a schlep from Boston with no real military experience, but I can honestly say I thought the folks in that mountain behind me had what it took to get the job done.

Fuck 'em. They're all dead now.

"So, which way?"

"South, Tim ole pal, south."

"What's south?"

"The Gulf of Mexico and the biggest damn human being you'll ever see."

"That's a long way."

"Then we best keep moving."

SOUTH OF BALDY

We drove for about an hour at maybe forty miles per hour, so my advanced math told me we were about forty miles south of the facility, which Tim had called simply; Baldy. It would be getting dark in a few hours. An older house, complete with barn, up a long paved driveway appeared off the road. After the day we had, I really wanted some quality rack time, and this looked like as good a place as any. I pulled off the road and drove up to the house. The driveway circled around and lead back in on itself, and there was a track to the barn.

The barn doors were closed, but the door to the house was wide open. Didn't bode well for the owners unless they were airing out the place during a zombie apocalypse.

Tim read my mind, not that it was overly difficult at the moment, "Uh… I don't really want to go in there."

"Me neither, but I'm still thirsty, and we're shit out of rations in here. We might have a quality ride, but without food and water, all it is is a metal coffin."

He nodded. "Damn."

"And then some."

I parked the behemoth, and shut off the engine. I immediately started it again to make sure it would start later, and began to formulate a plan.

"OK, so we just put about two days between the dead at Baldy and us. That doesn't account for anything that's already here, or heard us a mile or so off. We go up to the door, bang on it and make some noise, then wait it out. If nothing comes, we go in and see what's in there." Tim nodded, and I continued, "We grab what we can, bring it in here, put the truck in the barn, and sleep in the truck on the seats in the back."

"We're not sleeping in the beds in the house?"

"Fuck that noise. I don't want to get trapped in the house if we get swarmed, especially seeing as how we have what basically amounts to a tank at our disposal right here. Not to mention the house doesn't move, and this does." I patted the steering wheel of the MRAP.

He nodded again. "OK, let's do it."

So we did it. It went like clockwork. I pounded the door frame with my fist and we waited a solid ten minutes. I did it again, adding a couple of yells, and we got nothing so we entered, closing the door behind us.

Other than some dust and a single leaf on the floor, nothing seemed out of place. No blood, no boarded or broken windows, and no signs of struggle. These folks just up and left, or worse, they were still here.

We were greeted with quaint wooden furniture. A couch that my mom would have called a sofa. Fireplace complete with giant wooden mantle upon which sat photos of a younger man and woman with two small boys. Photos on the wall, the images of those boys grown, and more images of the couple older and retired. The guy liked to fish, and there were stuffed fish all over the place, and more pictures of him with fish and him fishing. The woman liked to crochet or knit, I dunno which is which (because I happen to possess a penis), but there were shitloads of doilies and afghans and pillow covers and shit. There was needlepoint of a guy fishing.

It was nice. After a year on the run, living on an oil rig, and then my time at Baldy, this was a slice of pretty. We moved to the kitchen and it looked like any grandma's kitchen. The only thing out of place was the moldy bread in an open bread box, rotten fruit in a bowl on the counter, and dead flowers in a skinny vase on the round kitchen table. Everything else looked as if the owners just needed to wake up and get on with the day.

We cleared the room, making sure the door to the basement and out the back were locked. Tim was about to open a cabinet, and I nodded no. We moved out of the kitchen and checked the other two rooms down the hall. Only dust welcomed us. Taking the stairs, we cleared the upstairs bathroom, and two bedrooms. Beds made, more dust. We checked every square inch of that house, including closets, but I wasn't opening the pull-down attic stairs, and F that basement, whatever was down there was staying there.

It was weird. Almost as if the owners were the victims of alien abduction. The nearest town was a half hour away, and I had no idea where the nearest homestead was. Not close, that's for sure. I wondered how many other houses across the country looked just like this.

Going back to the kitchen, on a whim I opened the fridge. It was nasty, and I closed it quickly. The cabinets were stocked. I mean totally full, like someone had just done the grocery shopping, except for the dust. There was dust on almost everything, but the cans and packaged goods were placed neatly.

Suddenly, I didn't want to be in this house anymore. What the hell happened to the people who lived here? They were in a better location than most to ride out the plague a little longer. No people nearby, secluded location. This was Montana, so it was probably some town ordinance that the folks who lived here had to possess guns, but unless they were in the attic or the basement, we missed them. There was a huge overgrown garden out back too, so where had the couple gone? To find their boys?

No kid would want to stay here; it was the middle of nowhere. They boys had probably found women at college and moved away.

"I don't like this place," Tim suddenly stated, mimicking my thoughts.

"Yeah, let's grab the food and book." No, Dear Reader, not the Bible on the end table, I'm from New England, "book" means leave, remember? Don't even get me started on accents either.

There were no bags or crates, and I wasn't going in the basement even if someone promised boobs and video games, so I grabbed a blanket off the couch, stuffing it full of vittles. We took everything. We dragged it out in two trips, then as an afterthought grabbed pillows and more blankets from the bedrooms. I was taking out two five gallon bottles of water for the water cooler when Tim called to me from the side of the MRAP.

I started getting a little pissy, because he was supposed to be less than five feet from me at all times, covering me. I let it pass this one time.

I put the water in the back, closed the hatch and strolled over to him.

He pointed down the road. "What's that?"

I could see something moving, and I didn't like it. I put my palm over my eyes, shielding them from the waning sun, and in a moment deduced what was on the way toward us.

I sighed. "That, my friend, is a small horde of infected."

"Shit."

"Your mastery of profanity is the stuff of legend sir. Get in the truck, bro, it's time to vacate the premises."

Tim put his hands on his hips. "You know, we could just park the thing right here and sleep for the night. They can't get in."

"And have them banging on the sides all night messing up our beauty sleep? Tempting, but until you turn into a hot blonde with a great rack, you need your beauty sleep."

Tim actually pouted. I don't know if it was my tone, or the fact that I had just told him I would prefer he was a hot chick. I felt like Ship should feel when he gives me that look of reproach. Big bastard can't say shit, but his looks are worse than those from that teacher you hated in high school.

We finished loading up, and the group of zombies...what is a group of zombies? A pride? A horde? A herd? A swarm? I know a group of crows is a murder, and that would be apt here, but it's taken. How about a legion? I like legion, but a swarm or flock of something is a group that moves together. Fuck flock, that's lame, so we have to go with swarm. Yup, a swarm of zombies.

Anyway, the *swarm* (yeah, that shit works) of zombies had gotten significantly closer, maybe a quarter mile, and Pouting Tim and I climbed into the MRAP and prepared to make ourselves scarce. I started her up, and I'm not afraid to tell you that sexy growl gave me a bit of wood. With a grin that would have put a shit-eater to shame, I pulled into the road, and Tim positively yelled at me to stop.

Wood gone, I jerked my head at him and he was pointing down the road at the mini-swarm. I adjusted my vision, and could not fail to notice that the lead zombie was frantically waving its arms at us. Something was amiss here. Zombies do not wave.

Well shit. That dude was just that; a dude. Not a dead dude, but a live dude. Fucker was close enough now that I could see he was big. Not Ship big, but certainly in the could-have-played-linebacker-for-a-pro-football-team category. He was limping too, and using something as a crutch. The pus bags were gaining, albeit slowly. There must have been fifty of the things, and they were in slow pursuit of said live dude.

Now my momma didn't raise no dummies. If we picked this guy up and he was the Charles Manson type, we were in trouble. If we left him, he was chow. Even if he beat them to the house, they would get in and get him, plus we had just raided it and swiped all the food. So it was pick him up or live with the fact that we had allowed him to be nosh.

I actually thought about leaving. One more mouth, (and it was a large one), to feed would seriously cut into our rations. Not to mention, he could be on the crazy, or *I need all your shit* side of things. I spun the wheel to move in the other direction, to leave him, and before Tim could even offer a surprised intake of breath, spun it back and floored the accelerator.

We drove the now eighth of a mile toward the hapless bastard, and I realized he never would have made it to the house. The dead were maybe twenty feet behind him. Jamming on the brakes, we kept the truck thirty feet in front of the guy, and waited. He redoubled his efforts, and climbed up the step and hung on Tim's window mirror, not unlike the dead prick that had been on mine some hours earlier.

The guy looked at the things advancing on us and looked at Tim pleadingly. "Open the door!"

I looked at Tim, "Not yet. Tell him to hold on."

The first of the swarm thudded against the nose of the MRAP. I didn't hear it, I saw it. Dumbass just walked right into it. I backed up, slowly at first, then picked up speed with the guy attached to us like a tick. I slowed and turned the truck around, driving forward with him still outside.

We got about a half a mile away from the swarm, and I stopped. Now half a mile doesn't sound like much, but you try hanging on to a mirror and travelling half a mile at about thirty miles per hour. Gotta be scary, and in my head I commended this big bastard for his strength of will. What got me on edge was his crutch. It was a fancy black combat shotgun.

"He has to disarm before he gets in, tell him."

Tim told him and the guy stepped down off the MRAP with a look back toward the swarm, inexorably making their way up the road. He put his shotgun down on the dotted yellow line and stepped back a little, putting his hands up and casting another glance in the direction of the dead.

Tim moved into the back of the truck and opened the back hatch, getting out. He picked up the guy's shotgun and the guy followed Tim into our mini-tank.

Tim shut the door, brought the gun up forward, and the guy sat down on one of the seats. "Thank ya, boys. I was a goner iff'n ya dint stop. They was gonna git me fer shore."

"What happened to your leg?"

"Wassat?"

"Your leg," I repeated, "have you been bitten?"

He looked at his leg, then back at me. "Nosir," (he had said it as one word), "took a bullet a couple months back, n' she's been weak ever since. Twisted it foragin' in a town 'bout six miles south o' here, and them pus bags found me. I been crawlin' as fast as I could, but I was jus' 'bout done when I came across you boys." He pulled his pant-leg up, and I could see he wasn't bitten.

I turned around and started to drive south again, toward the swarm.

"Uh…did, ah…did we jus' turn round?"

"Yes."

"Back *towards* the dead-uns?"

"Yeah, we're heading south."

He sighed. "There ain't nothin' south, son. I been up an' down this country in the past year, an' all I've seen is death. Been from the west coast t' the east an' back this far."

"Then we're in the same boat…er, truck, chief. So have I."

The guy stood up in the back of the MRAP, and Tim tensed, his hand on his pistol.

"I'm much obliged t' ya for pickin' me up an all, but I needs t' head north. Sorry."

I rolled the truck to a stop, but didn't turn to look at him. "You'd like to discuss this now?" I had purposely stopped fifty feet from the dead folks. The first hand slapped on the side of the MRAP in just a few seconds.

The guy looked out the side windows and sighed again. "Now's as good a time as any. I gots t'look for a friend. Actually, I ain't never met her, but I know her husband. He said she was there when th' plague hit, and he thinks she must be dead. I'm a find out and tell him or bring her back."

"Back where?" Tim demanded.

"San Francisco. Alcatraz."

A prison. Figures.

I put the truck in park, dead fists beating on the side. I clenched *my* fists on the steering wheel, and Tim tensed even more. If the poor kid was sitting on a lump of coal, we would have had one hell of a diamond.

"So," I began without looking back at him, "you're telling me that you've crossed an entire infected United States, to attempt a rescue mission for someone you've never met based on information that this person *might* be in a city with a population of ten thousand undead cannibals." I stated it, I didn't ask.

"Yep."

"OK then." I put the truck in drive and turned back around.

If it were possible, Tim clenched harder. "What the hell are you doing?"

"Dropping off our new pal."

He looked shocked. "But you know what's back there! We barely got away!"

I laughed. "Tim, old buddy, what's back there is small potatoes compared to what's south of us. There's way more people to the south, which means way more infected."

He still looked stunned.

"Zombies dude, fuckloads of zombies either way."

Tim didn't say anything, so I asked the southerner his name.

"Dallas. Name's Dallas."

I couldn't help it. I just couldn't. My comedic stylings get the better of me sometimes.

"Oh," I said, "are you from Texas?"

HAVRE

So he was from Texas. He began on a fantastical story about how he was caught in San Francisco when the plague hit. He met up with a group of good people, and they got to Alcatraz, where they were fortifying and trying to make it. There's apparently a military presence on the island as well.

What was really a great plot twist is that he had traversed the country from coast to coast with a group of Navy SEALs trying to find a vaccine for the plague, with a crazy CIA guy chasing them.

Sounded familiar to me.

We took route two-thirty-six west and hooked up with route eighty-seven north skirting Baldy Mountain, and the hundreds of infected that now called it home. It was weird not seeing as many abandoned vehicles and destruction or even undead, but then I remembered our location: Montana. Middle of No and Where. We reached route two at about eleven PM, and I pulled over. We got out of the vehicle, and I made a fire with a broken wooden street sign right on the middle of the road. I used the light of the fire to inspect the MRAP. Several fuel cans had been placed in racks under both sides of the vehicle. Eight in all, looked like five gallons each.

A shit-ton of medical supplies resided in the back of the MRAP, and Tim had dressed Dallas's ankle with an Ace-type bandage. The big man said it felt worlds better with just the wrap on it, and thanked us. He also thanked us profusely when we cooked up some noodles and had a can of peaches each as well. He was hungry, and while not out of food, he only had a couple of Slim Jims, and a bag of rice left, but he was out of water and had been for a day.

We continued trading stories, and he dropped a bombshell: He had come across some type of spook, whom he had had no choice but to kill. The spook's name had been Lynch, and that scared the shit out of me. Him too when I told him about my Lynch. I told

Dallas that I hadn't seen my Lynch die, but he had been bitten, and was surrounded in a small room by what had to be dozens of infected.

I was sipping a blue Gatorade pilfered from the homestead when I heard the tell-tale moan of an incoming pus bag. Our fire must have been a beacon to it. Tim stood when he heard the moan, drawing his weapon and looking terrified, pointing the M9 in every direction. The Texan's shotgun was strapped to Tim's back, and it slipped off his shoulder with each turn the nerd made.

Dallas looked at Tim, then at me and raised his eyes.

"He was in a secure location since the start of all of this…" I grew thoughtful for the briefest of moments and furrowed my brow. "Tim, is this the first time you've been outside the mountain since the plague hit?"

"Yeah. Where is the thing I don't see it?"

"Relax, Pard, I got this." The big man stood, pulling a length of rebar that both Tim and I had missed from his belt. The thing coming at us out of the dark hissed and Dallas turned to look at it. It was walking straight down the road, and now we could hear its step-drag as it approached. The Texan moved toward it with a practiced grace (and messed-up ankle). He sidestepped when it lunged, bringing the rebar down on the back of its neck. It collapsed, but wasn't done, and feebly latched on to Dallas' injured ankle. Dallas chuckled. "Peppy one, this'n." He swung the rebar down, impacting the back of the thing's skull with a sickening crunch. "Finito," he said. "Thas' Italian."

He sat back down and began drinking the juice out of his peach can.

"Tim, old buddy, why don't you give the big fella his shotgun back?"

Without a word Tim complied, still looking at the sack of death on the ground twenty feet away.

Dallas seemed touched by the fact that we would allow him a gun in our presence. "Now what madeja change yer mind if ya don't mind me askin'?"

"I think you could have done to us what you did to that," I pointed at the former human, "at any time. Never saw that piece of metal you're carrying."

"Ya dint ask me about it. Ya just tole me t' give ya my gun."

"We did. Tim, sit down. Our large friend here has diffused the situation."

"I'll sit down, but in the truck. If one of those things found us, there could be a hundred of them bearing down on us."

Guy had a point.

Dallas stood. "He's got a point."

I kicked the fire out, and we all got back in the truck. I didn't feel the need for a watch, as we were in what we were in. I let Dallas have my stretcher-bed, which I still hadn't slept in. His leg was feeling better, but I wanted him to heal it overnight if we were going into a town of over ten thousand.

I slept in the front seat. Or, rather, I didn't sleep. I fidgeted in that damn chair all night, tossing and turning and trying to get comfortable. I saw the sunrise, and the next thing I knew, I was regretting the idea of not posting a watch.

Penguins. I was dreaming about penguins. They were all walking toward me, swaying side to side as they do their little waddle. I heard something familiar, as the penguins waddled. It was a sound I should be afraid of, but I couldn't remember what it was. It was then I realized all the penguins were dead. They all had red eyes and huge, very un-penguin like teeth, and they were all hungry.

I sort of shocked myself awake. My mother used to call that "falling out of my tree." I cleared my throat and blinked a couple of times, kind of thirsty and having to take a leak.

I started to stretch, and looked out the window at the backs of a giant waddle of penguins. Yeah, I know some shit, a group of land-walking penguins is a waddle. Except this wasn't a waddle. It was a *swarm*. Yup, you guessed it, I was looking at the backs of several hundred undead, all shuffling past the MRAP as if it were a rock. All of them headed east on route 2. Directly toward Havre. Right where we had to go.

I got up slowly and made my way back to the sleeping beauties in the back. The stretchers they were using as beds were fit into frames on each side of the MRAP, over the seats. I put my hand over Tim's mouth and he freaked. I held him for a second whispering at him to *ssshhh* until he calmed down. Wait! Wait,

wait, wait! I don't hold him, I held him *down*, there was no cuddling. Anyway, I pointed out the front window and he nodded. Dallas had heard the commotion and was sitting up. "Damn," was all he whispered.

"They don't know we're in here, or they'd be banging the shit out of the sides."

"Trust me, all it takes is fer one ta start bangin' and they's all gonna be on us."

"Fuck 'em," Tim said, taking me completely off guard, "they can't get in, and we should just run them over. They're heading toward where we have to go anyway."

I looked at Dallas, and he at me. We both shrugged. Why not? Why not run them down and grind them up. It there was anything left of Havre, those people didn't want a few hundred dead coming down on them, so why not stop them here?

Tim was right again. Fuck 'em. I got back to the driver's seat, and buckled up. There were some stragglers but the main force of this small army was now ahead of us by an eighth of a mile. I looked in the mirror, but couldn't see any more than a few behind us. The weird thing was that every single one of them was on the road. Not one pus bag was walking on the dusty ground or side of the road; they were all crowded on the asphalt. Some random inherent memory maybe? Dunno.

I started the truck, and it turned over immediately, much to the chagrin of the always hungry undead that had just ambled by a canned dinner unawares. The humiliation didn't last long, and I could see it turn to irritation then downright anger. The scientists at Baldy had told me that these things have no emotion, but they were wrong. They didn't have compassion, or pity, or mercy, but they could get mad. Pissed, I had seen it.

I got into an argument about the *Alphas* vs. the *Betas* one day with one of the Baldy egg heads. Alphas being Runners. Runners were always pissed, nobody on the planet was going to tell me otherwise, but this woman had tried her best. Maybe they were irritated about the fact that we weren't infected. Maybe they were annoyed that we looked better than them, I don't give a shit. They were all mad, and they absolutely hated us.

Runners were way more terrifying than pus bags too, unless there was a huge group of the dead ones. Kind of like what was now looking at us.

OK, maybe they were incapable of humiliation, but they were sure as shit surprised. They all turned, and started toward us. I drove forward and smacked down maybe ten of them before the main mass of the swarm was in front of me. I backed up, running over several more that I had missed when moving forward. The swarm was bearing down on us, but I didn't care. What could they do?

The faster of them broke away gradually from the slower, and in five minutes of backing up slowly, perhaps sixty of them were thinned out in front of the rest. So I ran them over. Ground them down. It must have been icky outside on that road. There were still so many though.

I rinsed and repeated, and realized this was going to take all day. I drove off the road and circled around the swarm, getting back up on the asphalt and leaving them behind us. They were going to follow, but unless we circled for twenty miles, they would see us on the flatlands in this valley.

We saw the first signs for Havre a minute later, and ten minutes after that we saw the town. It was a fortress. We had to skirt an outer wall of useless vehicles, razor wire, and spike walls until we got up to the massive front gate. It was a school bus with welded plate steel eight feet high that sat in a groove cut in the road. Simple yet elegant. When the bus moved forward or back, the gate would open. I had seen this very type of gate before, at a hastily erected military wall in Tennessee, although this one was way better.

The inner wall was constructed of all kinds of stuff meshed together; telephone poles cut in half and stuck vertically into the ground, sheet metal, plywood, concrete Jersey barriers, crushed vehicles, more razor wire, chain link and stockade fence, and lumber. It looked haphazard at first glance, but upon closer inspection, it was a goddamn work of art. There wasn't a millimeter of open space to slip through, and hardly a place existed where you could get a finger hold, and those places were covered in razor wire or metal blades or spikes.

It was genius.

There were two towers made of shipping containers with aluminum sheds placed on top one on either side of the gate, and from this side I couldn't tell how the bus could move forward and back with those towers there. What I could see is that those fortifications, and quite a bit of the wall were bristling with gun barrels, all pointed at us. Not one, but two huge machine guns had their business ends trained on us as well, as did a nozzle on a swivel that I would bet dollars to doughnuts was a flame thrower.

"Sorry, folks, Havre is closed today." No introductions were made, and I could barely see any of the folks who could have shouted that.

Well shit.

"Uhh, Dallas? Any ideas here?"

"Yep. But I gotta get out."

Dallas stood, hunched over because of his height, and opened the back hatch. He stepped out and closed it behind him. He moved to the front of the vehicle, put his shotgun on the asphalt, and his rebar as well, and turned in a complete circle. "I'm lookin' fer Clara McInerney."

"Who's lookin'?"

"Name's Dallas."

"What do you want her for?"

"Got a message."

"Give it to me and I'll tell her."

"No."

"No?"

"No. Go git 'er, I'll wait." The big bastard actually folded his arms.

There was some commotion, although I could barely see it through the slits in the wall. "Gonna be a minute."

"I got time, but not too much, there's a..." he paused, obviously thinking. He snapped his fingers and said, "Swarm! A swarm o' dead folks 'bout three miles back on the road. They's headed this way."

"How many?"

"A lot."

"How many!"

"Hunerts."

There was dead silence until a woman shouted over the wall maybe fifteen minutes later, "Who are you?"

"Name's Dallas."

"I don't know anyone named Dallas."

A gigantic grin crossed the face of our new travelling buddy as he looked back at us. He turned back and spoke to the wall, "Your husband Kevin does. Captain Kevin McInerney of the USS Florida? He tole me that you was home here in Havra," (he pronounced it like that), "when the dead come back t'life. He was on board the Florida and couldn't get here. He's alive 'n well on Alcatraz in San Francisco, or was when I left a few months back. He's m' friend, an' he tole me to call 'im Kevin, not Captain, or Commander or any of that. He said he misses you and Clyde."

Dallas would tell me later he heard a loud sob, but all I heard was the sound of a bus engine. A smallish man dressed in coyote camouflage dropped over the side of the plate steel covered bus. He skirted right past Dallas when the big guy put his hand out for a shake. The little guy moved to the MRAP and climbed up on the driver's side steps. He showed me a large bundle he had, waving it slightly. "C4. If you turn hostile, you go boom." He nodded and I nodded back. He attached the bundle to the front windshield, and stepped away.

The bus moved forward, and a middle-aged woman, also in coyote camo, came running out and stopped in front of Dallas, looking up at him. A dog trotted out behind her and sat on the pavement, scratching his side. She slung her rifle, and threw herself at Dallas, her arms going around him in a hug. She couldn't reach all the way around the guy, but she tried like hell. The big guy, taken aback, didn't know what to do for a moment, then he returned the hug.

Seven men, all in that coyote camo, followed her out and looked us over. One of them hand motioned us to drive through the gate, and I did, stopping just inside.

"Gotta get out, buddy."

I opened the door and Tim did the same. I brought my weapon, and the locals looked at it, but didn't raise their weapons, which I thought was odd.

One of the guys came over and crawled up into the MRAP. He looked around and got out, nodding in approval. A different guy, older, with a beard full of gray stepped up to us. He shook Tim's hand and then mine. "Any of you bit or scratched?"

The dog, a bloodhound, and a big one, came and sat at my feet, his gigantic tongue lolling. He looked up at me and I scratched his head. "No, sir. No bites or scratches."

Two of the guys looked at each other, "Welcome to Havre, Montana, population just over sixteen hundred souls. Don't get in no trouble and you can stay for a bit. Get in trouble and we'll shoot you. Gotta get checked out by the doc and surrender your weapons before you're allowed to walk around."

I unslung the HK and checked the safety, then handed it to him. I gave him my Sig, and he looked at the suppressor, then at me with raised eyes, then sideways at one of his buddies. I unsheathed my SOG knife from my shoulder strap, and he put his hand out to stop me. "You can keep that."

I thanked him and stuck it back in the sheath while he disarmed Tim.

Dallas brought the woman over. "Boys, this here's Clara."

I shook her hand and so did Tim. "Thank you. Thank you for bringing word of my husband. You must be hungry! Let's get you to Eleanor's for some breakfast!"

She took Dallas' hand, pulling him down the street. Tim and I followed, me looking back longingly at the MRAP as the guys were now all over it like a flock of vultures. I heard it start up, and we turned a corner heading toward a small diner.

I smelled cooking, and suddenly I was starving.

BREWING COFFEE AND TROUBLE

When I had been on the road with Ship and Kat, we generally ate what we could find. Canned and dried stuff or MREs. The food at Atlantis, my new home, had been superior. Then I was a "guest" at Baldy Mountain, and the food had been standard cafeteria stuff. It was good. Reminded me of prison food. A lot of soups, cheese pizza, and pasta. Not a tremendous amount of meat, and the dairy products were substandard.

When Clara opened the door to the Havre House Diner and Grille, and the aroma of fresh breakfast food being cooked hit me; it was like a wet dream. Picture the unbelievable stench of a rotten zombie only in reverse. I realize you might think this is a terrible analogy, but it isn't. The smell did the exact opposite of what the zombie stink does. It filled me with thoughts of good things and better times.

The door had one of those little bells, and it rang when we came in. Clara moved to a diner-style booth and took a seat. Tim sat next to her and Dallas and I sat across from them. A couple of guys were at the bar, and there was a young couple at a table with a little girl, but other than that the place was empty. Clara waved to everyone, and they all waved back. They also all had weapons. Even the kid, maybe ten, had a small pistol in a holster hanging on a hook. It had to be hers; the gun belt wouldn't have fit anyone else in the room.

I heard the door to the kitchen open and Clara waved someone over. I expected it to be this Eleanor person, but she was behind me as she came to our booth. I was also expecting, much like you were, that Eleanor was an older woman with her hair in a bun, wearing an apron and wiping her hands on a dish rag.

Nope.

Eleanor was tall and tan and lithe. Auburn hair in a pony-tail, wearing jeans over cowboy boots with a button-down shirt buttoned to exactly the right position, no further no less. She was beautiful, and her smile made me feel like I was floating on a cloud of titties.

Fine, it may not have been her smile but this is my story.

"Mornin' Clara, who're your friends?"

"New-comers, they have news about Kevin!"

Smile vanished. Instant suspicion, "Do they." Not a question.

"Sure do," Dallas chimed. He stuck his big Texas paw out to her. "Name's Dallas."

She shook his hand and gave a curt nod to Tim and I. "Eleanor. What would you like and what do you have?"

Seeing the blank looks on our faces, Clara explained, "We work on a barter system. Money is useless, so we trade in goods and services."

I had a service in mind.

Dallas looked helpless, and I was thinking about a young lady friend on an oil rig a few thousand miles from here. Tim, with his ever-present logic and ability to totally pull shit off, pulled out a map of the area and a compass. Where he got that I will never know.

"Will this do?"

She looked at his stuff and told him it would work. "I don't need it, but there are other folks around that will trade for those. What about you fellas?"

Dallas continued to look helpless, and if he was half as hungry as me, he was about to start crying. "I got a bunch o' nuthin'"

Eleanor's beautiful brown eyes shifted to me. "Uhh...I have..."

"I like that knife."

She nodded toward my SOG. Now this girl was hot, but my knife? Nope. No way. I was absolutely keeping this knife. It was a Seal Pup for fuck's sake, quite possibly the best knife on the planet according to Lynch.

But...boobs.

I detached the Velcro and put it on the table. "For both of us," I said indicating Dallas.

She smiled and nodded. "We have fresh sausages and bacon to go with the fresh eggs. Milk or lemonade, and coffee, but it's instant."

Dallas and I both gave her our orders, and we didn't skimp. Tim ordered big too, and Clara had a glass of milk, stating (jokingly) that instant coffee was a construct of the devil. When Eleanor brought us our food, we dug in with gusto, and Dallas began his story to Clara between mouthfuls. The food was fantastic, and listening to Dallas's story again wasn't horrible.

When he got to the part about meeting us, Clara let loose with a small exclamation, "Oh! Oh, I thought Kevin sent them with you."

"No, ma'am. And beggin' yer pardon, but Kevin dint send me neither. This here's a favor, and he don't know nuthin' of it. Actually, he might by now iff'n Rick and th' others got back OK. Kevin wouldn't've asked me."

"No he wouldn't," Clara said quietly. "He would have gotten you situated and come by himself."

"I reckon that's true."

I heard the little bell on the door ring, and a shadow fell over us. It was the bearded guy from the gate, "Mind if I join you folks for a bit?"

Not waiting for an answer, he grabbed a chair from a nearby table and spun it around so the back was to us. He straddled it and sat, looking over his shoulder. "Can I get some of that coffee, El?"

"Be right out, Sheriff!"

Excellent. The law.

His name was Dimitri Sabotino, a name which fit a Midwestern sheriff about as much as a cat screwing a dog. He told us the story of his town, which was probably the same as every other town across the country, except with their remote location, they were able to cordon off a section of the town when the first of the plague hit, and remain in relative safety.

"We were almost done walling up the whole town when trouble started. We had one death in the beginning. One death, and overnight four fifths of our population was infected. We lost half the town area too, but were able to fight off our friends and neighbors until we got a makeshift barricade up, and then a wall inside that. The wall is damn sturdy, but we have issues."

I didn't look at him as I used my fork to spear one of the grilled tomatoes I was about to shove in my head. It was tasty. "What kind of issues?"

He looked at me. "Funny you should ask. We used to get deliveries from Baldy Mountain. Bunch of military types would come in and give us supplies. Medical stuff mostly, and they never asked for anything in return. That truck you're driving. It looks like one of the trucks from Baldy."

"It is."

"May I ask how you came by it?"

I sighed and pushed my plate away. Looking up, I noticed that the two guys at the bar were looking at our table.

"Baldy's gone. Infected from the inside. Actually, the geniuses that ran the place thought it would be a good idea to study the infected, so they brought hundreds of them there to check them out." I looked at the sheriff. "You seem like a smart fella sheriff. You can do the math on what happened."

He nodded. "How many survivors?"

"Me and him." I pointed to Tim, who was shoveling food in his face as fast as he could, probably expecting to be arrested or even shot.

He indicated Dallas. "And this fella?"

"Picked him up hitchhiking."

"Saved me from the swarm o' deaders that're gonna be knockin' on yer door in about an hour is more what happened."

Eleanor brought over the coffee, and stood next to the sheriff. "There's a swarm?"

Tim finished wiping his mouth with his napkin. "Couple hundred anyway."

"We can handle a couple hundred," Sabotino said, "but there's something else."

There always was.

"I need to borrow your truck."

I looked at Tim, then back at the sheriff. "What are we talking about here, sir? You want to go run over the crowd of zombies that are coming?"

"No. I want to take a quick ride to the hospital."

Sheriff Sabotino explained that when the town had been cut in half by the wall, not too surprisingly, the hospital was one of the first places to be overrun. The defenders had been forced to pull back, and were unable to rescue anyone in the hospital or the entire east side of the town. A municipality of ten thousand had been culled to less than sixteen hundred. All the rest had been infected.

"We need more medical supplies, and that hospital is full of them."

I looked at him hard, "You're damn right it's full of them. *Them* being things that want to eat you. What's your plan?"

"Drive the truck in, get the stuff, come back."

I shook my head. "Good plan. Why didn't the Baldy people ever clear the east side of Havre?"

"I asked them that. They said something about 'unacceptable losses.'"

I harrumphed and looked at Tim. "Typical bullshit. Where do you think those cattle trucks came from, Tim?"

Tim's eyes went wide and the sheriff asked what I meant. I told him about the trucks at Baldy, and he harrumphed too, "I'm wondering if the losses they were talking about were living folks or dead ones."

"Sheriff, I would like to help, but I need the truck to get home."

He nodded. "I understand that, son, I do. You have to understand I have a town to think about though. A lot of people depend on me, and your vehicle would help those people."

I hadn't noticed, but the place had gone extremely quiet. Everybody was looking at me, and I felt small.

Alright, don't think I'm a dick. I'm a fantastic human being, I swear, but c'mon. Do you really think this guy was ever going to give me my truck back? Either he was going on a successful trip to the hospital and would figure out that the MRAP was too valuable to give back, or, just as bad, he was going on an unsuccessful trip to the hospital, and would leave my almost-tank in the midst of eight thousand infected. I really didn't want to say no, but I needed to get home.

I looked at the two guys at the bar. One had picked up his rifle, and the other had his hand on his gun belt.

"Of course you can borrow my truck, Sheriff. But I want compensation." Out of the corner of my eye, I could see the two guys take their hands off their weapons, "First," I pointed at Eleanor, "I want my knife back. That means you have to come up with something to trade for it. And then I want six full diesel cans for the MRAP when I leave. Two hundred rounds of five-fifty-six would be nice too."

"Twenty gallons and your knife back. No ammo."

I knew this whole dickering thing was bullshit, and I'm pretty sure Sabotino knew I knew it, but what could I do? I thought Eleanor was going to be pissed, but she was all smiles as she handed my SOG back.

"Deal," I said and shook his hand, "when are you leaving?"

"Right now."

He stood, and the two guys at the bar stood and left with him.

Clara sighed. "The sheriff is a good man, he really is, but there's no way he'll ever give you your truck back if he thinks it will help the town."

"Not a chance in hell," echoed Eleanor, who sat down in the seat Sabotino had left at the end of our booth, "but I might be able to help get it back."

"Why would you do that? You just met us?"

"Because I want to come with you when you leave."

"Me too," Clara said quietly. "I would appreciate a ride at least part way to San Francisco. I have quite a few supplies we would be able to take as payment for a taxi ride."

I looked at Dallas who smirked. "Well, I ain't stayin' here."

The two guys that had been at the bar were our escorts. They showed back up about ten minutes after the sheriff had left and were very friendly. They said we had to see the doc and they brought us to him. We had gotten a once over when we were let in, but this guy was thorough. He noticed the bite scar on my leg, running his gloved fingers over it a few times, but the fact that it had healed threw him, and he didn't even question me about it. We were cleared just about the time gunshots echoed across the town from the western gate.

"A few dead ones hitting the gate is all," one of our escorts told us. "Nothing to worry about."

"Them's prolly the ones we drug with us."

"Agreed, my large friend." I looked at our guards. "What now, fellas?"

"Now you get to do whatever you want. Me and Tom will shadow you to make sure you don't get into any trouble until the sheriff says we don't have to anymore."

"Fair enough. Wouldn't mind a little rack time."

"They can stay with me," Clara told him and us.

The gunshots stopped as we reached Clara's house, and the guy who hadn't introduced himself yet reached for his radio. He spoke into it, asking if the western gate was clear, and we all heard that it was.

Dallas, Tim, myself, Clara, Tom, and No-name sat on a pretty couch and three chairs in her house for a few minutes talking, and then I asked if I could take a nap. Clara told me I could use the last bedroom at the end of the hall upstairs, so I excused myself, took a piss using a functional toilet with running water, and hit the proverbial sack.

It was dark when Tim shook me awake. Tom was standing with him.

"Whaazzzit?" I demanded groggily.

"Trouble."

I sat up immediately, well aware that my weapons were now in the possession of one Dimitri Sabotino, Sheriff of Havre Montana.

Tim put his hands up, palms toward me. "Whoa, we're OK! No infected attacking us."

That made me feel better.

Tom piped up, "The sheriff called on the radio. He and the scavenging team are trapped in the hospital."

That made me feel oddly better too. I let loose with a colossal yawn and stretched. This was the first time I had been allowed to sleep more than four hours in a row since my incarceration at Baldy. And no needles either, or probes or questions, or requests for other fluids.

I could tell Tom wasn't done. "And?"

Tom passed me my HK. "And we need help getting him back."

N.M.H. AND ZERO TOLERANCE

Now what would be comical about a group of cowboys, complete with cowboy hats, trapped in a hospital and surrounded by a few hundred living dead jonesing for some human flesh with a side order of fries?

They're trapped in the damn morgue.

Sabotino had taken four guys with him, one of whom was dead, and another unaccounted for. Three of them were trapped in the basement of the hospital, with half a town of undead roaming the halls. The yokels hadn't been found yet, but the sheriff said that the pus bags were getting close. The half-a-redneck also reported that he had a several huge duffel bags full of medical goodies, but no way out of the hospital. All of this Tom had related to me while we sat at Clara's table. Sabotino hadn't contacted Tom again since he first radioed almost an hour ago.

Tom ended his tale by asking me if I would help.

I looked at him dumbfounded. "What the hell can I do?"

"You guys can come with me to get the boys and meds."

"Wait a minute, dammit, don't you have almost two thousand people here? Can't a few of them help? Not to mention I've been here ten seconds and you trust me with your sheriff's life?

"The sheriff asked for you specifically."

I blinked. What? What did he just say?

"He said that you knew how to deal with the dead up close."

My dumbfoundedness continued. "Don't you? Haven't you had a swarm of them living right next to you for a year?"

"Yeah, but we don't go over the wall. At least not to the east. We haven't needed to until now."

"Fine. But where are your red-blooded American cowboy dudes that want to ride into the sunset after they rescue the sheriff?"

Tom seemed to find something particularly interesting on the floor near his shoes. "Nobody...ah...nobody else will go."

I was about to tell him that *I* sure as shit wasn't going, when I remembered my MRAP. "Your illustrious sheriff took my truck, didn't he?"

"Uh. Yeah."

I shook my head and started grumbling under my breath. Carla looked surprised at my language, and I was surprised she could decipher it. Dallas looked shocked too. "Uh, Pard? You OK?"

"Dandy!" I yelled at him, "Just fucking great! I was set to finally get home, and now Wyatt fucking Earp swiped my God damned palomino and lost it to the injuns!"

Best damn analogy ever considering our location and the circumstances.

Dallas stood. "So let's get 'er back."

I put my hands over my eyes and shook my head again. "Yeah. Yeah I'll go. Tom, I need you to show me where the hospital is, and the best way to get there. Most importantly, I want a map so I can memorize the best way back."

Dallas fingered his rebar. "When do we leave?"

"*We* don't. In case you've forgotten, you've got a busted wheel there, King Kong. And Tim stays too. I'll take Tom and that's it."

"Whoa there, Pard, I can help."

"Dallas, please don't be upset, and for Christ's sake don't kill me, but you'll only slow us down. You're not walking properly, and we will undoubtedly need to run."

He nodded. "You're right Hoss. Plus, if anything happens t'me, nobody will be aroun' t' take Clara t' Frisco." He sat down. "Good luck."

"People from San Francisco hate it when outsiders call their city 'Frisco.'"

Dallas looked thoughtful.

Tom left and came back in five minutes with a huge map of the town. "D.P.W. map," he told us. We studied the map, Tom drawing routes with his finger. The straightest path went unmentioned, and I asked about it.

"No way. That's where most of the infected hang out when they aren't attacking the wall. They just stumble around until they see or hear something, then they move like a flock of birds towards whatever it was spooked them."

Perfect.

We took two hours making a plan, with several diversions, and a run across the rooftops.

Soon Tom and I were standing at the wall, yet another piece of Havre artwork, staring down into the dead faces of about fifty infected scratching the wood and metal and staring right back at us with a malevolent hunger. The guys on the wall knew the plan and they started making noise. It was exactly nine PM when Tom and I moved a hundred yards south and dropped over the wall.

I was instantly petrified. Fuck bravery. Fuck doing the right thing, this was pants-shitting terror. Tom moved forward, and I followed him to a drugstore with a smashed front window. We crawled in, careful not to step on the glass and make a shitload of noise for any critters lying in wait in the aisles. It smelled of death in there. Tom had told me that there was rooftop access that we could use to get half a mile closer to our destination before we would need to hit the streets.

In the darkness, I looked around. The damn shelves were full. This store was fifty feet from the wall, but Sabotino had opted to go a mile and a half into the city to the hospital. Not being a doctor or a pharmacist, I didn't know what kind of drugs the hospital had over the drugstore, but this place should have been raided months ago regardless. There was a ton of shit in here, and not just over-the-counter drugs. Dozens of drinks in closed coolers, packaged food, all kinds of toiletries and sundries, and even small toys for kids. The back of the store was loaded with prescription drugs on metal shelves, and there were even some in yellow manila bags that had never been picked up by customers.

Tom was in front of me, and I was watching him closely. The floor was cheap shitty linoleum tiles, and I could make out the sound of his footsteps but just. What was weird was that for every step he took, I heard two, like there was an echo. I reached out and grabbed the back of his shirt. Probably not the best move, because he spun and pointed his gun in my face, his eyes wild. He mouthed *Sorry*! to me, and tried to turn back around, but I held him fast. He had stopped walking, but the steps hadn't ceased. I made a fist with my hand and he nodded. There was a scrape that sounded like someone was dragging something, then soft but deliberate footfalls.

I looked down, and we had moved off of the linoleum on to a carpeted area by the pharmacy. I couldn't see further than a few feet in the darkness, but I did see what was left of a body on the floor nearby. It had been human, but it wouldn't be getting up again. The top of its head was gone, and a huge pistol was on the ground next to it on a section of carpet that I could tell was significantly darker than the rest even in the low light. The corpse had no arms or legs, and the chest and abdominal cavities were empty. Poor bastard had killed himself and the fuckers ate him anyway.

I knew there had to be a way back behind the counter, but there was no way I was going to look for it. Tom and I moved forward and began to climb over the table. I slipped on some paper and went down on my knee. It didn't hurt at all, but it made a nice thump.

A low moan came from very close. It sounded like it was behind and to the right, but I couldn't see. More moans answered, and they were definitely in front of us.

We hopped over the counter, and not two seconds later I heard the sound of a body hitting the desk behind us. It started hissing, and I turned around to look at it. It had been a woman, and it was horribly emaciated and dry. The skin on the thing looked like gray beef jerky. One eye hung out of its socket and the other was so loose it looked as if it would be joining its brother at any time. It began to climb over as we did when I heard a sharp intake of breath from Tom. I spun and brought up my weapon, right into the looming pale face of another skinny dead thing. I pushed with the rifle, and the thing stumbled backward. Another one had chosen Tom as its late dinner, and moved in for a taste. He raised his weapon, a sawed-off, over-under shotgun, and prepared to remove the head of his attacker.

"No," I hissed, "that will bring every one of them that hears it!" He lashed out with his gun as I had, and his adversary went ass over teakettle, falling backwards. A loud snap punctuated its landing, bone protruding through its forearm. My zombie didn't seem to notice, and came straight at me. I yanked my knife from the shoulder sheath and brought it in a sideways arc into the side of the thing's dome. I had been aiming for the temple, but was a tad further back. A year of rot had taken its toll on this thing's cranium I guess because my SOG slipped into his melon easily. I tore my blade loose as the creature collapsed and I turned to help Tom with his adversary. I had totally forgotten about beef-jerky lady, and she latched a whole bunch of dried fingers on to my load-bearing vest. I'm not ashamed to admit that I panicked for a moment, and spun left with a tiny but masculine yelp. This thing had no weight to it, and it fell off the counter but remained locked on to me. I heard Tom stomping his size tens on the noggin of the one he had shoved down, and I ducked down and threw the thing over my shoulder. It did indeed go up and over, and when it landed on its back, its face (more importantly its teeth) were two inches from my nose.

That would not do.

It didn't take long for the thing to want to nibble my honker, and in slow motion it came for me. I whipped the SOG in another arc, but in my haste I missed and caught the creature in the mouth.

So picture this; I'm bent over, the monster on the ground in front of me on its back, its arms reached around the back of me, my knife in between its jaws as it struggles to bite my schnozz off. I pushed down as it pulled up, and the knife cut its face in half, the upper jaw, nose, and forehead of the thing falling away the instant the spine severed.

Eew.

It let go of me, but the eye in the socket wasn't done looking around. It focused on me, but with no body to propel it, it just stared. It had no way to eat or digest, but the bitch was still hungry, I could tell.

I stood up heaving and looked at Tom. He was heaving too. No more moans came, nor were there any footsteps, but I didn't want to take any chances. Tom brought me back to a small storeroom with a ladder to the roof. We climbed and sat up there panting. It was a good time for a rest. We were a hundred feet from the wall. A hundred feet and I was out of breath.

"All that shit in there," I said to Tom, thumbing toward the ladder. "Why didn't you ever get any of it before now?"

"Didn't have to. The soldiers from Baldy gave us all kinds of supplies to keep us going. We're only in here now because we're almost out of medical..." He looked at me funny, kind of a disgusted squint. "Eew. Oh that's wrong."

I had no idea what the hell he was talking about.

Tom reached his hand out toward me like he wanted to flick a spider off my shoulder, which immediately made me tense up because I hate spiders. I mean I don't give a shit who you are, from the Pope to Hitler, if you are OK with spiders crawling on you, than I am not OK with you. Tom had an appalled look on his face that I could make out easily under the mostly full moon. He picked something off of me and held it up for me to see before he tossed it away with a revolted gag. For a second, I thought it was a really small yo-yo, but then it hit me like a bug on a windshield: It was the eyeball from the dry, dead bitch that tried to chew on me. It had gotten stuck in my tactical vest.

At least it hadn't been a spider.

Fully ooged out, I stood and casually (very casually, because I'm effing cool) checked myself over to make sure no more of her desiccated ass was on me. I couldn't see any, so I stretched like it had been no big deal, etching my cool into the annals of awesomeness.

Tom wiped his glove on the gravel roof with a look of revulsion. Not cool. He didn't even *try* to look cool.

Looking across the roofs, I could see that un-cool Tom had known what he was doing during the planning stage of our little outing. The rooftops were quite close together, no more than a few feet apart for a quarter mile. We hopped the gaps, and used this impromptu bridge to get within sight of the hospital.

I pointed at a really nice-looking building, situated pretty much all by itself. "That's the hospital?"

"Yeah."

The building looked brand new. It certainly didn't look like a hospital, more like a space center or something. It was a damn nice-looking building. Wide, with three stories and tall vertical windows.

The parking lot, however, looked like something out of a war movie. Or a story about the zombie apocalypse. There were at least a hundred vehicles, some with doors open or windows smashed, others burned to metal husks. Trash was strewn everywhere, and some type of military helicopter was turned on its side, also burned. The remnants of medical tents were flapping in the breeze, and I could see dozens, if not hundreds, of wrapped figures piled in heaps next to a ten-wheel military truck also with its driver's side door open.

The entire parking lot was crawling with the dead as well. They moved in between the vehicles, stumbling over forgotten stuff on the ground, and shuffling in and out of the ruined tents.

I looked to the left of the lot, and noticed a school bus. I was happy when a cloud moved across the moon and shielded my eyes, and not a little bit of my sanity, from the tiny figures moving around in that bus. There was something about zombie children that really bothered me. The whole unfairness thing I guess. They never had a chance.

The dead also staggered in and out of the ruined front doors of the hospital. The cloud moved off and the moonlight illuminated the lot once again. One pus bag leaned against the Northern Montana Hospital sign off to the right. It looked like it was out for a smoke break. Something about it…

I sighed. "Aww shit."

"What?"

"Look there," I pointed, "near the sign, do you see him?"

The undead I pointed at jerked when one of his brothers got too close. He undoubtedly snarled, although I couldn't hear him from so far away. He launched himself at the other zombie, and my suspicions were confirmed. Infected, yes. Undead, no. A damn Runner.

The Runner slashed and punched at the zombie, then it did something I've never seen before. It leaned in and bit the dead thing on the shoulder. It bit it over and over again, and even from here I could tell it was chewing. The one on the ground fought feebly to get up, not do defend itself, just to stand, but the Runner kept knocking it back down. It even stomped on the dead dude's back a few times.

Suddenly, the onslaught stopped, and the Runner used its filthy sleeve to wipe its face. *That* scared the shit out of me more than anything else I had seen during this entire plague.

I went into sensory overload for a moment as my staggering intellect tried to process what was happening. Either this was a fresh Runner, meaning it had only recently been infected, or it had found a way to survive. It sure looked like it had been eating that zombie. If that were the case, and it was surviving by eating the rotten flesh of the dead, then not only did it contain more than just a rudimentary intelligence, it was exceptionally disease resistant. Not only could these things eat, and preserve their pathetic lives, but they could eat shit that would kill a normal human. Take away the fact that the zombie had been teeming with whatever shit had made it a zombie and you still have unbelievable amounts of nasty germs crawling all over its dead and rotting meat.

So Runners didn't starve to death, or just this one had figured out how to eat?

Fuck.

Yeah, my mind said back to me, *but you're forgetting that the bastard just wiped his face!*

Oh no, I didn't forget, mind of mine. I remember all too well. Why did the thing wipe its face? Instinct? Doctors at Baldy used to theorize that both zombies and Runners exist on instinct alone, but I thought that was bullshit. Now I know it. I agree that eating is instinct. Wiping your mouth is not. It is a *learned* response to having something uncomfortable on your face. This thing had *remembered*. It remembered to wipe its mouth. You could shoot this prick, or break his legs, but it would never stop coming at you. Self-preservation had no meaning to it, but it had wiped its mouth.

Double fuck.

What if it remembers how to open a door? Or use a knife? Or a gun? Or set traps? Or speak French? Ugh... Who wants to speak French? If this bastard had indeed survived, and was learning, then we were in a whole new world of shit.

Or it could have been a fluke. Just some weird shit that meant nothing. I filed it away in my head for later consideration.

Someone was talking to me. It was far off, but I couldn't help thinking it was also close. I blinked and looked at Tom. "What?"

"I said what the hell was that?"

"Just one more thing we need to be extra careful about. We'll have to skirt far around that Runner. Shit, I thought they'd all be dead."

"Runner? What's that?" He looked in a few directions.

"The Runner, the infected that just…" I looked at him, he was oblivious, "Tom, you've seen Runners before right?"

"What Runner? What's a Runner?"

Boom. If there ever was a God, and believe me I've thought about that a lot in the past year, even more than when I was in prison, then he had just targeted a nuclear missile on my nuts. My head actually hurt for a split second as I yet again processed something that shouldn't ever be processed.

I looked hard at him and asked in a very quiet voice, "Tom, you've never seen an infected that runs?"

He harrumphed. "Hilarious."

Triple fuck.

"Tom, this is no joke…"

He raised his eyebrows in that, *Look pal, I know you're bullshitting me* expression.

"So the dead can run too?"

"They aren't dead. Infected with whatever shit this is," I waved my hand across the parking lot, "but for whatever reason, they didn't die. Extremely resilient to pain, and don't give a shit about personal safety…or hygiene, but alive."

He still looked skeptical.

"Alright, have you ever seen a living person stand in a swarm like that, not only not getting eaten, but taking bites out of a zombie?"

He looked at the Runner, "He's dead. Just like the rest."

"Tom, why the hell would I… You know what? Forget it. If you see someone that just doesn't look right, or if somebody looks feverish and twitchy, or for fuck's sake if they scream all weird and loud, just run. Trust me when I say something will be chasing you."

He nodded smiling, "Sure, pal."

Idiot. Didn't have an issue with dead people walking, but running was out of the question. Suddenly, I didn't want Tom as my partner and guide, but I was committed now.

The front parking lot was as full of zombies as Tom was full of shit. The southern side barely had any though. The plan was to take the fire escape down from the roof of the barbershop/sewing supply business to the south, and traverse behind the little hill with the statue on it, bringing us right up to the ambulance parking area. Tom assured me there was a door there, and it would be open. He also assured me that the stairs to the morgue and his trapped cowboy buddies were twenty feet inside that ambulance bay.

He would not assure me that inside that door was a considerable lack of the living dead. It had been my experience that whenever you don't see zombies, zombies are everywhere. Oh, that and there's *always* a zombie in the bathroom.

Before any of that, we had to get to the Richie's Records across the wide street. There were no zombies that I could see in the road, but as I just mentioned, that's when I get really nervous. The music store had what we needed for a diversion.

We climbed down a fire ladder from the building we were on, and made our way across the street. The front window and door to our component shop were intact. I checked the top of the door for those annoying little bells that would announce our arrival, and finding none I opened said door. No stench of death of decay assaulted my olfactory senses, so I snapped my fingers once and waited.

Nothing came shuffling out of the darkness.

I held the door for Tom and he slipped inside, me following.

"You get some music, I'll get the batteries," he whispered and tried to mosey off.

I grabbed him. "I saw this movie. Everybody dies when they split up. We stick together. Don't move outside of a five foot range or we could end up eating each other later."

He blinked and nodded, wide-eyed, but most importantly he didn't move. I grabbed some D batteries, and Tom picked up a silver boom box that came straight out of a nineteen eighties break-dancing movie. I found a rack of CDs, and thought for a moment that the radio might only play cassette tapes if it were truly from the eighties. Bingo. It had a big old CD player right in the top.

"Put these in." I handed the batteries to Tom, and he ripped open the packages.

I started flipping through used CDs, shaking my head at the choices in the A section. Paula Abdul, Ace of Base, Air Supply. Air Supply? What kind of music shop was I in? Where in God's name was the AC/DC? Seriously.

"What are you doing?" Tom eyed the front window. "Just grab one and let's go!"

He grabbed the first disc in the first rack. Yup, you guessed it. ABBA.

He handed it to me and I almost puked. "Tom. There's a good chance we're going to get dead in a few minutes. I will not die to ABBA. Jesus, don't you hicks listen to anything good? This is the damn country! Where's all the country?" I came across something that had no right being with the rest of this shit: Aerosmith.

I held it up. "Now this? This is the shit." I used my knife to open the disc, because everyone on earth knows you can fight with your thumbnail trying to open a CD case and it will just smile and tell you to screw. I placed the disc case back on the rack. "Now we can go."

We got back to the ladder without seeing a single creature. I handed Tom the disc, but didn't let go right away. "Track number four, and crank that shit to eleven, buddy."

"It only goes to ten." He pointed at the knob.

Jesus, who are these people? "Ten then," I told him shaking my head. "Alright, get up the ladder, I'll turn it on." He climbed, and I tried to crank up the volume a little louder, but it wouldn't go. Of course I hadn't turned the damn thing on yet, I just wanted to see.

I put the boom box on the sidewalk and set the selector to CD. The blue light read number one, so I pressed skip three times and climbed up the ladder like a monkey with its ass on fire. I didn't get three rungs before the awesome sticks of Joey Kramer started beating the shit out of his drums. The song Walk This Way had begun, and it was LOUD. When I was halfway up the ladder, I turned to look down the street. At least thirty dead had decided to fight for the front row of this gig. Funny considering the musical choices in the record store.

I scuttled over the ledge, Tom helping me, and we stared down. The street was filling with undead. We moved two buildings over, and that might not sound like a lot, but it was probably almost an eighth of a mile when you considered the corner and the way the road was situated. Pus bags were stumbling past us down below, all headed for the concert.

"That, my friend, is a fucking diversion."

He nodded, smiling, and we made our way to the fire escape a few more buildings east. We belly crawled up to the edge and looked at the hospital parking lot. Sure enough, dozens of them were moving off toward the music. The Runner was gone too, but I didn't see him sprinting anywhere. When the coast was clear, we climbed down the iron ladder. We had to pass several inky black windows, which concealed God only knows, but nothing attempted to eat us.

Keeping low, and skulking between abandoned or crashed vehicles, it took us just under an hour to make that last quarter mile. The trip had been scary. I checked my watch and it was almost three AM. The sun would be up in two hours, compromising our stealth, but I didn't want to hurry for fear of making too much noise or being seen.

The caterwauling howl of a Runner froze my blood appropriately. That little shiver that most people say runs down your spine, but actually scrunches your balls (sorry ladies) hit me, and Tom looked absolutely terrified. I had no idea how he could have lived this long and not heard that scream. The scream had been close.

Tom looked like he was about to break radio silence, and I ran my finger over my own throat and then held it up to my lips in one of those desperate *Don't utter a sound!* gestures. He got it and kept his teeth together. No. Dear Reader, there was no radio, but that sounded great didn't it?

We were hunkered down next to an ambulance with open back doors. I peeked under it to make sure no feet were on the other side, or crawlers were down there. What I did see was the giant sexy rear tires of my MRAP. It was backed up to the ambulance bay, and it too had the back door open.

That royally pissed me off.

Morons brought my truck into a dangerous situation, and then left it completely vulnerable. It was no great wonder that these assholes were trapped.

I didn't have tons of time to remain angry because those feet I was looking for a moment ago shuffled into view. They were wearing cowboy boots, but that was no surprise, we were in shit-kicker country. The boots moved toward the back of the ambulance, and I pulled my SOG from the shoulder sheath once again. The thing moved past the end of the bus (that's what paramedics and EMTs call an ambulance, and I think it is just as cool as radio silence), and stopped, sort of looking about.

It didn't look in our direction though, and I crept up behind it and tapped it on the shoulder. It turned slowly to see what had touched it, and before it could moan, I drove the point of my blade into its eye.

This corpse was fresh, still dripping. It had been savaged, and most of its important morsels had been removed, although it still had its arms and legs. With my knife in its eye, the thing grabbed me and made a noise like *raaaaahhhh...* before its remaining eye rolled back in its skull and it collapsed. The sound it had made was more or less quiet, and we hadn't attracted any other critters. I was hoping most of them were listening to Aerosmith a few streets over.

I heard Tom sigh. "Jesus, Jimmy..." he said under his breath.

"Was this one of the guys that came in with Sabotino?"

Tom nodded. It had gone bad for this guy, but I also understood the need for the supplies they came for. We wouldn't disappoint.

Tom and I moved around the front of the bus, and I looked at my truck in all her beautiful glory. I stepped up on the passenger's runner and looked in the window. Nothing was amiss. Moving to the back I could see that the MRAP was empty, devoid of living or dead. I climbed in and made sure both the passenger and driver's side doors were unlocked, then hopped out the back and looked into the forebodingly dark maw of the ambulance bay doors. Both doors were propped open, one with a big trash receptacle, and the other with a corpse. I couldn't see five feet in with the darkness though.

Decision time: Turn on my tac light for a moment and shine it in there, illuminating the zillion or so shuffling corpses, and also telling them that dinner had arrived, or don't turn it on and go in blind.

Fuck that.

I turned it on for a moment and swept back and forth. Several corpses littered the area, but two steel interior doors twenty feet in were closed, and there was nothing else moving. I shut the light off and Tom pointed to a side door about ten feet past the exterior doors. This was the way down into the basement and the morgue. It was across the hall from an elevator which was undoubtedly used to bring deceased down to the basement. There were bullet marks in the concrete and brown arterial spray on the walls. Old brass littered the floor as well and a fluorescent light dangled broken from the ceiling. All of these things indicating a stand had been made here, but it hadn't been recent.

Scared shitless, I made my way inside the hospital and turned my light back on. My mouth was totally dry and my nuts were clenched. I was on edge, and Tom wasn't any better, looking every which way, pointing his shotgun at every possible location. I pushed the door open, and looked into the stairwell. More corpses. Three of them, and put down for good. Two landings down was another door, this one with a window. Tom and I crept down the steps, me turning my light off. I looked through the window, and I could see several shapes moving in the gloomy hallway, and there were lighted windows at the end of the hall.

I couldn't tell how many, but there were more than a couple, and they lurched and staggered. We were in the basement, a floor below the street, with a couple of doors between us and anything that could hear us. I was hoping if this went bad that nothing above would hear the shots down here. I pulled the suppressed Sig but it didn't have a light on it. I passed Tom the HK. "When I open the door, turn the light on and shine it at their faces. Don't shoot. If they start getting too close, or if I run out of ammo quickly, give me the rifle back and get ready to use your shotty." He swallowed hard and accepted the rifle. "You turn the light on here with this thumb switch." I indicated the pressure switch on the magwell grip. "You ready?" He nodded, looking terrified.

I pushed the door open, and the smell was pretty awful. The door hadn't made a sound, but the moment Tom hit the light, thirteen dead faces looked right at us. The moaning started, and so did the shooting. I dropped two before they moved. They came at us quickly then in the confined hallway and I took my time shooting. The suppressed rounds were loud in that hall, and my ears were ringing in just a second or two.

There were about fifteen left at thirty feet, and that math didn't work for me. Had I created zombies? I fired the Sig until it was empty and slid in another magazine. I fired that one empty too, but there were still plenty left. I'm not gonna lie and tell you every shot was a head shot, but I did pretty well. When the Sig's slide racked into the open position, I knew it was about to get louder.

Dutiful Tom passed me the HK and aimed his shotgun, but didn't fire. I chose the closest target, putting my red-dot on her forehead, and let the dead broad have it. Now *that* was loud. Way, way louder than the suppressed weapon. It sounded like a friggin grenade, and the sound bounced all around the corridor, instantly making my ears ring twice as loud.

Those dead bastards never made it within five feet. I dropped them all. Two more came from side rooms down the hall, and I ejected my magazine and shoved in a fresh one, yanking the charging handle and taking aim. Two shots later and the moans stopped. I could barely hear them anyway over the ringing, but I could tell they were done.

We moved down the hall, and I looked into the first open door: janitor's closet, and empty. Second door was closed, and the third door was an office in a complete shambles, but devoid of bad guys. I closed the door anyway, and Tom got the janitor's door.

The morgue was at the end of the hall, and it was all glass windows with that chicken wire embedded in it. There was also a light on in there and that didn't make sense. Heavy curtains covered all the windows from the inside, and I knew this is where Sabotino and his two guys were holed up if they were still alive. I could hear something moving around through the double doors at the end of the hall, but there's no way whatever it was hadn't heard the shots and the moaning, so it was either incapacitated or blocked from getting into the hallway.

I shined the light back and forth down the corridor, but nothing more was coming for us. That didn't mean that there weren't eight thousand ambulatory corpses bearing down on us from upstairs though.

I looked at the curtains again. If the boys were in here, those curtains had saved their lives. The twenty-five or so undead that I had re-killed might have overwhelmed the living men had they tried an escape. Granted there were three cowboys and only one of me, so if I could do it alone then the shit-kickers should be able to do it too.

I asked Tom if he would be kind enough to click the radio twice, wait, then twice more, signaling Sabotino that we were outside the door. He did, and we received four clicks in response. I knocked on the morgue door, and I heard something heavy being moved out of the way behind it. The door opened a crack and someone I didn't know looked out at me. He let loose with an audible sigh, and opened the door to allow us in, shutting it immediately after. "Heard you shooting."

The light was a camping lantern, and I almost laughed at that. These dumbasses were lucky the dead hadn't wanted to investigate the light, but if it had been on when the zombies got down here, I get why they didn't smash the windows in. The mortuary looked like any one you would picture, with the steel fridge doors to store horizontal chilled corpses against the wall, a couple of examination or autopsy tables, file cabinets, a desk, stainless steel sinks, and coroners tools.

Sabotino and his two remaining stooges did indeed have seven bags full of pilfered medical shit, but on their best day, they wouldn't be able to carry it all out in one trip. I wondered how they got it all down here, but I didn't want to spend the time to ask. Stooge Number Three was on one of the tables, very dead. "He got bit," said Stooge Number One. "Zero tolerance policy. I had to shoot him."

The sheriff put down his beautiful lever action rifle and stuck his hand out. "Thanks for coming," he said to me.

I shook his meaty paw. "It was my pleasure, but I'm driving us out of here. That, of course, assumes the entire ambulance bay isn't full of them by now."

He nodded, and I wanted to get this show on the road, so I shouldered a duffle and made to leave. The other guys did the same, and we all moved back out and up the stairs as quietly as possible. We didn't encounter anything scary all the way to the MRAP, and we loaded the stuff. Tom was getting in the passenger's side door when he somehow shut the door on his fingers. I heard them crack, it was gross, but to Tom's credit, he didn't make a damn sound. I would have screamed my head off at the pain.

I looked at his hand, but I couldn't do anything right then. We would have to button up first. "Alright, let's get the hell out of here; we'll fix your hand up in a minute."

The sheriff looked at me. "We need those last two duffels."

"Are you out of your fucking mind? We need to get as far from this place as we can, and now's the time, the dead are all a few streets over listening to a concert." I thumbed in the general direction of the tunes.

"Those bags have some critical supplies like drugs and bandages. We lost two men getting them, I won't have them die for nothing."

"Fine, go get them."

The stooge that opened the door folded his arms. "I ain't goin' back in there."

"Yeah, that's not happening," the other guy said.

"Then I'll have to make two trips."

"Oh for Christ's sake! You and me then!"

He looked at me and grinned. "You're a big damn hero, son."

I hopped out of the truck, and Stooge Number One took the driver's seat. The back hatch was open and stooge number two would close it if anything got close, "Tom, use some of this shit to wrap your hand while we're in there. We'll be back in five minutes."

Not waiting for an answer, the sheriff and I went back into the hospital. We went down the stairs, into the morgue and I shouldered one of the last two duffels.

"I'm sorry, son."

"Sorry about wha…" I turned around and the sheriff had that gorgeous lever action pointed at me. "What the hell are you doing?" My hands were on the duffel, and there was no way I could get to the HK on its single point sling before he drilled me.

"Son, my town needs your truck. That thing is the perfect vehicle to keep doing these runs. We screwed up this time, but it won't happen again. I'm really sorry, but nobody would understand me appropriating it from you, especially after you came in here to get us."

"You son of a bitch! This is why you asked for me to come? So you could kill me?"

He nodded and looked truly sad. I would have felt bad for him if it were his dog he was putting down instead of me. He was still a sanctimonious prick though.

He raised the rifle, thumbing back the double action hammer, and I put up my hand, backing toward the door, "Wait, don't!"

Click.

We both looked at his gun. He levered it, but no shell came flying out.

Click.

"Shit."

I dropped the duffel and grabbed the HK. "Mine isn't empty mother fu—" Rotten hands pushed through the door and grabbed me. They didn't pull me toward them, but them toward me. The thing was on me quickly, and sank its nasty teeth into my shoulder. It got the pad under my sling, and pulled back, pinching me. I gave it an elbow, flipping it around, and shot it in the face. Before I could do anything else, the sheriff was on me throwing haymakers. He caught me in the jaw then yanked my weapon forward. He was trying to turn it around and shoot me while it was still slung around my neck.

I brought a knee up and knocked it away from him, but he threw another punch and stunned me. He got behind me and looped his substantial forearm around my windpipe and suddenly it was damned hard to breathe. I couldn't bring the HK to bear, and he was moving me around trying to choke me out or break my neck, so I couldn't get my Sig. I also couldn't reach my knife because his forearm was on it, digging it into my collar bone. I punched upward with both hands into his arm, and his grip slipped a little, his arm coming over my mouth.

So I bit down for all I was worth.

He took it like a man for half a second, but then the pain overtook his senses and he tried to push me away. He succeeded, but not before I took a wicked chunk out of his arm. Then I pushed him away and pointed my rifle at him.

"You…you bit me?"

I spit out the piece of him and wiped his blood off my mouth. "Fuck you!" I raised my rifle, and Stooge Number One picked that moment to burst through the door. Confused, he saw me pointing a gun at his wounded sheriff, so he pointed his exceptionally large hunting rifle at me.

"Thank God, Nathan, this guy was trying to kill…"

I pointed at the sheriff. "He's bitten! That thing got him." I pointed at the corpse on the floor. "Look at his arm!"

Stooge Number One, also known as Nathan, took a comical look at his sheriff's boo-boo, and shifted his aim toward Sabotino's noggin.

"NATHAN! WAI—"

Nathan's gun did not go *click*. It went *boom*.

His sheriff, missing most of the top of his head, collapsed.

Nathan picked up Sabotino's rifle and shouldered one of the duffels. "Zero tolerance policy."

BYE

"He was gonna shoot ya?" It had sounded like *shootcha*.

"Yeah."

"For the truck?"

"Yeah."

"So ya bit 'im?"

"I did, yeah."

"That was quick thinking," Tim said.

Eleanor and Clara were looking at each other funny, and I thought right then that it may not have been the best plan to tell the rest of my group of five what had transpired in the basement of Northern Montana Hospital.

Clara looked up. "The sheriff would have done anything to protect this town. I don't think murder is acceptable though, no matter how many he thought he could have saved." She took my hand in hers. "I'm sorry."

"Me too," I said, gripping her hand tightly, "but it was me or him, and I like me better. I'm not a murderer, but I've had to protect me and mine since this started, and while I'm very sorry the sheriff had to die, I'm not sorry I'm alive because of it."

"So what happened next?" Eleanor asked. I had her attention, and I liked it.

After Nathan, AKA Stooge Number one, had put a round through Sabotino's dome, he and I grabbed the last two duffels and quickly got back to the MRAP. There were no dead in sight. We chucked the bags in the back and climbed in.

Nathan sat down on one of the seats and looked at me. "I couldn't let you guys go back in alone. I had to come." He looked down.

"I'm glad you did."

Stooge Number Two looked back at the two of us "Where's…" was all he got out before he stopped himself.

Suddenly big, fat tears were dropping from Nathan's face to the deck of the MRAP. "I shot the sheriff…"

Oh shit, all I could think of was Bob Marley. "He was infected. He would have hidden the bite and turned when inside the walls. He probably would have killed some people, and who knows how far it might have spread."

"How do I start this thing," demanded Stooge Number Two looking for a key hole.

I was rummaging around in the MRAP supplies looking for a bandage for Tom's hand, when I just grabbed a newly appropriated duffel and opened it. Boom. Gauze bandages and medical tape right there on the top. "You don't. I'm driving. You're gonna take this," I handed him the bandages, "and take care of Tom's mitt."

The guy nodded and took the stuff. Tom and Number Two moved into the back of the truck with Nathan, and I sat in the driver's seat. I turned the switch from ENG OFF to START, and my baby started right up. The switch flicked back to RUN of its own volition, and the MRAP's diesel belched black smoke.

Fifty or sixty feet away, a few pus bags moved into sight, curious at the sound of the truck. It was time to GTFO. I threw the gear shift into drive and we moved forward. We made maybe twenty feet when something impacted the passenger's side door and window. A Runner had launched itself at us. It hung on to the mirror, screaming and smashing at the steel louvers over the bullet-resistant glass with its left fist.

All three of the guys in the truck asked, "What was that?" in varying degrees of shocked fear at the same time.

"That, boys, is a Runner. And before you say you don't believe me, look out the back in a sec. Hang on to something." When I could see that they were secure, I jammed on the brakes. We had been travelling at maybe fifteen miles per hour, but that was enough to send the Runner flying forward off the truck. He bounced away and got up immediately, with significant amounts of his skin on the road.

Apparently neither he nor I gave a shit about his scrapes because I accelerated away, and he sprinted after us. Stooge Two stood up and looked out the double back windows. These were not louvered, but were like two windows stacked on top of each other, like a double pane with eight inches between them, and they stuck off the back of the truck maybe a foot.

"Hey! Hey there's a guy back there! He's running after us, we need to stop for him!"

Jesus. I mean, are you kidding me with this shit?

"He's infected, God damn it!"

"But he's running!"

"Because he's a fucking Runner!" All three of them looked at me like I had just shit diamonds. "Christ in a sidecar!" I slowed the truck down and stopped. "Do not open that door or we're all dead!" I put the truck in park and moved into the back. Stooge Two looked like he might open the door anyway, so I drew the suppressed Sig. I didn't point it at him, but I called to him, "Hey." I had said it quietly, but he got my meaning and looked back at me. Then, comically, all three of them looked down at the gun at the same time.

"What's your name?" I asked Stooge Two.

He swallowed, his eyes still on the pistol. "Mark."

"Mark, I will shoot you if you try to open that door."

"But that guy…"

"That guy will rip into you and turn you into one of them," I used the barrel extension on the Sig to point out the window, "and then where will you be?"

During the fifteen seconds it had taken for me to speak to this trio of morons, the Runner had caught up with us and impacted the rear of the vehicle with a dull thud. Stooge Two AKA Mark, turned and looked out the rear window. Then he shot backwards and landed on his ass. "Holy shit!" He looked at me, his face a rictus of stark terror.

"You two," obviously I was talking to Nathan and Tom, "look out the window."

They stood and did as they were told, Tom cradling his injured paw. The Runner had been a younger guy, but his anatomy was the only thing that was remotely human. His humanity was gone. Stolen, or eaten away by whatever shit was coursing through him. He was now just a shell for the red-eyed, slavering thing that was breaking its knuckles open trying to get in the truck. Remorseless and without mercy, all it was capable of was hatred, perpetrating horror, and spreading infection.

Wide, bloody eyes and a shaky, feverish look greeted the two humans staring with shock, revulsion, and not a little sadness at this creature. The thing broke its teeth as is smashed its face over and over into the window in an attempt to get at us. Infected blood smeared the glass.

Tom stared, and I saw his posture change a little. "Oh God, that's Al. It's Al Merrin."

Nathan looked too. "It is. It *is* Al."

"Was."

They all looked at me. "It *was* your friend. Now that thing is wearing him like a cheap suit. Everything that was your friend is gone, and the moment you show that thing pity, or anything but the business end of your gun, you're dead."

I turned around and got back in the driver's seat. All three of them looked out the back as we drove away, the thing that had been Al Merrin chasing us.

We took a route east out of eastern Havre, and looped around south and then west, and finally east again on Route 2. Yeah, a big circle. It was interesting that there were hardly any infected once we got outside the city. Inside the city it got dicey a couple of times, but I was never really scared. We had seen hundreds, maybe thousands during the trip through the plague-ridden side of Havre, but once we got past them and out into the flat lands, we saw two. An adult female and a dead little boy. They were walking together, and I hoped they were mother and son with some semblance of memory of each other. At least they were together even in death.

I might have mentioned this a couple of times, but seeing dead kids walk sucks. Kids represent our future and hope and good shit like that. To see them stumbling around dead and infected is horrible. Takes the wind out of my sails so to speak, and once I saw the kid, all conversation stopped.

Tom called in to the gate that we were coming, and they opened for us when we got there two hours after sunup. The gate folks had already heard about the sheriff, and to my eternal shame, they all congratulated and thanked me for saving two of the five stooges and getting the meds. Mark and Nathan thanked us too, and we all loaded the duffels onto a horse cart to be carried to the doc. Tom showed me how to get back to Clara's house, and then he went to see the doc as well to get his hand looked at. He told me he would get the fuel cans I was promised ready, and maybe some other sundries as well.

"And that's that." I finished.

Eleanor looked up. "So what now?"

"I'm leaving. Tim, I'm hoping you come with me, but you're welcome to make a home here if they'll have you."

"I'm coming with *you*," he said immediately.

Eleanor stood. "Me too. I have a ton of supplies we can take, and even some ammunition."

"I got nuthin'," the big guy interjected, "but I sure would like a ride a lil ways west. Clara too if she's comin'."

"I'm coming."

"Fair enough, there's room. But," I waited for everybody to look at me, "you haven't been out there, Dallas and I have. Once we leave, there's no coming back. I won't even entertain the notion of it."

Eleanor looked scared. "How bad is it really?

"Bad," both Dallas and I answered at the same time. We gave sideways glances to each other. "Those things are everywhere. I mean it too, *everywhere*."

"I used to pull up satellite scans of the cities," Tim added. "New York, Phoenix, Chicago. So full of the dead you couldn't see the streets. London, Mexico City, Paris, Perth, Delhi, all gone. Swarming with the dead. When I pulled up scans of open highways in Nevada, there were dead there. The bottom of the Grand Canyon, and the top of the Space Needle are full of dead. But I never really understood until they got into Baldy. It happened so *fast*, then everybody was gone, and they were everywhere."

"And that was just an installation of a few hundred. Imagine a town of twenty thousand, or a city of a million."

"I need to see my husband," Clara said, "I'm going."

Eleanor looked around sadly. "There's nothing here for me anymore, and winter is coming. The cold will kill at least a few on this side of the wall and I don't want to be here when that happens."

I nodded. "I understand, and I'm not trying to talk anybody out of coming, but I promise you, this place is pretty good compared with what's out there."

Everybody who wasn't standing stood.

"Alright then, we leave at first light." I had always wanted to say that, and it was epic.

"Tomorrow?"

"Yeah. Pack your stuff. I need to find Tom. He said he was going to the doc. Who can tell me how to get there?"

"I'll take you," Eleanor chimed. "I might need help packing some things anyway and my house is near the clinic. I really do have a lot of supplies." She smiled and it was a little slice of heaven.

We left for the doc's, everybody starting to bustle.

We took my MRAP, and we were almost at the doctor's place when I popped the question, "Eleanor, have you ever seen a Runner?"

"I'm sorry, what?"

"Have you seen a Runner, an infected that runs?"

She turned and looked at me horrified, "Oh my God, they can run now?"

"They've always been able to run. Well, not exactly... The ones that run aren't dead. They're infected, and will try to kill you, but you can kill them. The thing is, they'll be back up as one of the ones you've seen in a matter of moments sometimes."

She nodded slowly. "No. No I haven't seen or heard about them."

She looked scared. "Have you seen one?"

We kept driving. "Yeah. Yeah they're scary, but they tend to work alone instead of in groups like the dead ones."

"Which is worse?"

The clinic came into sight, and I could see a few guys moving some red jerry cans off of a horse-drawn cart. "Both are terrifying. Either can kill you. I guess I don't like any of them."

We reached the doc's place and got out of the truck. Two of the guys that were hauling my diesel shook my hand and thanked me for saving their buddies. I felt good, and that scared me. I was a magnet for doom and pretty much everywhere I had been in the past year had been attacked by the dead while I was getting comfortable. I wanted to get the duck out of Fodge, or in this case Havre, before this place became just another overrun haven for the undead. I didn't want to bring disaster to this place; they were doing well.

The two dudes and I loaded nine diesel cans of varying size onto the MRAP. It got to the point where I had to use a chain through the handles of the jugs to secure them to the side of the truck. Eleanor and I strolled into the clinic, and we saw Tom with a freshly bandaged hand.

He saw us and smiled. "Hey."

Tom was a disbelieving dumbass, but I liked him. He had gone over the wall to try to save his friends and get meds for sick kids. That was aces in my book, even if his sheriff buddy was an almost-murderer.

"Hey yourself, how's the paw?"

"Doc said I busted a couple of meta-somethings. My fingers are OK, but the hand is broke."

"Tom, you're so damned tough, I expect you to shrug this shit off and get back to work by morning." I reached out my hand to shake his, but I realized that his shaking had was the injured one. We both chuckled, and I nodded and said good-bye.

"Good luck," he said.

"You too, buddy."

The lovely Eleanor and I got back in my truck and she showed me where she lived. It was a quaint little ranch-style house, nice. We went in and it was nice inside too. She brought me through the kitchen and into a garage-turned-larder and I almost shit myself. She hadn't been kidding when she said she had tons of stuff. Lots of food, some of it in a few glass soda machines, lights off, but I could tell they were cool from the frost on the glass.

She deciphered my raised brows and vacant expression. "Solar power."

We packed several large boxes full of all kinds of food items, both perishable and not, but there was so much we had to leave most of it behind. "My waitress Stella is going to take over Havre House." She looked around. "I can't wait to get out of here."

So that's what we did. We picked up the others, a few more supplies from Clara, and one more mouth to feed; a giant bloodhound by the name of Clyde.

Clara and Eleanor said good-byes to folks around town, but it didn't take long, and in another hour and a half we were at the western gate. Three gunshots later, the bus was moving forward. Only three dead had been near the gate, but a huge, still-smoldering pile of corpses, with a greasy steam coming off of them was fifty yards outside of town. These must have been the zombies that had followed us down the road when we first got to Havre.

Tom, Nathan, and Mark were waiting at the gate for us, and for a moment I got nervous as they were all armed to the teeth. I thought, perhaps, that they too envisioned my truck as their property. They only wanted to say good bye though. Stella, Eleanor's friend, was there too, and both she and Eleanor began to cry. Soon half the town showed up as the gate was opening to wave to us as we drove out. I got about a hundred and fifty yards away from the gate, and I stopped, looking back in the side mirror. "Huh."

"Havin' second thoughts 'bout leavin' there, Pard?"

"Nope. I'm waiting for the inevitable wave of zombies to begin to tear into Havre and kill everyone. This time I'm going back if it happens and I'm gonna kill every damn zombie first." I heard sharp intakes of breath from the ladies, and I realized what I had just said. "Look, I'm sorry, it's just that Lady Luck has left the building when it comes to me and the undead. Most places I visit are overrun while I'm visiting."

Clara stood and looked back out the rear windows. "Well I'm glad we left then."

I shot the back of her head a glance, not knowing if she was serious or kidding. I realized it didn't matter and stepped on the accelerator. Havre disappeared in the side-view as we moved west down Route Two.

TIME TO GET YOUR GEEK ON

All I can say about today is *holy shit*. Less than one day on the road, and we get in it deep. I mean, *deep*, like bottom of the ocean, whale shit deep. I've mentioned that things can fall apart in seconds, and they can. They do.

We took Route Two west for a bit, then eighty-seven south quite a while. I saw sixteen abandoned vehicles in four hours, nobody was around, living or dead. I blinked, and realized my eyes were burning. I hadn't slept since I crashed in Clara's spare bedroom back in Havre, and that was before I engaged in legendary heroics that could quite possibly elevate me past Achilles or Hercules or even Bruce Willis in awesome status. Now I was just plumb tired. Yeah, I just wrote that. *Plumb tired*. I sound like Dallas. Whatever, forgive me if I ramble, I had a bad day.

I stopped the MRAP in the middle of nowhere, in the center of the road. According to our map, which was the map that Tim had traded to Eleanor for some food, we were about ten miles north of the city of Great Falls Montana. Yeah, I said city. Havre had a population of about ten thousand. Great Falls was eighty thousand. Screw that noise. We couldn't safely get through Great Falls, even with the MRAP. Plus, at some point we would have to cross the Missouri River.

There are several very important things I had learned during the zombie apocalypse. One of them, and this is a biggie: Stay the F away from bridges. Unless there is no other option, you go around. Bridges are either jam-packed with abandoned vehicles, which means shitloads of infected, or they just aren't there. The military blew them up early on to stem the tide of infection. You could get trapped on bridges, and zombies seemed to like them. I don't know if they just liked the feel of a bridge, or if they somehow knew that food would come to them if they hung around, or maybe just stayed where they were when they died.

None of that shit matters. What does matter is that bridges suck. We planned a route that would take us along the river and we would move steadily south west until we hit the mountains. That was something else: there were more friggin state parks around here than living people. A couple zillion square miles of state park, and that would mean little interaction with the living or the dead.

Or so we had thought.

Growing up in the northeast, I had a different understanding of roads than the folks out west. A highway was something with a ton of cars on it all travelling at sixty miles per hour, and there was no real way off the road other than an off ramp. An interstate was worse for both congestion and exits. Both were elevated for runoff from precipitation.

In Montana, at least the part of Montana near Great Falls, if you wanted off the highway, you took a right or a left anywhere and you were driving on dirt, or maybe a secondary road. Few trees, few houses, and fewer neighborhoods.

We started seeing our first signs of infection and destruction at that ten mile mark I mentioned a few paragraphs ago. When I stopped to look at the map, we were just outside a destroyed neighborhood. Most of it had burned to the ground, but there were quite a few infected roaming the ruins, and they were all headed in our direction. We collectively decided to keep moving, and turned west on West Portage Road. A dinky little paved thing that was almost a road. In fifteen minutes, we were at the gates of something called Benton Lake National Wildlife Refuge. I say gates, but it was a sign with a bird on it.

We soldiered on, and soon were surrounded by some gorges and marshes and a whole lot of nothing else. There was supposed to be a lake further north, but that was out of our way. The place was pretty, and soon we came across a red structure with white trim. We were not the first people there.

The circus was in town.

Three eighteen wheelers and a dozen other vehicles, some with small amusement rides strapped to them, some with empty animal cages, and some regular pickup trucks sat quietly in the parking lot. All had *Harrod Shows* logos and were parked in varying locations throughout the lot. OK, so it was more a carnival than a circus, but the bottom line was that in either venue, you have one thing in common: Carnies.

I must profess to always liking the idea of carnies. To have no real ties and move around a lot appealed to me. I never had the balls to pull the trigger on joining, and in retrospect it might have kept me out of prison, but either way we were about to meet a bunch of circus folk. Hopefully they wouldn't want to eat us.

I didn't want to shoot anybody, and I really didn't want to get shot, so we stayed put for a moment.

Nobody came, living or dead.

OK, so maybe I would have to step foot outside the MRAP. Dumb right? But I had to take a piss, and I wasn't alone.

"OK folks, here's the skinny. I need to use the facilities. Anybody else?"

Four hands shot skyward, and I realized we all needed to stretch our legs. We were a good distance away from the vehicles, and further away from the structure, so I shut the engine off. "Nobody goes anywhere alone," I looked at Tim, "not even for a second. Ladies, I realize you have to pee too, and one of us strapping young lads will accompany you, but we won't peek, I promise."

Clara looked at the red building. "You mean we aren't going inside?"

"Inside there," I asked pointing, "no friggin way. You do whatever you need out here behind our truck. Like I said, we won't look, but there's no way we're going in that building with all these vehicles out here." Clara started to protest, but I held a hand up forestalling her. "Clara, think about it; either those people are in there alive, and they are looking at us right now with who knows what intentions, or they are all dead and we know their intentions. We gotta stay out here and we gotta stay together."

She nodded. "You're right, of course. I'm sorry."

"No apologies necessary. When you came with us, you became my responsibility. The likelihood is that we're all going to die out here someplace, but I'll try to prevent that as long as possible."

"Dallas, would you kindly escort the ladies to the bathroom? That would be the ground to the rear of the truck. Keep the door open. Any trouble, and you can fire a shot, or get back in the truck and make some noise."

"I got it, Pard. Where are you goin?"

"Tim and I are going to check the vehicles."

Tim looked dumbfounded. "We are?"

"Yeah. I want to see if there's anyone here."

"But you just said—"

"I know. Still not going inside, but I need to see something. Tim, make sure you're going in weapons hot." *Damn* I sounded cool. I wasn't entirely sure what weapons hot actually meant, but I assumed it meant loaded with safeties off. *Weapons hot* sounded way cooler. I mean say it. Right now say it out loud. Cool right?

Tim and I moved to the nearest truck. It was a blue Dodge Ram 2500. It had been towing a bunch of what looked like rolled up tents on a trailer. The truck was locked up tight, and there was dust on the windshield, but all four tires were inflated. I had no idea if this thing pulled into the lot today or a year ago.

"Cover me," (Again, wicked cool) I said and unzipped. When I was done, Tim did his thing, and we moved on.

The next vehicle was a big International. Behind it was a huge empty animal cage. A couple more pickups, and an eighteen wheeler later, and I realized that everything was locked. I was getting an eerie feeling, and had decided to bug out, when psychic Tim told me he didn't like it here.

"I'm with you buddy, let's go."

I heard Clyde going absolutely ape shit, barking and doing that howling bay that he does, and Tim and I looked at each other worried.

We got two thirds of the way back to the truck when we heard the first BOOM! from a shotgun. We got to the truck before the second one went off, and rounded the corner as Dallas was closing the door. There wasn't a zombie in sight. We looked in all directions, but the only thing we saw was the tall marsh grass. It looked like a wheat field right up to the road. I scanned a second time, and was greeted with nothing but the swaying of the marsh in the breeze.

I went left and Tim came with me. My intention was to get back into the truck and ask Dallas what the hell he had been shooting at.

At that point, several things happened at once. The MRAP started, Tim had time for one of those sharp intakes of breath, and something exploded from the grass to the right. Whatever it was hadn't made a sound, but it hit us like a hammer. I went flying and the thing was on top of Tim.

Now it was making noise. Not the moaning of a shambling pus bag. Not that inhuman shriek of a Runner. It was making the deep guttural growl of a friggin' lion. In the half second it took me to process that we were being attacked by lions, Tim started screaming.

The thing had his arm in its mouth and was backing up, trying to drag him into the grass. Blood was streaming down my friend's arm and he was fighting like a…well…like a tiger. Punching the cat in the face and kicking for all he was worth. The lion was winning.

Not wanting to hit the human, I fired my HK into the air, and the thing looked at me but didn't let go of Tim's arm. I had to shoot it. I had to. I know it isn't fair, and if the Humane Society was still around you would report me, and you are calling me awful names right now, but this thing was going to eat my buddy.

Three black holes stitched across the side of this skinny creature, and it howled in pain letting go of my friend. It limped back into the grass leaving a trail of blood on the stalks.

Did I feel like shit for killing that cat?

Nope.

Did Tim feel like shit with his arm flayed? Damn skippy. I ran over to him, and Dallas opened the back of the MRAP, big shotgun out in front. "We dint see you fellas! Heard the yellin' and I come out to see if that damn lion was still around!" Dallas noticed all the blood, and me looking at Tim's arm, and he did something rare. He swore. "Aww shit…"

He saw me dragging Tim over to the back of the truck. "Lemme help ya, Hoss." He started to get out of the truck.

"No! Cover us, I've got him."

Tim stood, gritting his teeth, and I got a good look at his arm. The skin was pulled down in a band around his bicep, and I could see deep puncture marks in the red of the exposed muscle as it bulged out of the bloody wound. Blood streamed down his arm and saturated his jeans. The poor guy didn't have big arms, and I don't know if that was a good thing or bad, but he was looking poorly. I got him to the truck and Dallas pulled him in, me following. I slammed the door and then began rummaging through the small cabinet thingies on the sides of the MRAP looking for something to help him. I found gauze and stitches (they were called sutures on the label) and a curved needle. There was also some hydrogen peroxide and some green packets with KWIK CLOT on the side.

"Tim, there's no drugs."

He looked at me, but he was fading into unconsciousness. "I gotta clean this and sew you up, buddy." We got him on one of the cots, and I went to work. Or I tried anyway. I put some peroxide on a gauze pad and pressed it against the wound. I thought he would go bonkers and start screaming in pain, but he had passed out.

"What are you doing?" demanded Clara. "Give me that!"

She took the stuff from me and began to clean his wound with water from a squirt bottle and a cloth. Clara actually lifted up the torn flaps of skin and rinsed his muscle. She was making faces and they weren't nice ones. In fifteen minutes, she had him cleaned and was finishing stitching him up. I was amazed. The bleeding had totally stopped, and his pallor was better already. Clara put the back of her hand on his forehead.

"Good."

"What?" I asked, "No fever?"

She looked at me like I was a moron. "No, I was making sure he wasn't cold from either blood loss or shock. He seems to be OK. We'll need some antibiotics and pain killers though for sure." She moved her fingers up and down his limb. "His arm doesn't feel broken."

All four of us were looking for the drugs when Clyde sat up looking around. We all looked at him, expecting him to start growling or something, but all he did was let loose with a tremendous fart.

It was atrocious. Given the choice between that eye-watering dog-gas or lions, I bordered on opening the door. The big bastard lie back down and put his chin on his paws, and I swear to Christ he smiled.

We came up empty on the drugs. Tim was in for a painful night, and who knows what that lion had been eating lately, so I did what any prudent plague survivor would do; I tied him to the cot. This lion bite could be as serious as a bite from an infected if the lion had been gnawing on zombies. Time would tell.

I had wanted to see what the circus trucks had in store for us, and I guess I found out. Stupid. Just stupid. I glanced back and saw Eleanor cleaning Tim's blood off of the floor of the MRAP then threw the truck into gear, pissed at myself.

We travelled west, and in about five minutes I saw entrances for Interstate Fifteen. We drove under the elevated interstate and kept moving west, entering small neighborhoods. All of the street names were numbers, like 4th Rd NE or 7th Rd SE and the neighborhoods were set up like perfectly square city blocks. Other than the overgrown lawns and lack of home maintenance, the only thing out of place here seemed to be the occasional shambler. I saw the name Choteau a few times and figured out that was the name of this small town.

Tim woke up in extreme pain when I juked around an overturned baby carriage that came out of nowhere in the middle of the road. He wasn't happy, and gritted his teeth when he told Clara he was fine. Tim's a friggin' bona fide hero.

The first signs of destruction leapt out at us around the next corner. A mail truck had been hit by a pickup and they had both burned, as had the house on the corner. Three big cement walls surrounding boxy front yards held the vehicle corpses tight, and I was unsure if the MRAP could make it through without damage. I turned the truck around, but then I saw a red S on a white store in my side view. It was a CVS. A drug store. I circled the area, moving up some streets and down others, but it seems this part of town was where a lot of fighting had occurred, and every route to the store was blocked.

Reader, old buddy, you've made it this far, so you and I both know what had to be done. I parked the truck near a pretty ranch style house with a broken bow window. I couldn't see the CVS, but I knew it was only a couple of blocks away.

"What we stoppin' for, Pard?"

"There's a drug store up the road a little." I looked at my shoes and sighed. "I'm going for some drugs for Tim."

Tim tried to sit up and realized he was tied down. "No! No you can't!"

"Got to, buddy. You're tore up pretty bad." Damn that had sounded like Dallas too, but it had come out of me. "The store looked untouched from what I could see and..." Dallas started checking his shotgun, and the shells in his bandolier. "Uhh, what are you doing, Dallas?"

"I'm comin'."

"Nope. Your wheel is still bad. You can hardly stand on it. You'll slow me down, just like you would have at the hospital."

"I'm fine, now we jus'—"

"You're *not* fine. You're fucked up. If I don't make it, you need to get Clara back to San Francisco, and before that, you need to get Tim some meds." I moved into the back of the cramped truck and stood next to him. He was sitting on some cases of food, and his head came up to mid chest on me. Guy is big. I reached out and gave his ankle a tap with my boot, and he hissed an intake of breath. "See?"

"That was uncalled for," he said through clenched teeth.

"Well here's the good part: if I get eaten, you get the truck. It's a damn pretty truck."

"It is."

"I'll be back in a half hour. If I'm not back in two hours, I'm not coming, so leave."

He stuck his paw out to me. "Good luck, Hoss."

"You too, bud, get her home safe and take care of Tim if I get dead."

"Please don't," Eleanor said and stood.

"Yes," Clara added, "we need you."

"That's why I'm doing this." I looked out the rear windows, but you really can't see straight down, so I moved up to the driver's side door and checked the area. There was nobody there, so I opened the door quickly, got out, and shut it again.

Nothing in sight was moving, but that didn't mean every house and car in the area wasn't teeming with pus bags. That thought got me moving, and I headed out toward the CVS.

Cats and ninjas had nothing on me. I was as quiet as the wind.

I was passing another of those concrete and brick yard dividers (yeah a wall), and it hit me that I couldn't die. I mean I *could* die, sure, but I really had to strive not to. OK, so *everybody* strives not to die, but I was special. Shit I sound full of myself, but you know what I mean. But you're also thinking that I could quite possibly be a huge part of stopping this damn plague in its tracks, and I was out here, alone, trying to save the life of one insignificant guy.

Well fuck you. Yeah, that's right, screw. Who are you to decide the fate of my friend? He has as much right to live as any of us, including you or me, and if I choose to risk my life for his, then it's my decision. And if I don't try to help, then what the hell are we all fighting for?

I had already been with umpteen doctors and they didn't find out shit. Lynch would have killed a million people if it would have protected me, but for what? A chance? Every one of those million people that would have been killed for me also deserves a chance.

I'm not him. I'm not Lynch, and I wouldn't kill anybody that didn't need killing either. I intend to live, but not at the expense of everybody else.

Unless those people are trying to kill me.

So, those thoughts all plowed through my noggin in a heartbeat, and they hadn't quelled my fear but for a fleeting moment. When I got my reality slap, I heard something moving on the other side of the wall. It didn't sound friendly, so I kept to my crouch and moved on.

It was weird that this section of the town looked like a warzone. Bullet casings littered the ground, a Hummer with the doors open and a fifty cal on the roof stood abandoned, and there were stains and bullet holes everywhere. But there wasn't a single body or pus bag in the vicinity. One of the damn infected must have been killed. At least one. They don't get back up if you shoot them in the dome, and humans certainly wouldn't have moved them in the middle of a firefight, so where were all the bodies?

I moved down the center of the road, between cars and a pock-marked fire truck, scanning for anything odd. I made it to the front doors of the CVS without incident, and put my hand above my eyes, pressing myself to the glass to peer inside.

Nothing looked amiss other than the store appeared to have been looted. Shit was on the floor, but I didn't see anything moving, so I pushed on the door. It was one of those automatic types that opened when you stepped on the pad, but the power was out, so it needed persuading. It opened quietly, and I stepped inside.

It was darker than what you would have seen pre-plague, but there were tons of windows, so they brightened the place a bit. One of the windows must have caught a stray bullet, the only thing left a few clear shards in the frame. The breeze blew some type of banner, making it sway, but other than that, I was the only thing moving.

I was still effing scared. If you're reading this, then at some point you have been out there, hopefully not alone, but out there avoiding them. Skulking in a place you shouldn't have to be skulking in, like a gas station or a convenience store trying to find some spam. You get it. You understand the feeling I had in that CVS.

I checked every aisle, and there wasn't a single infected. No bodies, no drag marks or directional spatter. No bullet holes that I could see either. Sure the place had been looted, but barely. It looked as if this place had been hit hard and fast, or with a specific goal.

I got to the back, where the pharmacy was, and it was just like in Havre. I pushed through the half door that separated the counter from where the patrons would be, cleared it, and looked through the shelves. There was a whole section for antibiotics, and I took everything that would fit in my bag. There wasn't a lot, but I got most of it.

I got to the pain killers and found tons. Oxycontin was a winner, as was Oxycodone. I took it all.

Then I left back the way I came, grabbing some OTC stuff like aspirin and Neosporin. I even had the foresight to grab a big tube of SPF 30 sunscreen. Easy-peasy. I got outside and left the door open, thinking I would never come back. I had an epiphany, and turned around going back inside. I grabbed a couple of boxes of stuff and put them in one of those red plastic hand-held shopping thingies, then made my way back to the doors, and then out. This time I closed them, I dunno why.

I began my skulk back towards the truck when I realized something had changed. All the cars had been about the same height when I went in, but now something was different. I turned and focused on that different and was a little surprised at what I saw. On top of a cranberry Toyota Camry crouched a man in rags. He was on his haunches, his ass almost touching the roof, his fists on the top of the car between his feet. He looked at me with one eye, as the other had a black patch over it, his head cocked a little to the side. I had seen this stance before. It was on a trailer in New Hampshire.

It was the first time I had experienced a Runner.

The man looked at me for a second longer then stood from his crouch, his head tilting a little more.

I did that sharp intake of breath that is repeated countless times in this text, and that was all the impetus the thing needed. Its eyes went wide and it let out that awful shriek. It propelled itself off the car and landed on all fours scrabbling. Up very fast, it sprinted at me. I had my pack full of stuff, and a red shopping thing full of more stuff.

Going hand to hand with this thing wasn't out of the question, but I had a bunch of shit with me. He was thirty feet away when I was finally able to get the Sig out and shoot him in the chest.

Silencer. Bullshit.

I'm going to find they guy who coined the term "silencer" and punch him in the friggin' nose if he isn't dead already. Shit is loud. More than that it *doesn't belong*, and that is what tipped off the pus bags. It echoed through the formerly soundless cars and houses. Or maybe it was the shriek from that Runner. That brings them too. The moaning started. That wet gurgling cry or the hacking scrape that they do. It shrinks my nuts when I'm by myself. Hell, it shrinks them when I'm in an armored convoy. There were a shitload of moans. A shitload.

When I had crept down the street a half an hour ago, I hadn't seen any of them, and they hadn't seen me or they would have been on me. Now they came from under vehicles, out of doors and windows, from between houses, from the back of the burned mail truck…they were everywhere.

Back the way I came was not an option. The road was thick with them and they were coming my way. I ran back to the CVS and got inside. There was nothing more than a cardboard sunglasses display to bar the door with, and all they had to do was push on it and it would open.

I ran to the back but before I got there, they were already inside, stumbling and smashing their way toward me. I ran by the drive through window, and noticed it was relatively clear of infected outside, but I couldn't fit through the receptacle, so I had to opt for the door that I had missed. Yeah, I know, I'm a dumbass. In my defense, it was painted the same color as the wall, and had an eye-chart on it. And I was scared shitless and just above panic mode.

It wouldn't open though. It had one of those push bars, but nope, not opening. I descended into panic, and was about to start futilely pounding on the door until I saw the little silver turn-lock. I turned it and ran out into the parking lot behind the store. They were out here too, but not nearly as many. I ran across the lot and into a big school playground, them on my tail, the mass of them maybe two hundred feet back.

The things were in front of me too, and they came from the other sides of the park stumbling across the pavement. They were everywhere, and I could see where this was going. I was trapped. I was going to die on a yellow hopscotch court. Had I not returned to the store I might have made it. More than that, the reason I had gone back into the store was for feminine hygiene products for the ladies.

Yup, I was gonna die for tampons.

It started to thunder, and I realized I was going to get eaten alone and wet. I had been hoping to go when I was a few years older, in the midst of banging the A-list celebrity actress of my choice, but that wasn't going to happen. I was about to be eviscerated by the nails and teeth of two hundred undead flesh-eaters. Hopefully the feminine goods would sop up some of my blood. I had a horrible image of me stumbling around as a zombie with maxi-pads permanently stuck all over me, but with this many of the dead, there wouldn't be much left to re-animate.

The thunder pitch had increased, and it now seemed to come from everywhere, like an earthquake. God had a funny way of sending me off, with his angels playing bass. The zombies were hearing the rumble as well, and not a few of them turned to look in all directions, but most were focused on me.

I was totally encircled, no way out, and they closed in. I hoped the folks in the truck would make it, they were all good people. Maybe Tim would go with them to San Francisco. That would be the smart choice. None of my friends at Atlantis would ever know what had really happened to me, and that made me sad. I hoped they were alright as well, and would live long lives, but in this world that was getting harder to envision. I put down my bag and shouldered my rifle. I had almost two hundred rounds of ammo, and there were probably two hundred undead, but with reloading and missing some noggins, I knew I was screwed. Time to man up.

I dropped to a crouch and took aim at a particularly fat dead man with no face. My finger tightened on the trigger and the thunder, which had gotten exponentially louder, came into view.

It was not a tank. It was not the MRAP. It was about fifty armored horses, with all manner of people on them. The front ranks were dressed like knights, (no shit) with lances lowered. They were in various types of mismatched and homemade armor, looking like something out of a Mad Max movie, and they plowed through the lines of undead in front of me like the Reaper mowing souls. Dozens of infected were trampled down by the horses or impaled by the long wooden lances, and then the second rank of riders were in amongst the dead, swinging swords and axes, some shooting pistols or rifles. One guy had a big ice scraper and was thrusting it at the zombies, taking off the tops of their heads from the eyes up. Two riders on heavy horses rode fifteen feet apart with some type of wire between them. They didn't decapitate any of the dead but they sure as shit fucked them up as that wire hit infected in the face or neck. Some of the riders had bows, and they shot into the crowd behind me, and suddenly there were small explosions, the dead being tossed around.

I was so stunned I hadn't begun firing and that changed quickly. The riders in front of me were totally wrecking the zombies, so I turned and was surprised to see the dead behind me were only twenty feet away. Nearly shitting myself, I began firing slowly, picking targets as I backed up toward the knights. A pickup truck that looked like something out of the Road Warrior (shut it, I'm a fan) came into view and guns opened up from inside the armored bed. Four men got out and ran to stand beside me, shooting shotguns and rifles into the crowd. I swear to Holy Christ one of them was yelling *Yee Ha!* They were efficient, and within moments only the living were standing.

The dead never made it to within ten feet of me. One of the four that had jumped from the truck, dressed exactly like a cowboy, with hat and chaps and spurs. Holstered one of his twin six-guns and began to reload the other. "Mornin'," was all he said.

Another one, a fifteen-year-old kid by the look of him, looked at his over-under shotgun and cracked it open, shoving fresh shells into it. "Saved your ass, didn't we?"

"Uhh…"

"Yeah, you were about to have a bad day. What the hell were you doing coming in here anyway?" He looked at me sideways as the horses came trotting over. "This is where they all came when Great Falls burned."

"I needed…" He turned and looked the other way, and I could see that the right side of his face was covered with what looked like scales, and his right eye was a yellow color.

He looked at the bag, then at the red shopping basket I had dropped and he smiled. "Yeah, I hate it when Aunt Flo shows up too." He started to chuckle, and so did I.

He shouldered his weapon and stuck out his paw. "Name's Carter."

I shook his hand and started to tell him my name when, a guy in medieval armor carrying a gore-spattered, double-bladed battle axe got off his horse, raised the visor on his motorcycle helmet and looked at me hard. "You bitten?"

"No, they never got close to me. Thanks."

"Sure. You scavenging? Got anything good?" His eyebrows lifted. "Any beer?"

'Sorry, just antibiotics and some pain killers."

Carter stuck his face in the conversation. "And tampons!"

The knight took his helmet off, and a gunshot made everyone turn toward the south. "We can't stay here. I'm assuming you're with the folks in that armored vehicle a couple blocks over?"

I really didn't want to answer that question, so I didn't.

He smiled and snorted. "I don't blame you. Trust is a hard thing to come by these days." He looked back towards another gunshot from the same direction and then radio chirped on his belt. He picked it up and we all heard through the radio that another sizable horde of dead were on their way. "Copy that, Mark. Stay high, we'll come back for you in two days. Out." He looked back at me, "We can take you to the vehicle if you want, they won't answer us or move when we try to talk to them. Do you want to go?"

I nodded in the affirmative.

"Carter, get him and his tampons on the truck and back to his vehicle." He got back on his horse and looked at me. "You're welcome to come home with us, or you can be on your merry way. If I wanted you dead you'd be dead, so consider that. We'd love to have you, but if you want to stay you have to contribute."

He turned his horse and trotted off with the rest of them, back toward the west. Carter looked at me sideways. "You're taking this well. Whenever we meet somebody new, they kind of freak out at our little group, at least at first."

We moved to the pickup. "Well, it is a little…"

"Odd," he finished. "Hell, I used to be the Alligator Boy, and we live in a world of walking dead people. I grew up a freak, I'm used to odd."

He got in the back of the truck and reached a hand down to help me in. I hesitated, and he brought up the same point the guy with the axe had. "You see all the weaponry? If we wanted you dead, or if we wanted your shit, what could you do?"

"Like your friend said, it's hard to trust people nowadays." I grabbed his hand and he pulled me in the truck.

"Yeah, but you should never look a gift lizard in the mouth." He seemed to get a kick out of himself, and we both laughed.

We got back to the MRAP, the pickup at the back of the column of riders, and I hopped out. Dallas was smiling at me through the bullet-resistant glass behind the armored louvers of the driver's side window. I held up the bag of drugs. "Got them!"

His smile faded and he pointed to all the folks that were around me. "They saved my ass, big guy, you can open up."

He did, and Carter followed me over to the MRAP. "If you want some hot food, you can follow us back to our camp. You're all welcome. If not, best of luck, and don't get your asses bitten off out here." With that, he got back in his truck and drove to catch up with the horses.

Eleanor hugged me and Dallas looked out the window as I passed the drugs to Clara. "I seen some weird stuff, but...ah who cares? Can I drive?"

"Yeah, follow them, how's Tim doing?"

Tim craned his head to look at me. "It hurts, but I'm OK."

Clara looked through the bag, "Oh well done!" She was reading off some of the names of the drugs, "Augmentin, Cephlezxin... Ibuprofen. This amoxicillin will need to get mixed..." She opened a bottle and lifted Tim's head as she gave him two pills which he washed down with water.

"What was that?" he asked weakly.

"Percocet. That should help you out with the pain. I need to check the expiration dates on the antibiotics, but this is what we have, so we'll need to use them even if they're expired."

"Can I drive?" Dallas asked again.

"Sure, I could use a sit-down."

And that's just what I did. Dallas put the MRAP into gear and we followed the rag-tag group of weirdoes that had pulled my fish out of the fire.

CARNIES AND TOUGH GUYS

A group of carnies and some folks from a renaissance faire walk into a bar after a long day on the road. One of the ren-guys orders a beer and sits down at the bar, the other folks looking at menus or using the bathrooms. The faire guy begins a polite conversation with the pretty young bartender, food and drinks are delivered, and merriment ensues. The creaky tavern door opens, and the renaissance guy doesn't even turn around, because things are going well with the bartender. The drink slinger leans to the side to look behind the hot guy she's working up, who works as a knight in the show, and is the hero of the faire. Her eyes go wide and her mouth opens in the shape of an O. Naturally, the knight (who is not in his dress clothes), turns to look and sees this bloody, disheveled guy stagger in. Another member of the faire, the king, stands up to render assistance to the obviously injured man, and the man latches on to the king and tries to bite him. The king starts yelling, and the knight, true to his station, attempts to rescue his liege. The crazy man maneuvers in and takes a big chunk out of the king's forearm, so the knight sends a beefy roundhouse right crashing into the side of the offender's noggin. The biter is unfazed. Everyone keeps yelling at the man to let go of the now bleeding king, a couple of folks stepping in to help. They are bitten as well. Not seeing any way out of this, the knight realizes that this particular individual is either bat-shit crazy, or on drugs and bat-shit crazy. He draws his knife, utters a threat to the man, who pays no heed, then drives the knife into the man's side. While the man is still unfazed, the rest of the bar is extremely fucking fazed, and they all realize there is more at work here than bath salts. Benny the dwarf, one of the carnival workers, decides he has had enough, puts down his cigar, pulls out his .32 pistol and drills the guy in the forehead. Benny calmly sits down and says to the bartender, "Might wanna call your sheriff for this one."

The pretty bartender, removes her hands that were covering her mouth in shock and replies, "That was the sheriff."

Shitty punchline, I know, but there isn't a lot that's truly funny anymore. I was sitting around a campfire with a bunch of carnies and faire folk and people they had taken in. We were swapping stories about our time post-plague. Most of the folks told exactly the same story with little nuances in the details. When my turn came along, I related what had happened. Of course, I left out the minor detail on why the government wants me; they didn't need to know that. When Dallas related his tale, one of the guys that didn't look like he belonged with a group of carnival people scoffed and said one word, "Bullshit."

"Was' that?"

"I said bullshit. There's no way you traversed the entire country from west to east, then halfway back again. I've been out there, I've seen what it's like." The guy stood, chucked his coffee in the fire and stormed off.

"Don't mind him," Carter told us. "He's one of our military guys, and as such is skeptical that you were able to make it as far as you did."

I looked at Carter. "Military guys?" I don't have to tell you that where there are army guys, the government isn't far behind.

"Oh yeah, you don't think we could have done all this without help, do you?" He spread his arms out, indicating his camp.

The camp housed almost two hundred people. Built into the side of a mountain, they had augmented a natural cave system to fit their needs. There were dozens of "rooms," including a great room where everybody gathered for meetings. The cave was complete with hot and cold running water in the form of an underground stream and geyser. Outside the caves was a fort-like structure the likes of which you may have seen if you watched old movies about cowboys and Indians. It's what I would think Fort Apache would look like with high wooden walls that were trees jammed into the earth, the tops cut to points. Three towers made of the same wooden poles were at mismatched intervals down the wall, catwalks running between the towers. The whole thing encompassed a motor pool area with several cars and trucks, including two buggy-looking things that I had never seen before.

One of the guys called them "Flips." They were armored and looked really cool. Also in the large area was a huge circus tent under which we now had our fires.

These people had done well for themselves.

Dallas looked at Carter then at the back of the guy who was walking away. "I guess I can see 'is point."

A big guy came and sat down in the spot the army dude had just left. It was the guy who had been riding the horse and had saved my ass earlier. He had presided over the inspection of our bodies for bites when they brought is in. Absolutely everyone that came back in the fort remained in a quarantine zone, which was a mini-fort in and of itself, until they were checked out. They had no doctor, but a couple of the military guys had some medic experience.

He told us his name was Michael, and he was the knight that had tried to save his king that I mentioned above. He had a girl with him, and she was the cute bartender. They had been travelling as faire-folk do and hooked up with a carnival out of Florida called Harrod Shows. The plague struck when they were in Mercy's Bar in Great Falls, and they had escaped out of that hell and into the mountains to the west. They had suffered losses as has everyone, but the biggest loss was their friend and leader, the king.

A group of mix-matched military had stumbled across them, and they had pooled their resources, doing well in the year since the dead had begun walking.

"Of course we still have issues," Michael told us. He related a story about how when the group was on a run to collect and scavenge, they came across a group of bikers calling themselves the Devil's Reapers. Apparently the Reapers were not the friendly type, and moreover did not like to share, so naturally a gun battle ensued. The four Reapers were killed, but there must have been more of them because since then on several occasions when the carnies went out on a run they encountered groups of well-armed Reapers who always shot at them on sight. On one such run, the survivors had seen about a hundred and fifty bikes riding down the highway. A few of the carnival group had been lost to zombies, and some more to the Reapers, but for the most part this was a thriving camp.

I figured this was a good place to hole up while Tim was on the mend, and Clara was a better medic than anyone else in camp, so we decided to stay for a few days. I was able to earn my keep by helping fix some broken down stuff, Eleanor helped cook, Clara as stated, helped with the medicine, and Dallas did some repair on the walls.

The lion that had attacked us had been one of two that were released into the wild when the carnies had reached the red and white ranger's station in Benton Wildlife Refuge. Michael gave a personal apology to all of us, especially Tim, who had to be under lock and key with constant monitoring for the first two days we were in the compound. Michael said they just couldn't leave the lions to die in the cages, but they obviously couldn't bring them along. The carnies had met the hodgepodge group of military guys at the ranger's station as well, which is when they had all decided to throw in their lot together. It had worked out for the most part.

There were questions on who should be in command, and Michael had come up with the idea that all things non-military would be commanded by one of the civvies, and the military ops would be commanded by Captain Berry of MARSOC. MARSOC pretty much means Don't Fuck With Me. They are Marine Special Operations Command. There were also a few Army Rangers, two Air Force guys, and some Green Berets, who tell me they are Army Special Forces. Twenty-three guys altogether if you include some National Guardsmen. Oh yeah, and Remo.

I asked Remo what he did and he simply replied, "Teacher," shouldered his rifle and took off. That's the only word he's really said to us or anybody else since we got here. I got into a conversation with some of the Rangers about the baddest of the bad in the military, and soon all the other military guys were in on it. It was yet another friendly conversation around the fire with some boasting and bragging and exaggerated facts. Remo was, of course, not present.

So in the midst of hearing about how the Rangers would beat the crap out of the Marines in a game of "Tango Down," I asked what Remo really did.

"He's a Marine Scout Instructor," Dex, one of the MARSOC guys, said.

"Yeah, he told me he was a teacher, but what does it mean?"

Dex looked at me. "It means if you get the option of picking a fight with him or a pack of wolves, you choose the wolves."

"I disagree," Berry said and spit in the fire. "Dead quicker with Remo."

Everybody at the fire nodded in agreement quickly.

Dallas joined in the conversation and we got to talking about how tough truckers are. Everybody was having a good time, and then Dallas mentioned Alcatraz. He had mentioned the prison before, and how there were dozens of people there trying to fortify and make it, but this time he added that there was a group of military there as well.

Every single man and woman sitting around the fire stopped talking and looked at Dallas.

"What?" he asked looking around. "Was' wrong?"

Captain Berry shifted in his seat. "There's a group of military on Alcatraz?"

"Yeah, thas' why I'm here. I'm collectin' the wife of one of 'em. Clara's Commander McInerney's wife."

"There's a Navy *Commander* there? How many men are with him?"

"I dunno, maybe a hunnert and fifty? The Florida had her own crew and there was a buncha SEALs with 'em."

"The Florida? The USS Florida?"

"Yessir. If thas' the same as the sub, then yeah."

Then oh man did the questions start flying: Why didn't you tell us this before? Do they have communications? Are there any other vessels? What was the condition of the sub and the crew?

I felt it best to vacate the premises, and escaped to go see how Tim was doing. Tim was up and speaking to Clara about his boo-boo. Can you really call a lion bite a boo-boo? If you want to emasculate your buddy who just got attacked by a lion you can. And that shit works.

"How is he?" I asked Clara.

"He's fine. A bit of a baby, but he's fine." She looked right at me. "Thanks to you."

"Um, yeah. Pretty sure a *lion* bit me. Have you been attacked by a *lion*? No? Then I reserve the right to bitch about it." He pointed to the bandage on his arm. "*Lion*?"

I smiled in spite of myself, and Clara laughed out loud. "Well, you've got me there."

We chatted for a bit, and an hour later Eleanor brought her endless legs by to see how Tim was doing. An hour after that, Dallas showed up with Captain Berry and the shorter of the two Air Force guys, and it was a party.

We all sat down in folding chairs outside under the tent. It was warm, and I could smell the smoke from several fires. It was great. Then Dallas dropped the bomb.

"Clara, we's leavin' tomorrow."

Everyone looked at him except the Air Force guy, who was looking at Eleanor, and Berry, who was looking at his shoes. "We have a plane," he said. "It's a C-17 Globemaster III. It can take a contingent of up to fifty four people who want to go to San Francisco." He looked up. "It will have to be tomorrow though. The Reapers are close to the airfield, and it's only a matter of time until they find the plane. The airfield is hidden as well as you can hide an airfield, but the Reapers are branching out from wherever their base is, and they'll find it eventually. There are also two Black Hawk helicopters, but they can't make the trip, fuel would be an issue. Then there's landing. We don't know where we could land safely."

"I do," Dallas piped up. "I know where we can land."

Everyone was looking at him again, and he shrugged. "I was on my way there in a different plane when we set down ta find a friend, an' I come up here lookin' fer Clara. I know where there's a place t' land."

"Is it free of infected?"

"Dunno."

"Is there a clear runway?"

"Dunno."

"What *do* you know?" demanded the Air Force guy.

"I know where the airfield is."

Captain Berry shook his head. "Alright, stop it. We have a possibility to link with US forces, one of whom is a senior officer, in a secure location," he pointed to Dallas, "and you need to get to Alcatraz. I will send a squad with you, and we can possibly get some communications going."

Tim coughed and actually timidly raised his hand. "You will need a communications satellite."

"We have several, but with no ground crews or codes we can't access them. We *do* have access to older HAM radios in the Ranger stations at Blackleaf and Ear Mountain."

Like I knew where those places were. I looked at Tim, and he looked back at me. Would he keep his NSA-ness a secret, or would he pony up the fact that he had access to spy satellites?

"Um... I have codes."

Boom.

Berry turned from Dallas. "What? Codes to what?"

"I have access codes to the Sentinel satellites. I will need a transmitter capable of—"

Berry cut him off, "Sentinel? You mean you can access com-sats?"

"Well, they're not communications satellites per-se, but they can piggy-back any signal, or bounce between if you need. But I still need the transmitter."

"Let me worry about that."

He went off on how this camp would be able to communicate and coordinate with a west coast compliment of soldiers and sailors, and how it was of the utmost importance to establish links with them because we might be able to coordinate strikes against the infected and blah, blah, blah.

Did I dare tell these guys that there was a manned destroyer anchored next to my house in the middle of the Gulf of Mexico? What would that mean to them? I didn't even know if the destroyer was still there, or what their intentions were with my Atlantis friends. Shit, what's a boy to do? In the end I thought about what had happened to me and why. I had been stolen from my friends because I might have some type of cure or vaccine for this plague inside of me. I also remembered thinking that I had to live. Not just to see my friends, but to work on this plague vaccine thing somehow.

Fuck it.

"Captain," I had interrupted him from his tirade on saving the good old US of A. He looked at me and I sighed. "There's a destroyer that looked like it was fully manned anchored off of an oil rig in the Gulf of Mexico." He opened his mouth to ask me a billion questions, but I held up my hand forestalling him. "That rig is my home, and I don't know anything about the destroyer other than it's there."

In the end, it was decided that the Montana group of military guys was going to split up into three squads or groups or platoons or whatever you call a small group of military guys. Berry called them "Fire Teams" and that was awesome.

The news was brought to the attention of the general populace, and honestly I thought everyone would want to go, but only six civilians decided to take the plane ride. Nobody wanted to come with me on my MRAP ride south, which was great as far as I was concerned. Nobody except four military guys and Tim. Clara and Eleanor would go with Dallas, and I found myself sad at the prospect of losing them. I had only known them a few days, but they were all three great people.

Plus Eleanor was shit hot.

I gave her a long, perhaps inappropriate hug when it came time to split up the next morning. Clara's hug was much more appropriate, and she thanked me and cried a little. I tried to give Dallas a manly handshake, but he enveloped me in a hug that would have made a grizzly jealous.

He put his hands on my shoulders and looked me in the eye, "Ya saved m' life, Hoss. I ain't gon' forget that. Y'also got me t' where I needed t' be. Won't forget that neither. Be safe."

I still couldn't friggin' breath from when he crushed my lungs a moment ago, but I squeaked out a weak *good luck*, and we parted. I liked that guy. With so many dickheads in this post-apocalyptic nightmare, it was great to meet some nice folks.

Tim and I were sitting in the MRAP, nose pointed toward the gate when our detachment of badasses showed up. We got three MARSOC guys and to my utter surprise; Remo. Each of the Jarheads had a bag of gear and a bag of supplies, but Remo (who was also technically a jarhead, but his jar was made out of awesome) had two bags of gear and no supplies except for a water bladder attached to his tactical vest. I asked him why he wanted to come and he told me that the main force of the Reapers had been seen moving south. Actually, what he said was, "Reapers are south."

That was four words I had now pried out of him. I would have pressed for more, but honestly I believe that he could have melted my eyeballs with just a look. I really wanted to see a steel cage match with this guy and Lynch. I would have no idea who to bet on, even though I hadn't seen Remo in action yet. Except Lynch was dead.

They opened the wooden gate and we were off. I saw the two buggy-looking things go left with Dallas and company, and we went right. I surely hope I see them again. We drove for a while, talking back and forth, the occasional pus-bag in the road. We were in central Montana, coming out of the mountains, and there was really no way past either Butte or Helena, two of the larger cities in this godforsaken state. Taking Route 200 south west, it was our plan to turn south on 141, and hook up with Route 1 south. From there we would wing it. As it happens, we never made it to 141.

LINCOLN

We passed the turnoff for Hooper State Park at just before ten in the morning. We had gone over a small river, and yes we used a bridge, if you could call it that. The river was called Grosfield Ditch, and that's pretty much all it was. A small ditch in the ground with a trickle of water running through it. The bridge wasn't a scary bridge loaded with zombies; it was a two-lane piece of road laid over a concrete culvert.

The streets in Lincoln, the town we were about to pass through in less than a minute, were all numbered as they had been up by Great Falls. So much for originality. Lincoln hadn't escaped the plague, as there were a signs and evidence of it everywhere. The abandoned vehicles, broken windows, scattered bones, and burned buildings were a testament to how powerful this epidemic had been. Even a tiny (and I mean tiny) town like Lincoln had succumbed to the evils of the undead.

The growl of the MRAP was like ringing a dinner bell, and soon we found the town's entire population of zombies. They came at us as with that shambling stagger. Both of them. One was a guy in ragged business suit that was as rotten as you can imagine after a year. The other was a teenage girl, and she was fresh.

Didn't make a lot of sense. This whole town didn't make sense. If everybody was dead, where were they? Why didn't they come out?

"Stop," Remo said, and that was enough because I couldn't get my foot to the brake pedal fast enough.

We slowed, and he shouldered a bag of gear. "Pick me up on the other side of town in an hour."

WTF? Complete sentences?

He popped open the back hatch and was gone from sight before I knew what was happening. Brick, one of the MARSOC guys, shut the hatch and told me to keep going. The two zombies hadn't seen Remo either and they plodded along after us, reaching.

We drove for a full four minutes before we came over a hill and saw 1st Ave running perpendicular to us. It was a road like all the other roads, with trees on each side and a small structure to the right. The odd thing was that there were an electrical truck with a cherry picker bucket on it, and a tow truck across the road nose to nose. It looked exactly like a roadblock, and before I could even think that, one of the MARSOC guys yelled at me to stop and back up.

I jammed the brakes, and threw the MRAP in reverse. Before I was able to step on the gas, a guy in jeans and a black leather vest stepped through the gap in the vehicles, with a tube on his shoulder. Two guys popped out from behind trees on the left with rifles and ran toward us, and I could tell by Ray-Ban's (another marine, sitting in the passenger's seat) expression, that some were coming from the right as well.

"Fuck," was all Ray-Ban said.

"Is that…"

"Yeah, that's an RPG."

I heard engines, and saw in the rearview that four motorcycles were coming in fast behind us. Brick was looking out the back windows. "Contact, rear, four bikes!"

Ray Ban didn't take his eyes off the guy in front of us. "RPG up front!"

"They all have military gear," Brick informed us, and flipped the safety off his M4. "We can take the ones in back, but that RPG will waste our MRAP, and it's a long fuckin' walk to Texas."

Our MRAP? Whoa. Just whoa.

Ray-Ban got up and joined Brick, the other marine Kinga, and Tim in the back of the truck, "What's up, boss?" They were all checking their weapons, even Tim.

"Business as usual, we kill them all."

"That RPG is a game-changer."

"Doesn't change the plan, those are Reapers. Come out shootin' and don't get shot."

I joined them in the back just as a guy on the driver's side yelled in to us, "Yoo hoo! Do you have any Miracle Whip?"

I checked my HK416, fear making my heart pound. I have no idea how these guys did this kind of thing every day even before the plague. They were dropped into situations where everybody wanted to kill you, and they did it for shit pay.

Ray-Ban pointed at Brick then pointed left. He pointed at Kinga, and pointed right. He pointed at the two of us and whispered, "Stay behind me, don't fucking shoot me."

We nodded, and I stood from my crouch, the guy who had asked for salad dressing (yeah, Miracle Whip is a salad dressing, if you find a rotten jar of it someplace look at the label) called out again, "You comin' out or are we comin' in? Any chicks in there?"

He knocked on the door. "Don't worry, we can open this up, we have a can opener."

I looked out the front window at their can opener. The guy with the RPG was looking bored. He got a sudden smile on his face, and I knew we were screwed. I was about to turn and scream to Ray-Ban to open the door, when Remo stepped out from between the two trucks, pulled the big dude's hair back, and jammed his big ass knife into the guys Adam's apple. He didn't slice across, he jabbed down and sawed right for half a second, more or less decapitating the guy. Fucker was dead before he knew he was under attack. As he fell, Remo grabbed the RPG, spun to his left and fired it. We all heard it streak to wherever he pointed it. There was a significant *BOOM!* followed by small arms fire from outside.

Screams started before Ray-Ban pushed the door open, leapt out and fired into the guys that were looking in all directions behind us. They did a little dance before falling to the ground clutching at themselves. The other two marines went right and left, but the RPG and Remo's M9 had already taken the rest of the bad guys out. One of the guys in the RPG blast zone was screaming, but I hadn't seen what he looked like yet.

Remo was leaning against the MRAP unwrapping a stick of gum. I leaned next to him, and he held out the pack to me. I grabbed a stick and Remo pulled his M9 and shot one of the Reapers that had been trying to stand. The guy was a hundred feet away, and Remo drilled him in the chest. The best word I can think of for the way he had shot the guy is *nonchalantly*. Yeah, I can rock an adverb.

"Clear," he said as he chewed his Big Red.

"Clear!" I heard from the other three marines almost in synch.

Brick ran over to the guys who had been hit by the RPG. One was goo, and the other had stopped screaming and was just kind of rasping. It was this ragged breath/cough thing, and I will never forget that sound.

Ray-Ban trotted up to the guys he had shot, and I heard two more shots as I made my way to the RPG guys. It was bad. I had seen this kind of thing before when I had first met my pal Ship, and these redneck douches had been ravaged by a few claymores.

I heard retching, and turned to see Tim with his hands on his knees back by the MRAP. The goo guy looked like…goo. There wasn't a lot left. The other guy was a real mess, but was at least recognizable as human. His right arm and leg were hamburger. Think about that for a second. Hamburger. It is exactly what his arm and leg looked like, strings of meat with some bone fragments sticking here and there. He was a good twenty feet from where the RPG had hit the ground, and his other leg was bent under him. He was holding his guts in with his left hand, and was doing a shitty job because a purple loop of intestine slid out and hung like one of those strings of hot dogs you used to see in the deli section of the supermarket.

The guy made this sound like *ug-guh* about three times and he died. Fuck him. What do you think he was going to do to us? I doubt a game of checkers was an option. We checked all the other bodies, and took care of them before they turned. One had started to stir, and he put one hand out to push himself up before I drilled him. They all had these cool black vests with a scythe and the words Devil's Reapers on the back in red and white. Remo strode back to the bikes and sat on one. He looked it over then got off and scrunched down next to it. It looked like he was working on it.

He strode back to us and said, "My bag is back there." He thumbed over his shoulder back towards town. "And there's something I need to take care of. Don't touch the motorcycles. Fifteen minutes."

He began walking down the street toward town and moved off the road into the trees. I thought about dragging the Reapers' bodies out off of the road, but screw that. They could rot or be eaten by whatever. They did have some good shit. Three M4s, a

Squad Automatic Weapon, various pistols, and the RPG. There were no extra warheads (grenades?) for the RPG, but there was considerable ammo for the other weapons, and we took it all plus the guns.

I strolled back to the bikes with Kinga. "Remo said not to—"

"Not gonna. Just checkin' shit out."

We got to the bikes and looked at them. I couldn't see anything out of the ordinary, but Kinga got down on one knee and inspected it. He huffed and gave a low whistle.

"What?"

"Remo booby trapped it. He's got a frag on the head with a wire to the spoke, look."

Indeed, there was a wire, but I had to get down and look closely to see it.

Kinga looked at me with a half-smile. "Boom. He he."

Walking back to the MRAP, we heard a series of small explosions from Lincoln, and noticed some oily black smoke pouring into the air. We waited inside the truck for almost fifteen minutes, and suddenly Remo was there, knocking on the back door.

"What was that about?" Brick asked Remo when he was inside with us.

"Three trailers full of rotters parked back there. Looks like the Reapers were waiting to find the camp and then drop an infected bomb on it."

"Well, screw them then."

"Yup."

I went to get in the driver's seat, and Brick stood up, getting in my way. "I was thinking I might take a stab at driving."

"Think that and you might just get stabbed," I told him and brushed past. He was looking at me wide-eyed when I looked back into the cabin. "Buckle up, jarheads, this train is rolling."

Remo wasn't looking at me, but he did have the slightest hint of a smile on his face.

WHEN YOU'VE GOT TO GO, YOU'VE GOT TO GO

Brick was under the impression we should take the heads of the Reapers and put them on posts for their buddies to find with a note that told them to fuck off. Ray-Ban thought it would just incense them instead of scare them, and Remo said it would take too much time. Brick then said we should mess up their bikes, but Remo put the kibosh on that too, citing that he had left them a present, and he wanted someone to open it.

In the end, we just moved west on the 200, following the road through the mountains, and then south on Route 141 until we hit Route 12 west. 12 intersected with Interstate 90 south. This would bring us eventually to the city of Butte, and we wanted to stay far away from that, so we decided to hook south until we reached Interstate 15.

The little town of Deer Lodge was on the route, and we thought that might be a good place to find some fishing rods for some fresh fish. There were rivers everywhere, and a fishing excursion with the toughest men on the planet watching my ass sounded pretty nice. We took a left on Beck Hill Road, which the map told us would bypass a few miles of highway, including a bridge. Freeze Out Lane (no shit) continued where Beck Hill turned under I90, so we took that, and then a few other roads until we saw smoke in the distance. The smoke was coming from behind some low hills, so we parked the MRAP and went forward on foot, Tim and Kinga staying with the vehicle.

Ray-Ban, Brick, Remo, and I snuck up the side of a small hill and looked down on the town. The smoke was coming from barrels with fires in them. The entire town looked to be an armed encampment like I had seen in Havre, and my heart actually jumped a little. If two pissant Montana towns could hold out, then maybe there were more with many more people. Maybe we could eke out an existence, waiting for the pus bags to rot away. I started to stand, feeling some genuine joy for once, and Brick grabbed my load-bearing vest and yanked me back down. I looked at him all pissy, and he pointed to some of the people, obviously human, walking in the town.

They *were* human. They weren't stumbling or lurching. They were walking around like humans would. I didn't get it until Brick gave me his binoculars and pointed again. I peered through the glasses and then I could see what he was on about.

Most of the people walking around had black vests on. This was a Reaper town, probably their home base. I heard, "Son of a bitch," come from Remo. He was looking through his own binocs, and I followed his gaze. Two of the Reapers were dragging a guy out into the street, hitting him with black clubs. When he would hold his hand up to protect himself, they just clubbed him harder. They hit him and hit him until he stopped moving.

Looking at the small town through the binoculars, more of the same was happening, albeit not as bad as the stick beating. The streets were mostly empty, but every now and then some Deer Lodge citizen someone would need something, and they would have to brave the streets to get it. Often times, someone in a black vest would shove them, or swat them.

There wasn't a zombie in sight.

So the Reapers had taken over the town and cleared it, or they had taken it after it had been cleared. Either way, you took your life in your hands walking out into the streets as much from the bikers as from the zombies in another shitty town.

"Thirty six that I can see," Ray-Ban said as the lowered his binoculars. "It should be tonight, when they're drunk."

WTF was he talking about?

"Yeah but there could be a hundred in the buildings that we don't see. Look there." Brick pointed toward a large parking lot near what looked like a hotel. There were dozens of motorcycles parked there. Maybe Brick was right, maybe there were a hundred bikers. But what did we care? We were going way, way around this crappy town.

Brick took his binoculars back from me. "I'm not crazy about the ones we can't see."

"I'm not terribly fond of the ones we *can* see," Ray-Ban huffed, "Remo?"

Remo was looking through a larger pair of binoculars. "We fuckin' kill em all."

So I guess we weren't going around the town. We got back to the MRAP a few minutes later, and Kinga was asking how it looked. Now, we had been looking at the place for maybe ten minutes. I had seen that there were buildings, and bad guys between the buildings, and no zombies. That's what I saw.

These guys proved their badassery to me once again when they hunkered down, started drawing in the dirt and citing that this was a hundred meters from there so it would be a good cover spot and that this rock is the water tower and it's twenty meters high, with two Reaper spotters on it. This is a possible barracks because we saw this dude come out and when the door was open we saw a bunch more of the Reapers in there. There are guards here, here, here, and here, don't know about a rotation schedule.

These Marine dudes were legit. I looked at Tim, and he at me, and we must have looked a little nervous because three of the tough guys told us not to worry about it at the same time. Remo was shockingly silent.

Ray-Ban got up off his haunches and pitched a rock into the dust. "We can't just roll in there and nuke the place, there's civvies. I doubt they have NVGs, but we should still be cautious during the incursion."

Once again, I don't want you, Dear Reader, to think that I'm a total douche. I've done some badass shit in the past year; you know that because you've gotten this far in my journals. I am not a pussy. I am also not a friggin' Navy SEAL, or one of these MARSOC boys. Hell, I wasn't even a boy scout. I was getting better at the whole military thing, but the bottom line is that I didn't think I would survive a running gun battle with these Reaper assholes. There were just too many.

Don't get me wrong, I know that my escorts are more than capable of killing ten bad guys each in the blink of an eye, but all they need is one stray bullet, and their force is cut down by twenty five percent. Not to mention, that while I consider myself somewhat capable now, I can't compete with a hundred well-armed dickweeds that have probably been killing people for fun for a generation or two. I didn't want to complain, and I certainly wasn't about to tell these guys that I was taking my MRAP and going home, but come on? What could I do?

Turns out the decision was made for me. We ended up pulling the truck back, and parking it in the garage of the deserted, ramshackle local fire station. Why was there a fire station on the outskirts of a small town sans fire truck? No idea. "You two stay here," Ray-Ban told us. "If we aren't back in twenty four hours, you take off and head for the Gulf."

Damn he sounded cool.

The four of them took off without so much as a backward glance. Not that I could have seen said glance in the dark. As soon as the professional killers were outside of ass-saving distance, the creepiness of a rickety old fire house in a pitch black, post-apocalyptic world amped up to a gazillion. Tim and I decided we would be better served waiting inside our bullet-resistant, zombie-proof truck. We heated some MREs right in the MRAP, Tim got chicken pesto, and I got sausage with gravy.

People in the movies are always bitching about how airplane food and MREs are awful and they taste like dust or worse, but that simply isn't true. Try prison food. Ketchup on something that looks like spaghetti. The sausage with gravy MRE (from the Menu H case) is effing delicious.

We cleaned up, played a couple rounds of Crazy Eights with a deck of cards I had traded for in the last camp, and I realized that the delicious sausage meal I had eaten was wreaking havoc on my innards. I told Tim I had to drop a deuce, and he laughed like hell telling me he had never heard that before. I didn't think it was funny, but grabbed some toilet paper, checked our surroundings, and went to look for the toilet in the fire house.

The bathroom was on the second floor, and I creaked up the stairs with Tim close on my heels. No way was I going anywhere alone, possibly ever again. We passed the fire pole on the way to the bathroom, and I thought that there was absolutely no chance I was not sliding down that to get back to the truck.

The bathroom door was stuck open with one of those little rubber wedges when we found it. There were two stalls and a urinal. The first stall had no toilet, just a hole where one used to be. The second one did have a toilet, but it was so disgusting that I opted to poop outside. I thought about using the hole in the floor, but that just didn't appeal to me. We exited the bathroom, walking back to the unsteady stairs. I tested the fire-pole by shaking it, and we both slid down it. It was epic.

I checked out some windows, the area looking particularly zombie free, and we moved outside. Being in prison with a cellmate, there isn't even the illusion of privacy, so I was used to squatting with other guys around. Tim kept a lookout while I took care of business. When I was done, we made our way back to the MRAP. I opened the door to the firehouse garage, heard this whooshing sound and inky blackness took over as the ground rushed up to meet me.

REAPERS

Thirsty. In this friggin' apocalypse, you would think hunger would be the biggest issue, but I always seem to be thirsty. Pain throbbed through my melon before I could attempt another thought. The just-bumped-your-head-on-something-extremely-solid-and-unforgiving kind of pain. The one that sucks for a minute and subsides so that you have a dull throb. This didn't subside. It threatened to turn me into a quivering pile of jelly. This was bad, and remember, I've been shot in the head.

I opened my eyes (mistake) and light assaulted my senses through my rods and cones in the form of a sharp spear of torment. The little bastard in charge of the pain shut off switch was looking to get a raise, and he threw that damn lever as far into the *ON* position as my optic nerves would allow. It hurt so bad I was nauseated for a moment. Yup, you guessed it, sausage and gravy came out all over the floor. I had the nerve to turn my head to the side to puke, and that sent further requisitions of suffering to the pain guy. In triplicate.

I rolled back on the cot I was on and waited for a moment for everything to equilibrate. I dared to open my eyes, and then wished I had kept them the F closed. I was in jail. Bars on the window. Bars for a door. Bars for a wall on one side of me and several other cells, all occupied. For a split second, I felt extremely safe. Every person in the cells looked to be in the same shape I was in. I could see through the cell next to me and into the one beyond, and the two guys in there were bloody and beaten. Another three cells were across from me and the inhabitants were in the same state.

I heard a door open, and two guys strode in laughing and talking. They sauntered down the corridor between the six cells and came to look at me.

"Hey, he's up!"

"Yeah, I thought he was gonna wake up dead."

They both chuckled.

Pricks.

"Water…please."

"Oh man, you must be really thirsty. We're sorry about that. Have to take precautions and whatnot." He produced a key ring and began thumbing through the keys. "Diamond and Giggles are really sorry about the whack to the head. They did a number on your buddy too, but he wouldn't tell them where you were coming from or where you were headed. At first."

He found the correct key and unlocked my cell.

"You see, this is our town. If you live here, you have to pay taxes. If you're passing through, you have to pay a toll." He got down on his haunches next to me on the bunk. "You understand that in today's world things are different from before? I mean you get that right?"

"Yeah," I croaked.

The speaker, a guy of average size and curiously absent of tattoos, stepped into the cell. The gigantic guy with him leaned against the cell door frame looking exceptionally mean.

"Here," he passed me a bottle of water, "drink up."

"Thanks." I took the water and took a giant pull on it. It was cold, and that sent spirals of agony through my freshly smacked melon.

"So my boss wants to know a few things. First, what's your name?"

"Where's my friend? Is he OK?"

"Whoa pal, that's not how it works. Not only is it rude to answer a question with a question, but I'm the one who needs to report to a higher power here. Any further instances of non-compliance will be dealt with in a manner in which you will not be pleased. Have I made myself clear?" The huge dude snorted.

"Yes."

He pointed at my arm. "I see by your ink that you've bumped the proverbial head with the law in the past. Where'd you do your time?"

"Cedar Junction, Walpole Mass." It wasn't true, I did my stint in a medium security prison, and Walpole was for the bad boys.

"Ah. May I ask what you were in for?"

"Armed robbery with a side order of beating the shit out of a couple of cops." Again, a lie, and I'm sure you can see where this was going and why.

"Interesting. And why are you riding around in a military vehicle? Where did you get it?"

"Took it off some National Guard in Idaho. They didn't need it."

"I see."

He continued with the questions for another ten minutes or so, never once asking me about Lincoln, or dead Reapers up there. He never asked me about Tim either, and as he got up to leave, I asked him where Tim was.

"Ah yes. Tim. You see, I was a litigator in a previous life. A defense attorney. The Devil's Reapers were my largest account. When the dead came, I kind of ran out of clients. And food. And safety. The Reapers took me in and made me one of their own. I realize that the backstory is a little boring here, but it's important. As a lawyer, I was able to spot lies a mile away, and while you seem to be telling the truth, your friend was as full of shit as a Christmas goose. My brothers were going to persuade Tim to speak by removing his fingernails with a pair of pliers, but I asked them to hold on, and found this in his pocket."

He held up Tim's Baldy Mountain ID badge.

Crap.

"Young Tim finally acquiesced and told us about his escape from the facility, grabbing that vehicle, and how you saved him from a throng of those things on the road and have been inseparable ever since."

Good work Tim!

"Minor here," he thumbed at the guy with him, "was...upset? Disappointed?"

"Hurt that I was left out," the huge guy added.

"Ah yes, *hurt,* that he was unable to attend the questioning. So he decided that Tim should lose at least one fingernail. Who am I to prevent that? After all, I'm still a probie. Your friend is sore, but he'll live. At least for a bit longer."

"What does that mean?"

"Oh, you needn't worry about that," the guy told me and shut the cell door. "What you should worry about is the next line of questioning. While you appear to be telling the truth about things, you were still caught sneaking around in Reaper territory." He made a show of looking me over. "I don't see any Reaper ink or colors. Pure and simple, you were trespassing, and there's only one penalty for that."

The huge dude snorted again.

"Actually, there's only one penalty for anything."

They locked the door and laughed and talked on the way out.

I lay back and put my head back on the cot, the realization of a biker enforced death penalty sinking in quickly.

"They're going to kill you, you know that right?"

Someone had read my mind, or I was hearing my thoughts louder than usual.

I didn't even open my eyes. "Everybody dies."

"Yeah, well, they're going to make you fight a bunch of the dead in a ring. You like that smartass?"

"No. I like quiet. Shut up and let me think about fighting zombies." I didn't mean to sound like a dickhead, but I just wanted to sleep until they killed me.

"Screw you, pal, I'm just trying to help you."

This time I did sit up on an elbow. "Help me? If you want to help me, break me out of here." I looked through the bars to the cell directly across the corridor from me. The guy in there looked less beat up than the rest. "I appreciate the heads up, but it doesn't change my situation."

The dude squinted at me. "You look like one of them anyway. I heard you telling them you were in jail before. Where did you really get that big truck the guy was talking about?

This guy was not about to let me get any rest, and my head was killing me. In addition, his questions and demeanor screamed *informant*, which I had seen before, so I played it up. "You should drop your eaves better, chief. I met the guy with the truck on the road. He was taking a piss and almost got overrun and I saved his ass. He asked me if I wanted a ride, and I said yes. He's a decent guy. That's it."

"Why didn't you just let the dead get him and then take the wheels?"

I rolled my eyes. "Because then I would have had to sort through his infected parts to get the keys all the while fighting off the ones that ate him. As it turns out, the thing doesn't need keys. I thought about just taking the truck from him, but like I said, he ain't a bad guy." I put my head back on the cot and turned toward the wall. Other than some whimpering down the cell block, the place grew silent, and sleep took me soon.

The sounds of a scuffle and a guy shrieking *No!* over and over woke me that evening. The bikers dragged him away unkindly, smacking and pulling him while he fought to escape them. I sat up on the cot, and my head throbbed. They guy in the cell across from me, the inquisitive one, was gone.

Two of the bunch of Reapers stayed behind and came to my cell. Both were armed with shotguns. They stood in front of the door and looked at me, then at each other.

"Him?"

"Yeah. C'mon, *Chief,* somebody wants to meet you."

I stood, and waves of pain undulated through my noggin and the back of my neck. It passed rather quickly, and I shuffled like a zombie to the now open cell door. The darker-haired one, short but powerful-looking, pointed to my right, and they escorted me down the corridor. A guard waited for us at the reception area, and I noticed two DLSD vests hung on a metal coat rack, forgotten and dusty. Deer Lodge Sherriff Department.

We left the police station, moving into the street. It was lit up with fifty-five gallon drums with stuff burning in them. The air was warm, and the fifty-five gallon streetlights made the place look pretty, the flames creating dancing shadows on the quaint brick structures. Armed Reapers were walking the streets talking, but not many average citizens were around. In about a hundred steps, we were in front of what passed for city hall in this tiny town. It looked like an old brick school.

The smaller of the two bikers pushed me from behind. It was just a little push, *a move your ass*, type of thing that tagged me on the shoulder and made me take an elongated step forward.

It *really* pissed me off. My head hurt. It hurt a lot, and I just wanted to go home and see my friends. Screw the government, screw the zombies, and right now screw these damn bikers. I wanted to see my oil rig and feel safe.

Really not expecting any trouble, the smaller one went to push me again, I could just feel it. He leaned forward to push my right shoulder with his left hand, and I twisted, moving forward and to the left. It was his turn to take an elongated step, and I turned around and folded my arms looking at him, "Look dickhead, I'm old enough that I can walk without your hands on me. If you're cruising for a piece of ass, I don't swing that way."

The taller of the two smiled, obviously entertained, but the little one did something I didn't expect. He scowled and pointed the shotgun at my face. Then he did something I never would have thought he would do, he pulled the trigger.

Nobody will ever *get used* to being shot, or even shot at. Anybody tells you different, they're full of shit. Speaking of shit, a teeny bit may have squeaked out of me when that gun went off. Yet again, the shot went wide. This time because the big dude saw the murder that I had failed to see in the little dude's eyes, grabbed the side of the shotty and pushed it to the right so I could keep my noggin.

So I kept my noggin. Most of it. The barrel of the weapon went off maybe ten inches from my left ear. It was loud. Fucking loud. I cupped my hand to my head (remember, I already had a throbbing melon), and fell to one knee. A colossal ringing noise made me think there was a jetliner touching down on my forehead, and then the pain stabbed through harder. Feeling something sticky and wet, I pulled my hand away from my ear, and you guessed it, it came away bloody.

"You out your friggin mind?" the big one asked (it had sounded like: *outcha*). "You kill him and Chains'll cut your nuts off."

"Fuck that. Prick was trying to excape."

I thought I had misheard him. What with my screaming head and newly screwed up sense of hearing. I hate assholes who can't say escape. It's pure laziness. For Christ's sake, didn't his mother slap him when he said excape? Or nuke-ular, or axe, like axe a question? Evil murdering biker assholes are one thing, but being grammatically lax is inexcusable, *especially* if it's on purpose.

I tried to stand, and the little one gave me a shove with his boot. I fell on my ass and rolled to the side, immediately nauseated. Damn my head hurt. I retched. It was a very manly retch. I looked up and the little one was on his haunches looking down at me.

"Aww. Little pussy gonna puke?"

The big one nudged his buddy with his boot, using his chin to point to a group of three guys coming toward us. The little guy stood and, as an afterthought, spit on me.

You know, I keep calling him little, but he wasn't. He was short, but the kind of short that you know is tough. He just had that tank-like build to him even if he was only, like, five-six.

I sat up, my palms on my throbbing temples. The other three Reapers had arrived, and they were wearing actual leather jackets emblazoned with the Devil's Reapers insignias and colors. The two douchebags that had brought me out of the cell only had leather vests. That said something to me, but damn if I could figure out anything with my melon in its current state.

The bigger of my two escorts said nothing, but Short Stack said, "Chains, this is the guy, right?"

The man he had addressed shuffled forward with a jab/cross that knocked Shorty down. It was like lightning. My dulled senses picked up on the fact that this guy was the leader. In total contradiction of what I wrote moments ago about not being able to think straight, I admit that I instantly reckoned this guy, in addition to being in charge, was also extremely fit, a fighter, and brooked no bullshit. He reminded me of the MARSOC guys.

He reminded me of Remo.

Then my mind exploded with shitloads of thoughts, synapses firing willy-nilly. Where were the MARSOC boys? Why hadn't they rescued me? Why wasn't this town a smoking ruin with bits of Reapers scattered liberally about? Was Ship OK? Was Tim OK? Was I correct in hating Lynch like I did? Would I ever eat those little cocktail weenies in bourbon barbecue sauce again?

All I heard was: "Alive." I looked around for the speaker; it was the boss, Chains. Turning my dome had been a mistake though, and I leaned over and dry heaved.

"I need him alive, Petey." He shook his head. "Dead is as useless as...you." He kicked the guy on the ground, formally known as *the little one*, in the balls so hard, I was fairly certain Petey would be coughing them up soon.

In a fetal position, Petey did cough, but nothing resembling a testicle came out of him. He just kind of moaned, and I thought immediately of zombies. Cut me some slack, this is a zombie story.

"Get him up."

I was hoping they were talking about Petey, so I could just hang out and collect my myriad of broken thoughts, but alas, it was not to be. The bigger of my two escorts, and one of the new guys each grabbed an armpit and yanked me to my feet.

It was my turn to moan like an infected. I nailed that shit too, even though I tried like hell to come off tough.

I managed to squeeze out a question through my throbbing dome, "What do you want with me?"

I sounded like some movie douche that would be in this exact situation. *Not* tough.

Chains didn't even look at me, but he got down on his haunches and looked at a writhing Petey, who was cradling his nuts and looking pretty miserable. "That's one."

Petey looked scared, but he nodded.

Chains turned on his heel, walking into the building we were in front of. The two dudes carry-dragged me in after him.

BOOM

They sat me in a chair, across a beautiful oak desk from Chains. He was engrossed in a file folder, some of the contents half-spilled across the wood. He put some in a pile, the others he would look at and then put them face down when he was through.

He didn't look up when he said, "Get him some water."

One of the dudes came back after a moment and tapped me on the shoulder with a bottle of water, which I graciously accepted. "Thank you."

The dude shocked me when he told me I was welcome.

I didn't feel welcome.

The boss came across something in the folder, looked at me, back at the folder, and nodded. He stood and came around to my side of the desk, leaning against it and folding his arms.

He reached behind him, grabbed one of the items that was on the desk, and showed it to me. It was a picture of me with a bandage around my head. I was in a make-shift triage area, one that looked familiar. I swallowed my water, probably a little too hard. I remembered where that picture was from. The photo had been taken in Tennessee, probably more than a year ago now. It had been taken by none other than my favorite spy-prick, Lynch.

Chains raised an eyebrow. "Is this you?"

"Nope."

He looked at me with simultaneous expressions. One part looked like he was my dad and had caught me lying to him. The other part was undoubtedly the spider looking at the fly in the web. I could see this guy's hunger. He stood, moving his hand slowly toward me. I thought for sure he was going to slap or punch me, but I didn't want to appear the pussy, so I let it come. I was surprised when he used two fingers to pull my T-shirt to the side, exposing a healed wound on my collar bone.

He looked me in the eye, a half-smile appearing, I looked right back.

"It's you."

"That guy is fuk'n ugly," I said pointing to the picture. "Clearly, I'm prettier than he is."

He reached down and lifted my leg, pushing up my jeans and pulling down my sock. "Definitely you. Don't fucking lie to me again." He held up his right index finger. "That's one."

It's not like I can claim *I couldn't help it*. It didn't *slip out*. One second I was processing *That's one* from Chains, and the next I was on the floor cradling my melon in even fiercer agony. I couldn't believe he had hit me in the head. Maybe he didn't know how damaged my noggin was. Maybe he did, and wanted to exacerbate my pain. A thought ran across my mind. It was a memory, a recent one. Realization hit me like a thunderbolt. I had said something… I had answered his *That's one* with a question.

"How many do I get?"

Surrounded by three bikers, who were probably itching to kill me, I had back-talked the meanest of them instead of keeping my mouth shut. What a friggin' dumbass.

The two guys were lifting me up again, and they dumped me unceremoniously back into the chair. "This asshole is public enemy number one?"

"Don't' worry about it." Chains got up and moved back around the desk. "Lot of people looking for you. Why?" He sat back down and pushed a laminated document, obviously water-proof toward me. I picked it up and tried to read it, but couldn't focus right away. When I was able to concentrate, I saw that the sheet had a photo of me and some information on who I was, even the scars I had, but not what I was wanted for. There was a blue and white seal with a bird carrying a plant in one talon and a bunch of arrows in the other. Department of Homeland Security.

What the fuck?

Lynch! That spook asshole had reported me! To who? The President? Why was the government, what was left of it, working with crazy-ass murderers?

I looked at him. "Where did you get this?"

"They're all over the place, flyers pushed out of a plane. Read the bottom."

I looked down and saw the word REWARD, and everything made sense. I nodded. "So I'm a payoff."

"Yes." He steepled his fingers with his elbows on the table. He looked just like my eighth grade biology teacher, Mr. Harris. I fucking hated Mr. Harris. "Why do they want you. What did you do?"

I was deciding how to answer that when Chains stood. Apparently, I was taking too long to come up with a viable answer. I held my hands up in supplication, and he raised an eyebrow.

"I can neither confirm nor deny that I may have appropriated some shit that wasn't technically mine. It was just laying around, how was I supposed to know it belonged to the government?"

That peaked his interest. He sat back down and looked at me, thinking. I could see the wheels turning. If the shit I had stolen was worth more than whatever Homeland's reward was going to be, I could be a lucrative find indeed. He popped the inevitable question. "What did you take?"

"You know, at the beginning I didn't know what it was. I mean, I got some guns and ammo, yeah, but there was this computer hard drive, and that's what they wanted most."

My best line of bullshit yet. There was no friggin' hard drive. I'm actually giggling a little as I write this.

"Where is it now?"

"Baldy Mountain in Northern Montana. I got picked up by some alphabet agency guys, they never told me which one, and they took me to Baldy. Then the place got overrun and I got out. I found Tim on the road, and then I met you wonderful people. And then you hit me in the head. A lot." I rubbed the back of my neck for emphasis.

"Tim is the geek you were with, the one with armored truck?"

"Yeah."

He crinkled his face a little, it wasn't dignified. "Why didn't the dudes at the mountain just tell the people who chucked out these flyers?" He pushed another flyer at me.

"I got the impression they didn't get along. Something about differing opinions on how to run what's left of the country. About who should be in charge. Apparently, they didn't like the President's orders."

"President's dead."

"Nope. Not as of a week or so ago anyway." I had no idea if the President was alive, eaten, or just mostly eaten, but I wanted to show as much confusion as possible.

"So do we need this prick or not?" That had come from behind me. One of the apes with guns.

"You do," I said immediately. "The assholes looking for me don't know the hard drive is lost at Baldy."

Chains raised his eyebrow again. "And the guns?"

"They took 'em. But there's a shitload of guns at Baldy, and a hundred years-worth of ammo. Problem is there's a shitload of dead fucks in there too."

A gunshot sounded from down the street, then another, then another. Chains didn't look at all disturbed. His eyes flicked from mine to one of the gorillas. "Check it. Be quick about it." He looked from his stooge to me and back. "And check the pens."

Pens? Writing implements? WTF was he talking about?

The guy left and the boss leaned back in his office chair and looked at me hard. "You met my lawyer. He can smell bullshit a mile off, and he says you're on the up and up." He folded his hands. "You also met Six-Pack. He was planted in the cell next to you," (I knew it! Told you!) "and he says your story didn't change." (This was looking better for me,) "Problem is…" (Uh-oh,) "I just don't trust you."

Another gunshot. Chains looked at the window. The second gorilla moved toward the window, looking down at the street. "Got one down there. Where's our guys?"

An explosion ripped through the night. It was down the road some, but still close enough to shake the building. Gorilla number two turned from the window, "That came from the west, I dunno if—" The top of his head all of a sudden ceased to exist. Actually, the sequence of events went something like this: He had said *dunno if,* his melon popped like an overripe grape, spraying his dome back across the floor and ceiling, the window he had been in front of blossomed a hole, then shattered, he dropped, and I leapt for his gun.

I know the hole in the window came first, I do, but I swear that's how it looked.

I spun the weapon to get the drop on Chains, but he wasn't there. He was on his belly on the floor, a HUGE pistol pointed at me. "Don't. What the fuck is happening?"

"How should I know? I'm a hostage remember?"

The door opened, and three guys came running in, one was Petey. "Get down," the boss yelled. The three of them dropped to the floor and army-crawled over to us.

"Chains," one of the dudes (not Petey) said, "we've got deaders, and somebody is shooting at us!"

"So shoot back!" His giant gun was still pointing at me. "How many deaders?"

"I don't know, but Danny and Big Red ain't answering the radio!"

Everybody was yelling.

And then Petey dropped the bombshell: "So, this asshole shows up in his armored truck and we suddenly have people shooting at us? Why does he have a gun?"

Now everybody was quiet and looking at me.

"Yeah, it's the fucking SEAL team I had hidden in the glove compartment, asshole. They were stashed next to the zombies that are hitting us. Airstrikes are next, you douchecrust." I rolled my eyes, perhaps a little overdramatically. "I was gonna help you pricks, but screw, take your gun." I slid it across the floor to Chains, who stared at it for a second.

I had thrown the "us" in there to see if I could buy some trust. Fat chance, I know, but still. If Remo and the Jarheads…holy crap, awesome band name…were here, lots of folks were going to die. Hopefully, Tim and I weren't about to be lumped into that group.

I felt as if I were actually on fire from the look that Petey was giving me, but if I was about to die, I wouldn't go down without a fight. Even if it was only verbal in nature. One of the guys got on his knees and looked toward the window. He crawled over to it and used the reflection in a piece of broken glass he picked up to see out the window while keeping his head down. Smart.

A bullet came through the plywood, sheetrock, muscle and bone, skipping off the floor and shattering a glass something across the room. The guy slumped forward chin on chest. Not smart.

Motorcycle engines were roaring up and down the street, gunfire was roaring from several directions, and my ears were roaring from the fear and tension. Another round came into the room, and it was way closer than I would have liked. Petey looked up at me, eyes wide, and began backing up. He rolled over next to the guy who had just bought it, his shotgun pointing at the ceiling. I didn't think this was overly smart, but I also didn't think Petey was overly smart, and I didn't like him either. A third round hit the desk, and Chains yelled something.

I heard a bike crash and then more screaming, as the remaining douche belly-crawled over to Chains, who was now talking into a radio, "Danny! Red! Where are you two assholes? If you're high, I'm gonna kill both of you, I swear to Christ!" Chains continued to yell obscenities into the walkie-talkie until screaming began from inside the building. The last guy suddenly rose quickly bringing the desk with him, standing it up on its end. It was a big desk, but this was a big dude, hopped up on adrenaline and who knows what else. He began shoving shells into his shotgun, but he only got two before he was out of ammo.

"Nobody's answering." The boss looked at the radio. "They're either dead or they're going to be. Sonny, Petey, let's get the hell out of here and figure out what's happening."

"What about him?" Petey demanded, looking at me.

"Take him, and if he gets out of line, fuck the reward, do him."

Petey actually looked like a nice guy when he smiled. Granted that smile meant he was absolutely going to shoot me. No matter what happened, I would get blasted trying to escape, or trying to get the gun from him or whatever, so that's exactly what I planned to do.

The smart guy, the one with the big hole in his chest, opened his eyes and expectorated a large gout of blood. His next move was to grab for Petey, but the live guy was having none of the dead one, and deftly brought the butt of his shotgun up under Mr. Holy's chin. The dead guy's teeth clacked together, and he bit off half of his tongue. Petey quickly reversed the weapon and turned the deceased biker's head into mist.

What with bullets flying from an unseen enemy, bikers shooting dead bikers, and undead moving about in their secure town, Chains looked only mildly annoyed. "Out the door, down the stairs, out the back."

Oh, and explosions, forgot the explosions. Another large blast came from somewhere close. Dust fell from the ceiling, as did some of Gorilla Number Two's gray matter, and Chains was the only one of us who didn't look around like his ass was on fire. He reminded me of every tough military guy I had met since leaving prison. He reminded me of Remo. He reminded me of Lynch. I had to wonder if he was military trained, and probably would have if gunfire, screams, and a few more smaller explosions didn't scare me. I didn't hear moans, so I was hoping that whatever undead force was on the hunt wasn't sizeable. A few dozen infected would cause chaos and I might be able to escape in the ensuing confusion. A few hundred and I was most likely chow.

The four of us inched our way to the stairs then made our way down. The back door was made of wood with a glass window taking up most of the top of it. The shade was drawn, and Sonny, the bigger of Chains' two goons, moved forward and peeked out past the shade. He backed up quickly, two sets of arms bursting through the glass to grab a snack.

Petey fired his shotgun into the two pus bags trying to gain entry and to his credit, he got both with his buckshot. Zombie A and Zombie B tumbled backwards, and nothing else came in. Sonny looked out the window, and looked back at us.

Now Chains looked a little nervous. "Is it clear?"

"No."

"How many?"

"Looks like a Raiders game just ended and everybody's heading for the parking lot."

Holy shit. I mean holy shit what a *fantastic analogy*. Why did these bikers have to be evil bikers? Why couldn't they be bikers that brought you cake? With analogies like that, Sonny and I could hang, we could be buds. Petey had that adoring smile, and Chains with his nonchalant attitude to his world falling apart…well these guys were akin to people I liked to be around.

Don't get me wrong, I was going to have to kill them all, but still, the point is valid.

"Well, we can't stay here, they'll tear this place down around us." Chains moved past us and out the door. He looked right and shook his head. "Not that way." We all exited the building and ran left. We were in kind of an open alley with a Harley on its side. That drag mark you've seen countless times came from under the bike and moved off into the bushes. Why some infected just hoark a guy down where he falls, and others like to drag their victims off is still a mystery to me. Maybe they like to eat in privacy? Regardless, we could hear that wet ripping sound, and we knew what that meant. The sounds of chewing, multiple chewers actually, spurred us into action.

We jogged down the alley-thing and turned a corner, right into a band of undead that were shuffling in our direction. Either we were in amongst them or they us, it didn't really matter once the biting started. Sonny was bitten almost immediately, but he still fought well. He fired four shots from his shotgun, and it clicked empty. There were probably ten plus a baker's dozen infected, and he had killed five before one caught his shotgun club and another got in close and tore his throat out.

Petey was jacking shells and firing at noggins as fast as he could, and Chains was using his massive revolver. Both were crazy loud, but neither was effective enough, and I realized the dead were going to reach us if I didn't act. I reached over and pulled the little automatic pistol out of the back of Chains' belt, the one that I had slid to him earlier. He didn't even turn around. Stepping between the douches, I began firing as well, and I didn't miss a single shot. When I ran out of targets, I turned to see Chains hand to hand with two dead bastards, and I shot one in the dome, while Chains broke the neck of the other. He looked at me, then at himself, then back at me. We had gotten them all, but more were on the way. Petey was loading his shotgun with shells from a bandolier across his chest. He looked up at me briefly, then back at his weapon, "I really thought you were an asshole. Maybe—" I shot him in the face, spun to shoot Chains, but he was already pointing his gun at me.

He lowered it. "You know, I really don't like you." He clicked the hammer back on his cannon. "Why do the alphabets really want you?"

"I told you—"

He held his left arm out. That circular mark of doom, just starting to bleed was on his forearm. I felt bad for a split second. "I'm immune."

He raised his eyebrows like we had been beer-buddies for twenty years. "No shit?"

"No shit."

He sighed. "Then don't fuckin' die." He put his weapon under his chin and blew his head off. Seriously, the top of his head came off.

I heard crunching behind me, spun, and saw two dead bastards coming for me across some gravel. I shot one, and the slide on the automatic stayed back. I discarded the weapon and went for Chains' gun. It too was empty, so I opted for Petey's shotgun, and did this super-cool roll to get away from the dead thing that was reaching for me while at the same time grabbing the gun. I brought it up quickly and only had time for a chest shot on the first one. It flew back out of my immediate field of vision, as I had to adjust for the second one. The shotgun's kick was again substantial, but so was its damage as the head of the infected on the business end of the weapon ceased to exist. The lifeless form collapsed and I swung the barrel of the gun toward the one I had shot in the torso. I pumped out an expended shell, a fresh one entering the chamber. I remember hearing the casing hit the ground, and thought it was odd that I could hear it over the din of the carnage near me. It was at that point I was hit by a freight train.

All teeth and claws, this thing tore at me like it was a tiger and I was a...a...well, something that a tiger would eat. My weapon clattered to my left, and it was all I could do to fight the thing off. It was strong. I heard screaming, and realized that it was both the infected on top of me, and me. I took a nasty punch to the nose, becoming stunned for a half second, and the thing wrapped both of its disease-ridden hands around my throat and squeezed. Fucker was choking me out.

Cool went right out the proverbial window and I began to panic. Air had taken a vacation from my windpipe, my lungs burning after just a moment or two. Where the hell was my adrenaline buddy now? I'm sure my eyes were bulging too. They must have been about eight feet out of the sockets, because that's the only way I could have possibly seen a zombie with ragged hole in its chest cavity staggering toward us, its entrails dragging behind it.

This was not the first time I had had a Runner atop me shrieking, but it *was* the first time one of them was trying to compress my esophagus to the thickness of a credit card. It leaned in to bite my nose off, so I felt it prudent to jam a forearm between us. I was starting to see stars (no shit), and the diseased prick astride me began to look like he was falling away down a long green tunnel. Or maybe I was. Either way seconds were critical here, so I didn't delay.

The last time this had happened to me, I had done something truly spectacular. This time I was in worse shape, so I brought my left hand around, grabbed the side of the prick's noggin and jammed my thumb in his eye. It was my turn to squeeze, (not that this asshole had let up) and I felt the eyeball go under the onslaught of my digit, goo squirting down on my face. Aqueous humor, if you remember from Baldy Mountain.

Dickhead could have cared less, and actually squeezed harder if it were possible. I noticed the dead one had gotten close enough to get down on his knees and was looking at me like an entrée, when everything went black.

PAIN

Ow.

Thud, thud, thud.

Ow.

Thud, thud.

Ow, dammit.

Thud. Thud, thud.

For fuck's sake OUCH!

"Is he bitten?"

"I don't know, but he's damn heavy."

"Pussy."

"Screw you! You carry him, he's dead weight."

"I can carry me…"

"What?"

"That was him, put him down."

The guy that had been running with me over his shoulder put me down. I was ecstatic to see that it was Kinga. I looked left, and through my haze and the darkness I could see Brick. Well, two Bricks, I was seeing double. That shit *can* happen.

I put my palms over my throbbing eyes. My head was throbbing too. Hell, everything was throbbing. My neck was sore and my throat dry.

I tried to clear my head by blinking, and realized that I couldn't see out of my right eye. That was unsettling, so I reached up to probe it with my fingers. I found it was crusted with blood, which is when the cuts on my face started to sting.

Not for nothing, but the damn zombie apocalypse really sucks.

"What the hell took you assholes so long?"

The two MARSOC guys looked at each other. Brick thumbed at me and spoke to Kinga, "This fuckin' guy." He looked at me smiling. They were both smiling. "We ain't the ones who got our asses handed to us by a teenage girl."

Nope. No. I did not battle a girl. It was a *man* infected with the most horrible disease ever. This particular man was the exceptionally massive mutant spawn of a couple of Lees. Bruce and Mohammad Ah. OK, OK, so you didn't get that. Bruce Lee and Mohammad Ali. It was funny, you're just dumb. Bottom line is that the infected ass wipe that had tried to make me dead was *not* a ninety pound chick.

Both of those dicknoses pointed to my left. I glanced over at an overturned fifty-five gallon drum that had been being used as a lamp-post. Around it, drenched in gore and full of holes were the zombies and bikers that I had just battled against, battled with, and subsequently killed.

One had been, in fact, a young, blonde girl.

Crap.

The fight felt like it was five years ago and five thousand miles from here, but the carnage was a mere fifty feet away, and the proximity spoke as to the time as well.

"We can't stay here," Brick said, and pointed. Shadowy forms were stumbling their way toward us. "Can you stand?"

"Damn right I can stand." I stood. Well, halfway. I promptly fell back on my ass. I dry heaved, sending tendrils of agony through my head and into my shoulders.

"Shit, help me get him up." Brick looked at his watch. "We need to be at high two in five." They helped me up, and I've got to tell you, I didn't like it. I would probably have enjoyed being eaten less, but this still sucked.

"Where's Tim?"

"Remo and Ray-Ban have him and a bunch of the townsfolk."

Townsfolk. Ha! He sounded lame for a professional killer. We crept along a low stone wall near a pharmacy, my arm over Kinga's shoulder. Brick looked in all directions at once, and it still awed me how these guys were so calm. My cracked melon had a thought, and it was that these guys aren't afraid because they don't know how to be. They're true heroes, and if whoever finds this journal and is undoubtedly standing over my eviscerated corpse was ever in the military I would just like to say thanks. Thanks for everything, and I hope you make it.

A small group of stumblers shuffled past us while we were crouched in the shadows, and I decided that I had been carried enough. I removed my arm from my date's shoulder, and he nodded, passing me a pistol, butt first.

There were plenty of dead roaming about, but we seemed to be running low on bikers. Apparently the Reapers had been reaped. We crossed in front of a few of those big, green recycle bins when Brick, moving like lightning, grabbed something, beating the shit out of it with about three quick punches. A gun went off, not in our direction, and then the thing was on the ground. It had been the thing's gun, and it was now disarmed. Brick simultaneously aimed his weapon at a new noggin while checking the new weapon.

Kinga looked around. "They'll have heard that, let's bug."

Brick made to shoot the man on the ground, but he put his hands up in supplication, "Please! I'm not one of them! I'm not a Reaper!"

It was obviously true. He wasn't a bad-ass biker. We were looking at a skinny guy who had never been in a fight in his life. He had probably never held a gun before the one Brick had taken from him. He had been a lawyer though, in another life.

"He's not a Reaper," I told them. The guy stood and looked at me. "He's worse." I shot him in the leg and the bastard screamed loud. Brick and Kinga looked at each other, then at me. The douche I had just ventilated was back on the ground holding his thigh. I got down on my haunches and stared at him, almost losing my balance.

"Maybe you can litigate yourself out of this one, counselor." I looked over his shoulder at the cluster of pus bags on the way to investigate the shots. He made a desperate grab for my pant leg, but was woefully short. I hadn't even moved. "I'll tell Tim you said hi."

The three of us left him there, us slinking away in the dark. "That was some cold shit right there," Kinga told me.

"He deserved it." I heard him pleading as we passed another dumped motorcycle, then that high-pitched screaming started from where we left him, but it was brief. Fuck him.

Should have covered him in marinade.

My head was really hurting as we made it to a bank on the east end of town near the water tower. Ray-Ban met us at the door, and Remo popped up from nowhere. He was chewing a toothpick and looked me over. "You look like shit."

The MARSOC guys had enough gear to supply a flotilla of naval units. Remo had his rifle, a sidearm, and a black t-shirt. "Yeah, well you need a knife."

I surprised him! He looked surprised, and thus had shown emotion. He also pulled a big-ass knife out of a sheath that I hadn't seen. Then he smiled, I shit you not. "So do you."

I made an automatic reach for my chest, and then my hip. My SOG! Those biker douche-canoes had taken my knife!

Ray-Ban told us to get inside, and we did, except Remo, who was gone when I turned around. Guy was an actual ghost, and I have no doubt that video games were based on his past exploits.

The bank was full of people. There must have been thirty of them. Townsfolk as Brick had said. Someone wormed their way through the crowd toward me. It was Tim. He had a bandage on his finger, and I suddenly felt no shame about shooting that prick lawyer. Not that I had shame-a-plenty up to now.

He must have just had a poop-sandwich because he was wearing a shit-eating grin. "You look like crap."

"I get that a lot."

Then he did something I didn't expect. He hugged me.

I've been in prison, you know this. The "hugging" they wanted to do in there was a tad different than what was happening to me right then, and in the joint, I was able to assert myself in such a way that nobody came near me. I'm not huge, but I'm big, and my particular prison was medium security, but you still had your tough guys. Tim was not tough. Actually, you know what? Tim is one of the toughest sons of bitches I know. I'm ashamed I just wrote what I wrote and would like to take it back. See? There's shame.

Anyway, I didn't fight him off. That was the point I just strayed from and took too long to explain. I hugged that little dude right back. It was good to see him alive. We sat down (I really needed it), Tim and Brick telling me their portions of what had happened to them.

Tim's story was the same as mine except without the head trauma. Nobody had thumped him on the dome with a wrench. They did question him and pull out his fingernail though. That couldn't have been fun, and having all my nails right now I don't want to try to compare my headache to his finger pain. Both suck. They were taking Tim to the pens when Remo found him. I'll get to the pens in a minute, and as you can imagine, it went bad for the bikers with Tim.

Brick's story was way better. Nobody hit him in the head or tore out his fingernails, and he got to smoke a bunch of bad guys, so it was win-win. They started by doing recon. True recon, not the *take a peek over the hill for three seconds* shit that they excelled at. They grabbed a biker and got the Reapers story too.

Apparently, there had been some kind of motorcycle rendezvous for all the chapters of the Devil's Reapers out here at a ranch when the pandemic decided to rear its ugly head. Everybody was dying, but the bikers sat back and watched it on TV and listened to it on the radio. After the cops were either dead or running, the bad guys came out in force and grabbed up what they could, arming themselves and killing anyone that got in their way, or looked funny, or was minding their own business.

When the story was done, so was the biker's usefulness, and Kinga ended him silently. They now knew what they needed to accomplish, and split up. Brick had gone with Kinga, Ray-Ban would take the guys on the tower when the time was right, and Remo just killed everything he saw.

Brick and Kinga found a bunch of the townsfolk (can't stop saying it now) during their recon and extracted them as they could, storing them in the bank like a week's pay. That's what took so long for them to rescue my ass: getting the people out. They couldn't get everybody, but they got who they could before they unleashed their nasty surprise.

Remo saw some bad guys pushing Tim around, making him walk in front of an infected. The thing and Tim were tied to a pole together, the zombie just out of reach of my pal, well, vice-versa really. They were apparently going to feed him to more infected, and that's when Remo found two more tractor trailers full of zombies. The pens that Chains had mentioned. He dispatched the shitheads, destroyed the infected hitched to Tim, and brought my nerdy buddy back to the bank.

They set some generators up to go boom, then killed the bunch of assholes who came to check on the hubbub.

Remo let the infected loose from the pens, radioed to the MARSOC boys that the feces was on the fan, and then the killing really started. They straight up murdered every biker they saw, using zombies to do the heavy lifting and wreak havoc.

Ray-Ban did the guys on the tower as silently as possible, then used his incredibly sexy M14 EBR sniper rifle to deal death from above. He still won't tell me how many bikers or zombies he killed, prick. He's the one who blasted the guys in the office with me. I asked him if he had known I was there. His only reply: *Nope*. But he had seen me come out into the alley and almost get eaten. He didn't want to smoke the teenage infected that had tried to choke me out for fear of hitting me, but he had shot one of the gorillas (not Petey) and I hadn't even seen it happen. He let Kinga and Brick know where I was and they got to me just before Ray-Ban would have made the Fuck-It call, and shot the little bitch that was killing me anyway.

Zombies and bikers and tough-guys. Oh my. The boys moved about, quietly removing threats, or wounding and allowing zombies to remove threats. So I told them my story. My story was lame.

As I was telling my lame story, a pack of undead had found us, and a woman pointed to the window and screamed. There were only a few, but these people weren't used to infected... Wow. That was a stupid statement. Like anybody is *used* to these things. Anyway, they started banging on the bank window, and all of a sudden a shadow shows up, kills them, and fades back into the darkness. It was like watching Batman. Not the 1970's or 80's or 90's pussy Batman, the mid-to-late 2000's Batman that killed everybody. One guess on who it was.

We sat there for a few hours and I got tired. Tim and Kinga had tried to keep me awake, stating that head injuries were bad, and sleeping with a possible concussion wasn't the best thing. I told them to screw, and that if I were going to survive a zombie apocalypse, giants, bikers, rednecks, rogue militaries, underground installations, and a super-spy, I would not allow sleep to kill me.

So yeah, with all this shit going on I took a nap.

WRAPPING UP AND MOVING ON

When Tim nudged me awake, the sun was shining through the tall glass-front windows of the bank. I sat up fast, reaching for my rifle, which was a tremendous error on my part, as I no longer had a rifle. In addition, the pain and nausea centers of my body decided to collaborate on a paper entitled *Don't Sit the Fuck Up*, and were looking to me to publish.

I put my head back down on the sleeping bag, and put my hands to my forehead. "Ow."

Tim looked at me like a stern, self-righteous physician. "You really should have stayed awake. Sleeping with a head injury can be a serious thing."

"Got news for you, Timmy," I said through my hands, "we're all already dead, and this is Hell."

Tim looked thoughtful for a second then smiled, "I'm glad you're still you."

"I'm not. Everything hurts." I swallowed, or tried to. "And my throat is…" I looked past my palms, noticing that Tim was holding out a cup of water and some pills. I graciously accepted them, and swallowed the pills on the first try with the entire cup of water.

I looked at my hand. "What were they?"

"Percocet."

Damn, Tim wasn't screwing around. He had given me the good stuff.

"So, Remo, Ray Ban, and Kinga have been out clearing the town all night. They have thirteen Reapers in the jail, and have taken care of all the infectoids." *Infectoids*? Whatever, he could have that one. "Kinga radioed back to Brick to let him know that a group of Reapers came in at about one this morning on their bikes, totally unaware that our guys had taken the town. MARSOC took care of it, and added some of the bad guys to the jail, and some to the morgue."

"And the town?"

"Totally safe and with the homeowners in control. Well, those that are left. The Reapers did a number on this place. Our guys found a bunch of girls in a room in their barracks." He looked away. "It was bad."

"Wait... Remo allowed prisoners?"

"It was his idea. He thinks that the town should have a trial."

I perked up at that. "That's a good idea. Although I can only see one penalty for those assholes."

A guy appeared to my left. "May I sit down?"

I palm-pointed to the floor next to the sleeping bag I was on. He sat. "My name is Ed Parsons. I was the town assessor. When the Devil's Reapers showed up after the plague started, they killed the sheriff and the three deputies he had."

It was almost like I had just heard this shit. Blah blah. Zombies ate my dog. Blah blah. Bikers killed my goldfish. Sorry, Reader, if I seem a tad insensitive, but my head hurts right now, I've heard all this guy's bullshit before, *and* I just re-figured out that if you're reading this then I'm probably dead, so I'm pissy.

Parsons was going to be the new mayor, death penalty for all bikers, thanks for saving us, will you please stay and help us. That last one was new. Usually people either couldn't wait to get rid of me, wanted to incarcerate me, or wished my demise. Deer Lodge was kind of nice, other than the cliché, Road Warrior-type biker gang. I was typically the one disaster seemed to follow, but this place had been pre-disastered by the Reapers, so who knew?

But I couldn't stay. I had to get back to my homies. I told Parsons he was out of luck on me hanging around, and he smiled and said he understood. No hard feelings, thanks, hand-shake, bye.

Remo showed up with Kinga a moment later and told people they could go home. Some were filing out of the bank when a beautiful apparition appeared on the other side of the glass. It was not a busload of porn stars, but it was close. It was my MRAP.

I smiled and put my head back down on the sleeping bag. This was going to be a good day. They let me rest for a day while the jarheads taught some of the folks in Deer Lodge some tactics. The bikers had appropriated an incredible arsenal, and the military guys showed the ordinary folks how to shoot as well. I thought for sure at least one of the MARSOC boys would stay behind, but they all said that wasn't part of the mission. Brick had radioed to the carny camp to let the other military dudes know that the Reapers had been dealt a huge blow. They weren't completely gone, but their numbers were now significantly lower. Brick wouldn't tell Deer Lodge where the camp was, but he told the camp that Deer Lodge could use some help.

My noggin felt better the next day. Kind of like a bad hangover, but not the throb session it had been. Baldy Mountain had seemed like a million years ago, but it had been only a few weeks past. All those people…all the people here… The death just kept coming.

Our gear and weapons had been stored at the sheriff's office, so I got most of it back. My 416 was fully loaded, with my extra six magazines. I laid her out on sleeping bag and cleaned her before it was time to leave. All the stuff from the MRAP was still in it, and the grateful folks of Deer Lodge gave us some more supplies, and we now had a shit-ton of ammo. I was sad I didn't get my SOG back. That was as important to me as my rifle, or even the truck. I didn't really know anybody as I had slept while the leathernecks schooled the townsfolk—damn, hard not to say that now—so I didn't really have anybody to say good bye to. That was good. I waved and got in the truck. Remo was on one bench chewing a piece of gum. Ray-Ban looked back from the driver's seat, not a little chagrined when he saw the look I gave him, but I smiled and told him the driver's seat was all his today. He nodded, and when the door slammed behind us, he fired that mother up and we drove off.

I-90 sunk south through the map for about twenty miles, (I wanted to sound cool and write "klicks" right there, but I don't know what a klick is. I will have to ask the boys), then hooked to the east and in another ten or so miles went right through Butte. Butte once had a population of about thirty five thousand the atlas told me, so we decided to head south on I-15 prior to heading into that particular nightmare.

I-15 had been bombed. Nothing else could have accomplished the destruction we were seeing. The highway was simply gone. We saw the occasional car, and the occasional stumbling corpse, but no crowds. Passing signs for Beaverhead National Forest, we saw a group of about thirty live people. They were heading down the forest road on foot, and hid in the grass when we drove by. We left them alone, and within the hour passed into Idaho.

We stopped the first night after Deer Lodge about fifteen miles north of Idaho Falls. It was dark, and we decided to eat outside with a real fire as there wasn't anything around us but the flat landscape for miles. We were tired of the MRE heaters, and had some of the provisions that the folks in Deer Lodge had given us as a going away present.

We pulled a big log, which had no business being anywhere around here as there wasn't a tree in sight, over onto the side of the road and sat on it. Brick built a fire out of some trash and a few choice pieces of wood hacked off the log. Remo was chewing on a piece of jerky when he sat down next to me. He looked at me and nodded, then reached into his webbing and pulled something out. He handed it to me, and even in the firelight I knew what it was.

It was my SOG. This Jarhead bastard had had my knife the whole time. Everybody, even Tim, started chuckling. Sons of bitches! Of course I started laughing too, and soon we had a great guffaw. Then we talked. Not about our current world, but about shit before. We *talked.*

It was great. These guys were guys I would have hung out with prior to this tiny little undead issue. Except I had been in prison.

Brick told us about his surfing buddies in California. He told us about endless parties and tanned legs before he left for the Navy. Kinga was on the opposite coast, and was at Holy Cross in Massachusetts before serving. Ray Ban had joined the military right out of high school. He's twenty-one years old. Tim told us what I already knew; he had worked for the NSA as a computer nerd for ten years now.

We were all laughing and joking when I caught Remo staring at me.

"What?" I asked between chuckles.

Everybody stopped talking and looked at us, the laughs slowly subsiding.

Remo reached into his vest, pulled out something and passed it to me. It was a laminated piece of paper. I looked at it and then at him.

He put a toothpick in his mouth, an elbow on one knee, and a hand on the other leaning forward. Then he raised his eyebrows.

Crap.

The other three MARSOC boys and Tim remained silent, expectant looks on their faces.

I handed the card to Brick, he looked it over, then passed it to Kinga. When it at last made it to Tim, Tim looked scared.

Everybody was looking at me.

"I'm immune."

Remo stood. "I need a piss." He strode into the shadows.

EXPLANATIONS

"Wait," Brick asked, "immune to what?" It was his turn to raise his eyebrows. "The plague? Bullshit!"

"Been bitten three times." I pulled my pant leg up and put my leg closer to the fire.

Kinga, Brick, and Ray-Ban all looked at my bite then at each other. It was an unmistakable bite wound. I pulled the collar of my T shirt down and showed them the scar there too, but that looked like I had lost a battle with a belt sander.

Kinga took the laminated sheet from Tim. "What the hell is this? Why is Homeland looking for you?"

"I may have mentioned that I'm immune."

"He did!" Tim added quickly. Thanks for the support there, Tim old sock. "A CIA spook found out, tracked me to Atlantis, and carted me to Baldy Mountain at gunpoint. Baldy fell apart, I escaped, and then I met you wonderful people."

Remo came back and sat on his log. The three MARSOC guys looked at him, and Ray-Ban popped the inevitable question: "What do we do now?"

Remo held his hand out to Kinga, who gave him the laminated paper with my mug all over it. The tough bastard didn't even look at it before he threw it in the fire. Then he spit. "We finish the mission."

Ran Ban thumbed at me, "But he—"

"Doesn't change the mission." Interrupted Remo. "What I want to know is how you let three of them get close enough to bite you." He hadn't asked, he just said it and expected an answer.

Now everybody's eyes (except you-know-who's, he was poking the fire with a stick he pulled out of somewhere) were on me, even Tim's.

"Well," I started, "the first time I was working on a broken down truck, and the fucker was underneath it."

"You didn't check first?" demanded both Brick and Kinga at the same time.

"No, I'm not a fuk'n SEAL. I wasn't trained to look under vehicles for undead cannibals. Besides, it was like, day two of the outbreak, and nobody knew shit yet. Anyway, that thing did the calf biting, and the group I was with decided that I was a liability and left me to die."

"Assholes," Tim blurted.

"You know," I said sympathetically, "I thought about that as I lay dying in a decrepit Airstream trailer. Initially I agreed with you, but after careful consideration, I came to an understanding of what they did. I could have turned at any time. They had kids." I shifted on my busted log and scratched my ass. "So after the thing bit me I got really sick. Like, super, gonna die sick. I had only seen a couple bites, but after day one, everybody knew a bite was a death-sentence."

Tim looked really intrigued. I had told him that I had been bitten, but we had never had a detailed conversation about it. "Then what happened?"

"I got bitten again. These two enormous undead bitches tried to eat me when I began to die on the highway. I passed out and the heifers were on me in minutes. The first one got me here," I pointed to my collarbone, "before I blasted her. The second one got close and I put one through her dome. Then I walked off into the woods, found the trailer, and climbed in to die. Then I got better. I met my buddy Ship a bit later, and the rest you know."

"You said you were bitten three times." I don't know who said that, it was either Kinga or Brick.

"Yeah, I got another one here," I tapped the one on my side, "in a struggle another time"

"I got sick every time I got bit, and when I was incarcerated at Baldy, they actually injected me with zombie goo to see if I would die."

Things like: *Those bastards,* and *Fuckers*, and *Assholes*, blurted out from everybody. Even Remo stopped his fire poking and looked up at me. He looked pissed.

"Well, I didn't die."

"But are you a carrier?" demanded Tim.

"Apparently not. The Baldy doctors, and there were a lot of them, told me that none of my fluids, and they took them *all*, had any trace of whatever this is. My liquids are the same as everybody else's. Then there's the fact that I bit one of the doctors," Remo whipped his head up at that one, he *whipped* it, "and he didn't die. Well, at least not from my bite."

Tim's eyes were the widest, but it was Brick that asked, "What did you bite him for?"

"He was a dick, and he was talkin' shit. All that stuff is in here." I pulled out my first journal, and then the one I'm currently writing in. "Read it if you want, but I need it back."

Tim looked at me funny, "You're keeping a log?"

"Yeah, why not?"

"I'm still having a hard time believing the whole immunity thing," Kinga said. "Everyone, absolutely everyone dies from a bite." He was shaking his head.

"Sorry brah, not everyone. Do you think I made those damn laminated wanted posters up myself, then littered the countryside with them so some military dudes would think I was cool?"

"Don't *brah* me, bro."

Remo reached for my first journal, nodding in acceptance when I gave it to him. "I'm going to get some rack." He stood up and got in the MRAP. What a line of bullshit. This guy was so tough I'm sure he thought sleep was for pussies.

Now the MRAP, having two fold-down stretcher bays, and two banks of seats you could sort-of stretch out on, was somewhat accommodating for sleep, but only for whoever got into a stretcher first. There were six of us, so five guys could sleep lying down if one guy was on the floor between the benches, but somebody had to sit in a driver's seat for the first watch.

I volunteered. I had gotten a good snooze with my busted head back in Deer Lodge. Tim said it was a good idea that I didn't sleep too much, even though I had gotten some sack time, if not quality, already.

We finished eating, and got back in my truck. Remo gave us a nod as we entered, he was stretched out and reading on the left side bench seats with a small light. Brick, Ray Ban, and Kinga threw one or two fingers, and Brick was odd man out. He got the floor. Tim and Kinga took the stretchers with Ray-Ban on the opposite bench from Remo.

Everybody was asleep in minutes.

It's boring and lonely when you're alone with your thoughts with nothing to do for a few hours. Reminded me of prison. I thought about my friends back on Atlantis, and couldn't help but wonder about the destroyer that I had seen tied up to her when Tim and I had used the spy satellite. I thought about Lynch, and what had happened at Baldy, both what they had done to me, and the cluster-fuck they had pulled on themselves. Lynch made me think about Dallas and *his* spooks. Dallas' Lynch and mine couldn't have been a coincidence. Then I went off on a *me* tangent. Did I have the right to keep myself away from those who could use me to figure out what the hell was going on and how to stop it?

With all the tests the doctors and nerds did on me at Baldy, they had never come up with anything. One of the doctors had said that if this thing was a virus, it was damn difficult to figure out where it was. It had to be in the bodily fluids, but they couldn't find it even in captured undead specimens. They had looked for odd bacteria and fungi in addition to viruses and had found nothing. That was about the extent of what I knew, but I still mulled it over until Remo scared the ever-loving shit out of me with a tap on the shoulder.

He handed me the journal. "That was some funny shit. How much of it really happened?"

I was groggy, but I got what he was asking. "All of it."

"And that Lynch guy was a real bad-ass huh?"

"He was. He called himself an *asset*. I prefer ass-hat. If you read the second journal, somewhere in there I say I wouldn't have minded seeing you and he duke it out."

"Huh." He nodded to the side like he wanted me to follow him.

"What's up?"

"Time you learned some shit," he said and moved to wake up Brick for second watch.

I got up and followed him out of the MRAP, as Brick woke up with alarming alacrity and took my seat up front. Nobody else even stirred.

We closed the door and it locked behind us. He pulled his giant knife and passed it to me hilt first. "Kill me," he said.

PLANNING

I lifted an eyebrow and looked at him in a *no way* manner. "I may be dumb but I'm not stupid. I try to stick you with this thing, and shortly thereafter it resides in my anus."

"Exactly. Don't you want to learn how to do that?"

Guy had a point. How had I lived on earth so long without learning the skill to put a big knife in some dude's pooper?

"How would you come at me? Do it slow."

I held the knife so I could come at him with a downward stabbing motion and did just that. He put his hands up in sort of an X and caught my wrist. Ever so slowly, he rolled one hand over the other gripping my wrist with his right hand and using his left forearm to push down just above my elbow. He did it gradually, so as not to hurt me, and show me what he was doing at the same time. "Grip the wrist here, and exert pressure above the elbow. Below the elbow and you lose most of your effectiveness." I ended up facing down, he took the knife from me and I was looking at the butt end of it half an inch from my face in half a second.

"Now you try. Slowly."

He came at me with an exaggeratedly slow attack, the knife coming down toward my skull the same way I had done it to him. I mimicked his movements, and to my surprise, had him face down with his arm bent up in a moment. "Now pull the knife from my hand with a slight twist, but don't grab the blade."

This last part was trickier, but he walked me through it until I had it. He sheathed the knife and we worked it without the knife, again and again, over and over until I could do it quickly and effectively.

It was awesome.

We worked few more *techniques* as he called them, until I could defend multiple forms of knife attack. He taught me to attack the weapon, not the man, if I could. He said that club attacks were almost the same thing, and we would learn those as we moved south.

And we did. We moved overland to bypass Idaho Falls to our east. Like almost everywhere else, the dead had claimed it. The Reapers may have been more evil than this plague, but at least they had kept Deer Lodge zombie free.

Moving southwest, we crossed over Route 26, west of a town called Blackfoot, then did the same to Pocatello where we crossed over Interstate 86 then swung south. There were small rural roads that we took until we reached Interstate 84. We stopped there to have a pow-wow. Salt Lake City was to the south, then Provo. Two big cities for the middle of nowhere. Provo had about a hundred thousand people pre-plague, but Salt Lake City, when you figured in all the surrounding boroughs, was a headliner with about one point two million. We hadn't seen any infected in two days.

We were cooking chow when we decided that we would have to go overland to the west then hook south and run parallel with Interstate 15. That was about two hundred miles of flatland to the west of the Rocky Mountains. State parks all over. That could be good or bad. Last time I had stopped at a state park, we had been attacked by lions.

Lions were better than a million zombies though, and Remo continued to instruct me on how to defend myself and kill bad guys at each stop.

Another issue popped up as well. We would have to swing east at some point, as I-15 moved right through Sin City. Las-effing-Vegas. We ended up deciding on south to Route 89, then east just north of Grand Canyon National Park. We would be immediately north of Arizona by then, and ironically, that's where we ran out of gas. Diesel actually, but you get the point.

Big Water was the town. Town. It had a population of less than five hundred. But it had diesel pumps. This shit place was about three miles from Lake Powell, and that was a big tourist trap.

All five hundred Big Water people seemed to have better places to be, and not a soul, living, dead, or undead was in the area except us. Yes, Dear Reader, I realize that the undead have no souls, but kindly shut it, this is my story. We didn't recon the buildings, as anything in them would come toward us anyway, and we had no intentions of entering any of them except the gas station.

We spotted the gas station on Route 89 just before noon. It looked like it had been buttoned up for the weekend not the better part of a year. No signs of distress. No signs of anything. We did a quick circuit of the joint and pulled over. Remo was the first one out of the MRAP, and we all followed him except for Kinga, who remained behind to charge the batteries on three of the spare ANPRC 152 radios using the in-vehicle charging station. I busted out the map, and Tim helped me spread it across the asphalt. The wind was such that we couldn't keep it on the ground, and we opted for a quick recon of the station itself.

Brick banged on the door five times and we waited for the obligatory stumbler to come...well... stumbling. Nothing came. Using a crowbar from an outer container on the MRAP, (actually it was a military tool that looked really fun to play with) Ray-Ban busted us into the place. We cleared it in under a minute. It wasn't that big.

It was also completely untouched. No power, so all the milk and other refrigerated items from the convenience fridges were gone over, but there was tons of other stuff, including...you guessed it: Mountain Fucking Dew. I grabbed a twenty ouncer and did half of it in one tilt. Nectar of the gods, I shit you not.

I put the Dew down on one corner of the map that Tim was spreading on the counter by the cash register. I snapped into a Slim Jim and we studied the chart. Route 89 to 98, overland to 264 through the Hopi Indian Reservation, south on 87, west on 40... holy shit. I remember Dallas talking to me about traversing the US from west to east, and that took three months. We were going north to south, and I had been away five months at least already. I looked out the window at the MRAP, then back at the scale of miles on the map.

Shit.

"Team huddle," I said aloud.

Everybody perked up and came over. I passed out Slim Jims. "We need a plane." They all looked at me, then at the map, then back at me. It was friggin' funny. "We have another thousand miles to go give or take, and we're averaging about forty miles per hour when we get good road. That's…"

I started counting on my fingers, but Tim piped up damn quickly, "Twenty-five hours."

I couldn't believe it. "Is that all?"

"Yeah, but the further south we go," Brick said, "it will be much harder to stay away from populated areas."

"Better think on a couple of weeks if all goes well. That's if we can keep in the diesel."

"Speaking of which." Ray-Ban dangled a set of pump keys from his fingers, but with no power we would have to figure out a different way.

"Place has got to have a generator," Tim said. "I'll go check out back."

Brick grabbed his arm. "Not alone. Actually, even with the wind it's quiet here, I don't want to start up a generator and tell anyone or anything we're here unless we have to. Let's see if we can find some hand pumps."

Tim nodded, and he and Brick moved off to look for a pump. "Hey!" I said, "I wasn't done." They all looked at me expectantly. "We should think about flying. In fact," I looked out at my MRAP again and let loose with a tremendous sigh, "we have to fly. Brick's right when he says that the population is going up as we go south. It will explode." They all looked thoughtful. "Besides, what happens when we get to the water? We're hoping there are boats, and there probably are, but what if there aren't? We need a plane."

"Nope," Remo said and spit out his toothpick on the floor. He looked *exactly* like Clint Eastwood in the Outlaw Josey Wales. It was uncanny. "How you going to land a plane on an oil rig?"

"Fine, a helicopter then."

Brick began looking at the map, drawing lines with his finger. "There's five of us. Better be a strong bird. No sightseeing news choppers."

A thought came to me, "You MARSOC guys can all fly helicopters right?"

"I played Call of Duty a couple times," Ray-Ban volunteered. "I was pretty good."

I blinked. "Wait, none of you guys can fly?"

"Why would *we*," Brick asked, emphasis on we, "know how to pilot a helicopter?"

"You're bad-ass military dudes! Don't they teach you that shit on day two of basic or something?"

I don't think anybody caught it except me, but there definitely had been the flicker of a smile on Remo's face. Microsecond timeframe, but it hadn't been my imagination. I looked at him hopefully.

"Don't look at me."

Brick, Ray-Ban, and I began to get into a heated discussion on why I thought they should all know how to fly at least something. A single-engine prop plane, a military helicopter, a fucking kite, anything!

Nope.

Remo tapped me on the shoulder and I turned to face him. He was pointing over my shoulder, and it was my turn to whip my head around. Tim had his hand up. "I can fly."

I was astounded. "You can fly what?"

"A helicopter or anything up to a multi-engine fixed wing. I have a commercial rating."

This guy! I love him, I shit you not. True blue, dyed-in-the-wool hero. Yay nerds!

"How many hours do you have in a helicopter?" Brick asked Tim.

"Almost a thousand. They didn't let us out much at Baldy, and one of the things they encouraged was training." He shrugged. "I liked to fly, so they trained me."

Brick pointed at Tim. "That's good." Brick looked at the map, then ran his finger in a line southwest. "Closest base to us would be Camp Navajo, and it should have a shitload of everything we need, assuming it hasn't been looted. It's a training facility for all kinds of shit. I did my crew-served training there, as well as M-203 and desert survival."

Ray-Ban nodded. "I did M-203 and M-249. Desert too."

"Sweet numbers," I said. "What the hell do they mean?"

"Grenade launcher and Squad Automatic Weapon. You've seen the SAW, they were on the walls at our camp."

"Oh, yeah, I've seen them in other places too. Sorry."

"Yeah, but Navajo is right outside of Flagstaff," Remo said. "That's a city with more than a hundred thousand people. Some of them must have tried to get to the base for safety, and that base is huge, so I don't see the base personnel being able to keep them out. When we did our desert training out in the middle of nowhere, the only deterrent I saw was a threatening sign on a chain-link fence as we drove in. No way Navajo could possibly defend the entire perimeter."

Holy shit. Remo had said all that at once. An entire paragraph. I mean, I think I got it all correct, but still, just writing it freaks me out. This was unnatural.

"So it will be a tough incursion. We'll have to plan and—"

"There's another base." Tim had interrupted Brick mid-speech, a small breach of etiquette, but it looked like Brick was going to overlook it. "Joint Base Jackson-Gray." Everybody was looking at Tim now. "It's here." He put his finger on the map just like Brick had. "Just north of Tuba City Arizona. We're..." Tim looked at the scale of miles on the map, "a hundred miles away, give or take. City had a population of about eight thousand, but the base is north of it, and it was a quiet area. We could head due south on Route 89, and be there in a few hours if 89 is clear."

"Never heard of it." Brick's brows were furrowed as he looked where Tim had touched the map.

Ray-Ban shook his head. "Me neither."

I looked at Remo expectantly. He nodded in the negative. Back to his silent self apparently. We all redirected out gazes back at the Timster. "It's there. We used to communicate with them all the time. We got spare parts for our helicopters from them; they have a huge machine shop way bigger than we did at Baldy. But... I was ordered to check on them using my Sentinel sats when they didn't respond to us a few months ago." He sighed. "It looked abandoned." He perked up a little. "There were several helicopters there though. Four Chinooks, and some other, smaller birds."

Ray-Ban looked at Brick. "Operational range of a Chinook is about, what, two hundred miles?"

"Yeah, easy. And," he looked at me, "it can carry your pimp mobile." He thumbed at my MRAP.

I got an instant stiffy. Not only would we be flying over hostile, infected territory, but we would be taking my baby with us? Best. Day. Ever.

"Yes, but carrying that," it was Tim's turn to thumb at my MRAP, "will seriously, and I do mean *seriously*, deplete the fuel. The Chinook is a transport helo, and can carry up to twenty-eight thousand pounds including cargo and crew, but heavy loads should only go for short distances. Also, I've never flown with a slung load." He looked at me and looked down, saying in a weak voice, "I wouldn't recommend carrying the truck all the way. Besides, what are we going to do, put it on the oil rig?"

There are several ways to just straight up wreck a woody. One is cold water. Another is imminent danger. The third is when the group smarty-pants-nerd tells you that you have to leave your sexy, zombie-proof, armored vehicle behind when a certified killer has just told you it can come with us.

Well, shit.

"OK," I said, "the MRAP stays at this base then. That's a bitch, but I think flying is the way to go."

Brick and Ray-Ban nodded. "Agreed," they both said at the same time.

Remo got up and left. I didn't see his face, but I knew he liked the truck as much as I did and was sad to see it go.

The four of us talked logistics for another two minutes or so until a loud thud came from the plate glass window right next to us. I can admit a little pee might have escaped right then. Yes, it was an infected. Yes, it was a Runner, and yes, Remo dispatched it in about three seconds from behind with his knife. He yanked its hair back and drove his knife down into its esophagus as it pounded on the glass, a great gout of thick crimson spurting on to the pane. Rather than fall to the ground and bleed out in a matter of seconds as etiquette demands, the thing spun and launched itself at our buddy. Nobody, not even Remo saw this coming. The thing grabbed him by his T-shirt, and tried to gnaw his face off. The uninfected got his forearm across the infected's ruined throat, and in only a few terrifying seconds, we could see through the blood smeared window that the thing's strength was spent. It collapsed/was thrown to the ground, no doubt gurgling, before we could get outside to help. Before we could react at all really. My eyes were still wide from the initial impact of the thing against the glass.

We got to him as he was coup-de-gracing the infected by driving his blade into the creature's eye. He stood, a disgusted look on his face. "Ripped my shirt."

He went to drag his forearm across his face and I screamed at him, "STOP!" which he immediately did. Frozen with his arm in mid-air he looked at me. I pointed at his appendage. It was literally dripping with tainted blood. He looked at his arm, then at me, giving me a curt nod.

"Let's wipe that shit off of you, OK Chief?"

He nodded again. That was about the time we heard the screaming.

BIG WATER.
POPULATION: LOTS.

When I was a kid, maybe eight, I went to stay with my grandfather for a week in Maine. It was a great trip. He lived alone on a lake in the middle of nowhere. We went fishing and hiking. We swam in the lake and he showed me how to make a fire and which plants were edible. I got to see some great wildlife that you just don't see in Massachusetts.

Round about nine o'clock on night two, we're sitting around the campfire, just he and I, cooking the fish we had caught in the lake earlier that day. (Not a lot tastes better than landlocked salmon and largemouth bass that had been swimming around not five hours before, especially when you had caught them with your granddad.) So I reach over to grab a Coke out of the cooler and I hear this caterwauling scream that scared the ever-loving shit out of me. I looked around as a terrified eight year old does when confronted with something that unnerves them. I half expected some horrible apparition to come crashing through the woods to gobble me up.

Grandpa put his rock-steady hand on my shoulder as I searched, and pointed to the tree across the fire from us. Perched on a branch not thirty feet from where we sat was a bird about the size of a beer can. It let loose with another scream, and I thought it impossible that such a loud noise could come from so small a critter. That was the year I learned about screech owls.

The terror I felt as an eight year old hearing that screech returned as I stood looking at Remo's dripping arm. The scream I was hearing now was not unlike that screech owl, but this time I knew what it was. Even though I had access to what was basically a tank against infected, and was surrounded by four of the toughest guys on planet Earth, my oversized nuts shriveled up into my stomach. I was, again, scared shitless. I wasn't the only one either, as everybody searched quickly for the source of the sound.

The scream was answered by another, then another, then two more. It seems we were surrounded by invisible runners. The really scary thing is that up to right then I had thought they were mindless. The calls they had just made certainly seemed like coordinated hunting calls, and answering hollers as well, but how could mindless infected be smart enough for that?

I didn't have time to contemplate this, as the first of them came sprinting around the garage side of the service station and headed right for us. (Good thing Tim hadn't gone looking for a generator.) One came from the other side, and two from a house down the road. More shapes were loping towards us from the distance. Brick dropped the first one with his HK416; single shot, center mass, then Remo and Ray-Ban started firing as well. They moved into a triangular formation with Tim and I in the center.

The MRAP isn't overly loud, but it's still a big truck, so why hadn't we been attacked instantly upon arrival? They must have heard us. In addition, we have all figured out that Runners aren't dead; they're infected humans that have lost the ability to reason or think rationally at all. Moreover, if these things weren't dead, that meant that either they had recently been infected, or they had been eating steadily. I instantly remembered the Runner that had taken a bite out of one of the dead ones back in Havre. Thing had chewed and swallowed, and that had been new. All interesting topics to discuss with the boys if we made it out of here alive. We hadn't even gotten the gas yet. (I know, diesel.)

My 416 was brought to bear, but I had been trained in the past few weeks only to fire if the MARSOC boys missed (didn't see) something, or when they were reloading. Oddly enough, even though I felt my nuts clench with every Runner's scream, I didn't feel that panic I usually felt creeping in.

A group of six of them were dashing toward us from town, and Ray-Ban picked that moment to shout, "Loading!" I stepped up next to him took aim, and fired at an older woman with running gear on. She had been prepared I guess. I could see her blood-red eyes from two hundred feet. I missed the first shot, but got her with the second. She fell, but got up and started back toward us much more slowly. She wasn't dead, but the round had fucked her up. I fired twice more, nailing another woman in the shoulder and spinning her, and missing with the last round. Ray-Ban shouted, "Ready!" and got back on the line. The dead ones were beginning to come out, and I had to wonder again why they hadn't attacked when we first pulled in.

"Negative!" I heard Brick shout. "Stay inside! If we need a quick out, we can fall back to you! Cover the back!" He must have been shouting into the radio to Kinga, who was still in the MRAP.

"Loading," Remo said almost casually, and I stepped up to his position. He did this tactical reload that was so fast it was almost done before he had finished speaking. I hadn't fired a round. Tim was standing in the center of us with his pistol, and to his credit he looked as not-terrified as I felt.

In about a minute, all the Runners were down. Not all dead, but hurt enough that they could no longer run. Brick switched magazines. "Pack it up and let's re-fuel before they get here." Several dozen undead were on the way, and it was then I realized that Big Water was as dead as every other place we'd been to. It just looked better. These dead things had flair.

Kinga had pulled the truck up to the pumps, and it was then we grasped the fact that we hadn't had the chance to get any hand pumps. Remo and Ray-Ban ran off to find a generator, Brick, Tim, and I setting the Jerry cans out and removing the caps. The vanguard of the dead would be on us in thirty seconds. Brick grabbed an entrenching tool off the side of the MRAP, passing it to me and he hefted his crowbar-like apparatus. Tim grabbed a piece of pipe that was lying next to one of the pumps. "Don't get too close," Brick told us.

"They're damn fast when they get near you," I reminded him. He nodded. The first to reach us, a fat guy and a thing so mauled I couldn't tell what sex it had been, received equally as deadly thumps on the noggin from Brick and I. I had used the side of the shovel end of the tool so as not to get it stuck in fat dude's head. We got through about six more before we realized that this wasn't going to work. There seemed to be many more undead coming from the surrounding area than the five hundred or so that were supposed to make up this town. The three of us heard shots, and soon Remo and Ray-Ban were running back around the side of the station. They both skidded to a stop when they saw what was shuffling toward us.

"We. Are. Leaving!" Brick yelled. We were sprinting back to the MRAP, Kinga waiting with the door open firing Ray-Ban's EBR. With the sound of the .308 rounds, he couldn't see the dozen or so stumblers that were right on him. I did the only thing I could think of. I shot at him. Well, I shot at the glass window with fresh Runner goo on it. It imploded and he jerked his head to the left. Seeing the pus bags that were already reaching for him, he fired into them and was able to get the door to the truck closed after a brief but victorious tug of war with a dead girl wearing only a bikini bottom. The dead bastards began beating their rotting fists against the side of the vehicle until they noticed the four meat popsicles in the middle of the road, then started toward us.

At the same time, dead began to flood around both sides of the station. We were in some deep shit. The MRAP fired up and Kinga took right off. He barreled down the road, turning anything in his way into bad-smelling strawberry jam. But while I was looking at the new stains on my MRAP, all the stainees and their pals were looking at me. They looked hungry. Except the ones that had come apart at the seams when they got run over, they looked like the aforementioned strawberry jam.

It didn't take long for Kinga to turn the truck around and flatten some more pus bags on the way back to us. He made it just as the main force got to us, but we had already dropped quite a few of the vanguard.

I had an extra two magazines on me, but we were starting to burn through ammo. A particularly skinny woman pushed up to Brick and he hit her with the butt of his rifle. She didn't give a shit and latched on to his forearm with her nasty paws. I was in mid swing with the entrenching tool when dead bitch's head snapped back, goo shooting out of her as Tim's .40 cal round exited her melon. I over-swung and took an involuntary step forward, right into the reaching claws of a half-naked young guy with horrible wounds on his neck and shoulder. This guy had no doubt been one of those dick-head tool-bags, complete with gold chains and fifty selfies on his phone of himself and the other shitheads he hung out with. Shirtless, muscles flexing, and baseball caps on sideways.

The claws were on the left hand only, the right arm was nowhere to be seen. I wonder if he was popping a selfie as the thing tore his arm off?

The thing fell forward, teeth first, to rob me of my schnoz. Off balance, I was able to get the blade of the tool in front of my face, and his teeth smashed into the other side of it, both of us going down in a heap. I kicked away and tried to roll back into the relative safety of my friends, but the dead douche grabbed my 416, and the sling choked me when he started pulling me back toward him. I spun and tried to fight him off, but Tim shot this one too, and it let go of my rifle.

If anything, there were more of the dead here than three minutes ago. Kinga drove right past us and skidded to a halt. The back door to safety opened up, and we rushed over to it, Kinga firing his rifle over us at the closest ones.

"Save it!" yelled Brick. "We're good!

We piled in the back of the truck, Remo closing the door in a bunch of dead faces. The truck jolted forward a little and we were off. No, Dear Reader, I haven't forgotten about the lack of fuel in our vehicle, but driving away from this particular event with almost no diesel in the tanks was better than hanging around being trapped in the MRAP with a thousand fists pounding on the steel.

The only road was the one into town, and we barreled down that for another quarter mile before the MRAP began to shudder. "Fuck!" Kinga yelled from up front. My Mine Resistant baby shuddered a few more times, sputtered, and the engine quit. We were smack-dab in the middle of the residential section of the crappy town, and its residents all decided to come out to see us. We grabbed what ammo we could, as the majority of the dead folks were coming from where we just were, and they were slow. We didn't want to hang around though.

Another scream rent the air, and there were scrabblings up front as a speedy infected climbed up on the hood of the truck like a four-limbed spider. It threw its head back and screamed so loud I thought it would pop, then launched itself at the front window trying to bite Kinga through the bullet-resistant glass. Its vile fluids spattered the window as it tore at the glass. Kinga recoiled appropriately, and moved to the back with us.

"Remo, how we looking back there?" Brick demanded

Remo, looking through the back door double window, spit out his toothpick. "Environment is target rich."

"How close?"

"Sixty meters."

Brick wiped his forearm across his ebony forehead, "Last guy out shuts the door, we might be able to get back with fuel. We head for those houses and see what we can find. You two," he pointed at us, "make sure your safeties are off and don't shoot unless you have to. Ray and Tim, you carry the food."

They each picked up one of the bug-out bags we had previously packed with food and water. Brick and I had the ammo bags, and Kinga was positively covered in ammo already. Remo had his knife.

"Remember the one on the roof." Yeah, like we all couldn't hear the bastard up there, trying to scratch through the steel with his fingernails

"Forty meters," Remo said like he was informing us it was tea-time.

"Do it!"

Remo threw the door open, and kicked out with his boot. He jumped down, leaned over and stabbed a pus bag through the eye, then let out with another side kick to the right. I heard a sickening crunch, and another dead woman fell forward into view, her leg bent wrong. She reached out to grab him and he shot her in the forehead with his sidearm. He spun, swinging the knife in an arc, catching what used to be a young girl in the top of her dome while simultaneously shooting out of my line of sight. An upward palm thrust sent the tongue of one of the things flying out of its mouth before he pulled the knife from the little girl and jammed it through the eye socket of now-tongue-less.

This had all happened before any of the rest of us could get out of the truck. "Clear. Well, for a minute." He casually lifted his handgun and shot the Runner that had leapt screaming from the roof of the MRAP. He had caught it in the throat, and it gurgled as we filed out of the armored rear door. It reached for him, and he kicked its filthy claws away, shooting it again just below the left eye.

We spread out and surveyed our surroundings. Ray-Ban took care of the last dead man in the area with his knife. "This way!" Brick said quickly, and we followed. We ran through a small housing development, the homes way too close together for a town of so few. The first house had an above-ground pool in the backyard, and it was occupied. A blueish-gray man with no shirt on reached for us over the pool wall. Poor bastard would probably be trapped in there forever. We continued on, not seeing any dead in front of us because, hopefully, they were all behind.

Continuing on blindly, we rounded the corner of the next house and my hopes proved fruitless. Brick ran into a group of six of them. Two latched on to him and leaned in to eat, but the MARSOC guy was having none of that, and fought them for all he was worth. Both were down before we could come to his aid, and I drilled a third that had grabbed his shoulder with my shovel, cleaving its rotten dome down the side. The front half of its face fell to the overgrown grass, the thing taking another step before collapsing. Brick destroyed another before Kinga and Ray-Ban were able to dispatch the remainders.

More were coming, and again I had to think that there were more than five hundred people in this shitty town. The place was eerily silent as well, except for the moans of the things that had given a slow, plodding chase. Our hushed voices echoed between the houses a little when we dared communicate.

We made it through the residential area only killing one more of the things. A structure larger than a house loomed before us. It was a brick school with no front door. We could see shuffling forms through the broken windows on both floors. Deciding to skip school, Brick brought us past a drugstore and a hardware store into a small parking lot. We caught our breath next to a green dumpster once Kinga had cleared it. "They don't give up," Kinga said, pointing. We turned to look, and noticed that a smaller group of infected were closing from behind the school.

"Circle back through the neighborhood," Brick told us between breaths. "Break into two teams, one to distract, and one to fuel up. Distraction team meets back up with the MRAP when it starts. One civvie with each group, my group gets to distract. You two, with me." He looked at Ray and me. He shook Kinga's hand and nodded to Remo. "C'mon," Remo said, and he jogged off to the right of the way we had come with Tim and Kinga.

I remember thinking right then that I hoped I would be able to write about what happened to us later that evening. "Hey assholes!" I shouted. "Eat this!" I extended my middle finger as high as it would go. I totally pulled something in my shoulder when I did it too.

"Did it now." Brick shook his head and we moved double-time in the opposite direction of Remo's team. We took a right between two houses, one with aluminum siding, and the other a brick frontage. The houses were, maybe, fifteen feet apart, which didn't make any sense to me as there was more land here than you could ever need. Why did these folks want to be on top of each other?

As I pondered the possible reasons for the proximity of the homes in this neighborhood, a mottled, filthy arm snaked slowly out from a broken window. Ray saw it and tried to juke around it, but we were moving quickly, and the thing latched on to his tac-webbing. The arm was attached to a dead teenager, and he came through the window without letting go of Ray. Ray-Ban gave the thing a side kick, but it didn't concern itself with the trivialities of a broken collarbone, and threw its other arm around his leg. This was enough for him to stumble, and they both went down in a heap. The dead boy really wanted a piece of my buddy, and he was lazily snapping his jaws as Ray held his rotten head in check with a hand on the kid's throat. I grabbed the kid's hair and stabbed down with my SOG into air. The boy's scalp peeled off like an orange skin. Tossing my nasty prize to the side, I stabbed a second time into bare skull, and my knife skidded off. The thing was still snapping as Ray jabbed his own blade into the right side eye socket. The dead teen stopped moving immediately.

I looked up and noticed that in the ten seconds the last paragraph took to transpire, fifty or so undead had shuffled close enough to the front of us that we wouldn't be able to make it between the houses to safety before they got to us.

Ray pushed the kid off him and I reached down to help him up. "Back!" Brick hissed, and he meant we needed to retreat the way we had come. Ray stood and started yelling. The re-killed dead kid wasn't re-killed and had latched on to Ray's leg. The thing pulled its mouth to Ray's calf and bit him. Ray kicked it off and stomped on its head. My knife had failed to penetrate the kid's dome, but Ray's size twelve made nasty black and gray shit spew out of three sides of a crushed skull. Brick began firing behind us, and right then I knew we were all dead. Ray wasn't thinking that and he grabbed me, pointing to the window the kid had come out of. He gave me ten fingers, and yelled to Brick, "First Sergeant! Up!" I didn't turn to see what was happening, or even think of what could be on the other side of that dark window. I accepted the ten fingers and pulled myself into the house cutting my shoulder on a shard of glass. I quickly cleared the room. It was a bathroom, small, maybe eight feet by twelve, and I was standing in a tub. The door was open, and I immediately closed it, spinning around to help Brick through the window. I got him in and reached out to help Ray. The dead had closed and they were reaching for him as he reached up to me. Ray climbed and I pulled like hell, but several hands began pulling him back. Ray didn't look scared, but crazy-pissed off as he kicked for all he was worth. Brick leaned out and shot the two pus bags that had grabbed our pal, and we managed to yank him through the window, falling on shards of glass that were littering the floor.

The dead outside really wanted in, and the ones that weren't fighting each other to futilely gain entrance through the window were beginning to bang on the side of the house. I didn't bother putting my ear to the door to see what was on the other side, I just yanked it open. We didn't have time to dick around; those infected bastards knew we were in here, which meant they would be in here in short order. I was really hoping the zombie teenager's folks weren't home. A quick pan right and left told me the hallway was clear. I took a step to the right, Ray limping out to the left. "This way!" I hissed, seeing the hallway in my direction open into a kitchen. The other way must lead to bedrooms and no door. I moved forward, trusting that my MARSOC buddies would cover my rear. The banging on the house was getting unnerving, but it didn't mask the creak of a floorboard around the corner to my left. I held my left fist up as I had seen these military boys do countless times, and although I wasn't looking at them, I'm sure they froze as I did.

I heard that odd rasping sound that the dead sometimes make just before a horror that used to be a younger woman stepped into view. She saw me at the same time, and lunged, grabbing me by the shirt, and my single-point sling before I could react even though I knew she had been there. I let go of the rifle and brought my right forearm crashing across my body into her forearms. There was an audible snap as her left ulna broke, and she let go with both hands. I brought my forearm up as her head came forward and I caught her perfectly under the chin. I gave her a right side kick to the knee and as she started to fall forward, I brought my left boot up catching her under her chin again. Her head snapped back, and her frail body followed. She ended up on her back. She tried to stand, and I kicked her as hard as I could in the forehead. Her eyes rolled back in her head and she stopped moving. I had just used some of Remo's training and I felt great. So great that I didn't see the second monster until he was pulling my face toward his.

The sound of Brick's sidearm was deafening in the hallway, and it was a dinner bell for the critters outside not already aware of us, but if he hadn't shot this thing, I would be missing a large chunk of face. Let's not forget I'm pretty, and I would like to thank Brick right now for preserving my pretty. Destroyed, the thing's legs just evaporated and it fell straight down. The bastard didn't let go even in second death, and I went with him, landing chest first (technically weapon first, then chest) on his stink. Dead guy was big. I fought with his clenched fingers for a few seconds before I was able to pry them off. We all heard a window break in front of us and knew that we had issues there. Brick pushed past me and into the kitchen, taking a quick recon. He moved left and we followed. The side door, now behind us, was wide open, but we could see what was out there and opted for the front door. What was out there had seen us too and was now doing the moan-shuffle in our direction.

Brick made it to the front door, but looking through the two small front windows, I could tell it was a no go. The penguins were waddling fiercely out front.

"Shit, back!" Brick yelled. Ray sprinted to the side door and closed it in the face of a fat guy with one cowboy boot on, big belly all but eaten through on one side. The glass in the door was pushed in immediately, hands reaching for us. The left side front window gave way with a crash, and this one was lower, allowing access. The dead began to crawl in instantly. The window over the kitchen sink was full of dead faces, as were the three small, diagonal panes in the front door.

I moved back into the hall searching, and just as the side door crashed in spilling infected on the shitty linoleum, I reached up and yanked on a string with one of those little cones on it hanging from a trapdoor in the ceiling. The door pulled down exposing a ladder-stair, and I yelled for the two jarheads to come quickly. Not waiting, I unfolded then climbed up the ladder thingie and panned my light around. A plywood floor covered the ceiling joists, and there was a cooler, camping light, and two sleeping bags in the corner. Trash littered the floor. I continued panning the light when Brick hit me in the ass.

"What the hell are you doing? MOVE!" I climbed the rest of the way up, Brick following. I stormed up onto the floor finishing my sweep of the attic. Six feet or so high, angled with roof joists and a plywood roof. Basic storage, not a lot, but decent room for stuff. Ray made it to the top of the slanting stairs, but had to kick off something that thought he would be tasty. It started to follow him up, but Brick drilled it with his pistol. It fell back into the crowd that had gathered, and we saw what deep shit we were in. "Here!" Ray almost yelled and passed Brick his multi tool with the Phillips head ready. Ray fired his M9 twice before I was able to join him. Brick got down on his stomach and began to unscrew the access ladder. There ended up being six screws on either side, and he was able to get four before one of the more industrious creatures luckily juked a shot from Both Ray-Ban and myself, pulled itself up and grabbed Brick's arm. Brick looked into its face, and was rewarded with a close up of its head snapping back when I popped it in the melon.

"Fuck this, get back!" Ray shouted. Brick scrambled out of the way. Ray holstered his Sig and pulled his HK416 around to the front of him on his sling, switched to full auto and gave both the dead things and the stairway an extended burst on full auto. He fired into the spot where Brick had been attempting to pull the screws, turning the hinge and the wood around it into shredded aluminum and splinters. The thing crawling up the ladder twisted slightly, but remained on the ladder. I shot it in the face, and Brick fired full auto into the other hinge while Ray yelled, "Loading!" I don't know how, but the stairs stayed attached. I got on my ass and began to kick, and on the second kick the right side came loose and the access fell away with two dead women on it. I looked into the sea of dead faces and they looked back, hungry.

Brick stared down too. "We're in some pretty shit now."

We heard something move behind us over the moans below. We all raised our weapons, aiming our tac-lights at two stacked steamer trunks. Something definitely had moved behind them. "Cover," said Ray, and he took two steps on the plywood. He gripped the handle on the top trunk, looked at us, nodded, and yanked it away. Two sets of terrified eyes stared back at us as we stared disbelievingly at them.

A little girl and a little boy. Filthy, skinny, and scared, they held on to each other as they looked at us.

"Are they infected?"

I let my rifle dangle, then pushed it behind me so it was on my back. "No." Both kids looked at me. "Hey, hey we're not going to hurt you, we're the good guys, OK?"

I pulled a granola bar out of a pouch on my belt. "You hungry?" The girl perked up and looked like she was about to stand, but the boy held her fast and narrowed his eyes. He had a ballpeen hammer in his left hand.

"Kids, it's OK," Ray said. "We won't hurt you, and we aren't infected." I looked at Ray-Ban as he took a step forward. On the plywood where he had just been standing was a bloody boot-print illuminated by the side window.

TWINS

"Roger that. Kids, two. Boy and a girl." Ray looked over at Brick, who had just put away his small med kit and was checking the bandage he had put on the boy's hand. "They're getting checked now. Negative, they'd be dead or worse. ETA? First light confirmed. Rogue One Copies all, out." Damn, he sounded like some dude from Star Wars. Ray sat on a steamer trunk and put the radio down. He rubbed his calf.

I pointed at it. "Want me to have a look?"

"Would it help?"

I looked at the floor.

"How long?" he asked.

"How long what?"

"You've been through this. How long until I'm useless?"

"I'm a different case…"

Ray froze me with a glare and I sighed. "You'll start to get sick in about an hour. You should feel something is *off* sooner. In five hours, you'll be wishing for death, but it won't come for another three to five after that. You won't be able to do much in about six hours." I looked at the floor again. "Nobody makes a day."

"Except you."

"Except me."

"What's so special about you?"

I harrumphed. "Dunno. Been asking myself that since my night in an Airstream trailer a year ago. If there is a God, He sure as shit picked the wrong guy to make immune." I pointed at his leg again. "Want me to have a look?"

Brick stood, ruffled the boy's hair and smiled. He came over quickly. "SITREP?"

Ray started to stand, but Brick put his hand on his shoulder, forestalling him. Ray nodded, drawing his wrist across his forehead. "Kinga says they have the fuel. They took out several

Tangos, but almost got overwhelmed at the pumps. That was the gunfire we heard earlier. They left the gas and bugged out to a house just like we did, but they lost the hostiles that were in pursuit. Most of them were on us. They can see the fuel cans from where they are, but they're going to wait until twenty hundred before they go get it and fuel up. Should be dark enough by then. They'll hole up in the MRAP until first light, then make some noise to draw the meatheads. Swing back, pick you all up and ride off into the sunset on some unicorns."

Brick smiled, his hand still on his buddy's shoulder. "Want me to do it?"

"Only if I puss out. He," Ray thumbed at me, "says I have a few hours yet."

Ray broke out in a smile that would have made a piranha proud and pointed behind us. The boy was standing in front of the open trap-door, pissing on the infected. His sister let loose with a giggle. "Richy, stand back from there, OK?" Brick asked him.

The boy nodded, shook off, and sat back down with his sister, who punched him in the arm. "Gross!" I heard her whisper.

The kids, Richy and Chloe Joseph, were eleven years old. Twins. Their story was the same as everybody else's. Their older brother Tommy had come home from a night at the movies with some friends. He had gotten into an altercation with a drunk in the theater parking lot, and the drunk had scratched him on the neck. He and his friends had pushed the guy away, and run for the sheriff. They never did find the drunk, but that night, there was something terribly wrong with Tommy, and Tommy's mom Lucy took him to the hospital in Paige, Arizona. The next morning, the neighbors were trying to break in the house. Their dad, a bit of a prepper, had gotten them upstairs and told them not to come down no matter what, until he came up into the attic for them. The poor kids had been up in this attic for almost a year. I admired their resolve not to go down and check things out. They wouldn't have made it if they had.

The kids were pretty much through their food and drink. Three cases of bottled water and eighty-eight MREs were all that was left. They would have begun to get thirsty in a week. The boy was prepared to go for a supply run, but they kept hearing movement in the house below them. Two more days and Richy was planning on a run anyway.

One of the more interesting things about these kids was that they had two moms. Tommy's mom was not their biological mother. All six people; the twins, Tommy, their dad, and their two moms lived in this house together. They didn't seem to think anything was different about having two moms and a dad, and who am I to judge? This is Utah.

"The scariest part was that we could hear the zombies making noise all the time," the little girl said. "That sound they make. And some of 'em are fast too!"

"Zombies?" I asked.

"Yeah." Richy said. "I seen Resident Evil. I know what a zombie is." He pointed toward the open trap-door. "Those are zombies. I saw Mr. MacRuder from the garage shoot Steve Joseph in the stomach with his Mossberg, and Steve just got up and bit Mr. MacRuder when he was reloading. Only zombies can do that."

"Saw it how?"

The kid pointed to the louvered vent in the side of the house. I moved toward it and the louvers were the type on little rods, and thus could rotate open and closed. I was able to peek outside. The dead were everywhere, spread out and searching. They usually grouped together, and what I didn't understand was why they weren't all in this house trying to get to us. Don't get me wrong, there were a fair amount looking to eat us, but I would think that with the racket the dead beneath us were making, all the others in town would be trying to chew on us. I could see some of them walking in and out of houses all the way up the street, obviously searching. It didn't make sense. Even if they were looking for Remo's group, everything I knew about them told me that they should all be here where the noise was.

I sat back down on an overturned Home Depot bucket. "Do you guys want to come with us when we leave?"

"No!" Richy almost shouted.

Everybody was looking at us. "OK, OK, we won't make you come. Just think about it, OK?"

"We're waiting for someone to rescue us," Chloe told me.

"Sweetie, that's us. We're here to rescue you."

Chloe nudged her brother. "See?"

"Yeah, but they're *strangers*. I need to protect you."

"They got guns, Rich. And food and a truck." That seemed to work into the boy's head.

He stood up and pointed his hammer at me. "Fine, but you gotta call the State Police in St. George and let me talk to them first. I want to speak to Sergeant Reed. He's my dad's uncle."

I looked at Brick, and he came over and got down on his haunches. "I'm sorry, kid, I really am. They," Brick pointed to the same louvered window the kid did a minute ago, "are everywhere. There's hardly anybody left. I swear I will try a call to the cops, but I promise you, they aren't there."

"Where are they?" he demanded.

Chloe stood and took the hammer with no effort. "Dead, stupid, and probably trying to eat each other. We're going with them. We can't stay here anymore."

Richy let loose a big sigh. "Where are you guys going?"

It was my turn for a shit-eating grin. "Atlantis."

SUNGLASSES DOWN

The kid reached for his hammer, obviously thinking that I was a liar. "Bullshit!"

"Rich!" his sister whisper-yelled, pulling the tool out of reach and looking back and forth from him to me. The boy took a half-step back and looked both chastised and menacing at the same time. He pulled that shit off too. I was in an attic with two tried and true badass killers two feet above a hundred undead cannibals, and this kid was the scariest part of the bunch.

"Atlantis is an oil rig in the Gulf of Mexico. Lots of people, lots of guns and food, no infected."

They looked at each other, then at me.

These two kids, not even teenagers, had survived a year in an attic waiting for a rescue that was never coming. They were filthy, and just about to starve, but looked healthy nonetheless. I was impressed. More than that, the jarheads were impressed, and that was hard to do.

Brick inspected our surroundings. He asked pointed questions to the kids: "How did you keep warm in the winter?" Richy showed us his array of sleeping bags, and two tents that were folded and put away. "It got pretty cold," he told us, "we had to stay in the tent together all the time unless we had to…"

Brick furrowed his brow. It was hilarious, because I knew what he was about to ask. "Where did you—" The kid pointed to the same louvered grill we had peeked out before. "We dump the buckets out there." I smiled, and so did the kid. Brick saw us and smiled too. Even Ray, doomed as he was, smiled at the thought of dumping poop out the window. It isn't even that funny as I write this. Had to be there.

Brick had found a four-by-eight piece of five-eighths plywood, and put it over the trap-door. Two skylights let in light, but it was still fairly dark and shadowy in the attic. The kids sat back down, and we let them know what was happening.

"A *year*?" Chloe asked. "We've been up here for a whole year?"

"I think so." I hitched my bucket a little closer to them, the noise from the infected below was beginning to get loud. "It was about a year ago that this started happening. I can only assume you came up here pretty quick once things started to fall apart." I looked around, marveling at what these kids' dad had done. "If you hadn't come up here quickly, you'd be dead. Actually, you would have been dead anyway if your dad hadn't had all this shit…er, stuff up here. You're luckier than most."

She began to cry.

The boy stood. "Knock it off! We finally get some help and you're gonna cry about it?"

"Stop it, Rich. Everybody's dead. Everybody we ever knew. Nana, Grammy and Gramps, all our cousins, all our friends." She looked up, tears in her eyes, and I swear to Christ I began to get misty. "Mom, Dad, and Tommy too."

He got down on her level, took her hands in his and looked her in the face, "Yeah, well, we're still on *this* side of the grass."

She smiled at him and I realized that I was in love with these kids after being with them for less than an hour. I would kill a hundred rednecks, a thousand bikers, and a million pus-bags before I let harm come to these children. Another realization hit me right then. Smacked me so hard I moved my head back a little: Lynch would have done the same to protect me.

Was I him? Were a certifiable psycho and I the same core person? I was prepared to force these kids to come with us just as Lynch had done to me. For their own good. Were that prick-spook and I the same? No. No we were not. I can't think of any good reasons that don't end up biting me in my hypocritical ass as to why, but no. I'm a nice guy dammit. I'm *nice*! If nothing else, I had that on him. He was a douche.

I suddenly wanted to hear some Led Zeppelin while spooning a hot fudge sundae into my head.

"Rogue One, Rogue Two, how copy?"

Ray grabbed his radio, "Two this is One, we're green, over?"

"Smoke 'em if you got 'em Two, be there in six hours. Be ready, over."

"Rogue Two copies all, out."

"Six hours until evac," Ray said to all of us.

Brick sat down, leaning back against two crates of stuff. "Get some rack. It won't be fun tomorrow. Kids, get whatever you want to come with you ready and get some sleep. We're leaving in a few hours."

Each kid had a Condor Assault Pack already kitted out, and they pulled them close, each using it as a pillow. They were out in just under a minute, sleeping soundly. How they pulled that shit off I will never know. Probably from being in an attic surrounded by undead for a year.

I got up off my bucket and moved to sit next to Brick. I looked at Ray-Ban, who was looking at me. "What do we do about him?" I asked.

Brick looked at Ray. "We shoot him in the head if he tries any monkey shit."

Ray looked away and chuckled. "Screw that. Blaze of glory for this operator. First watch is mine."

Brick was loading some spare magazines. "Let's share it." I saw him run out of shells three into the second mag.

I woke to the familiar sounds of retching. Ray was wiping his mouth when I spied him. "I'm good," he said. Brick was looking out the louvers, and both kids had their backpacks on. I stood and stretched, checking my SOG and ejecting the mag from my 416 for inspection.

Brick shut the louvered grill. "Sun's coming up."

We heard the guttural rumble of salvation over the noises from the pus bags. It came from the west, and we couldn't see that way out either attic vent. The kids looked nervous.

"Relax you two," I told them. "We do this stuff all the time." I pulled the charging handle on my rifle for effect. "Walk in the park."

"Last guy to walk through the park got eaten," Richy said as he adjusted the strap on his pack.

Shit. Unprecedented backfire right there.

Brick was standing next to us. He got down on his haunches, and we got down with him. "OK kids, this is how this is going to go: Above all, you have to be quiet. Don't say anything, nothing at all, unless you see one of them that's close and none of us sees it. I'll go first," he pointed at the plywood covering the attic trap-door, "get you two down, then the other two members of my team will follow. Always stay between me and one of them, and no matter what happens, don't run unless the three of us are all dead. Oh, and this is probably going to get really loud."

"Do we get guns? "

Brick smiled. "Not yet, we don't have enough to spare. And no more talking at all." He looked at Chloe. "Do you understand what to do?" She nodded, terrified.

"And you?" He looked at her brother. "We good?" The boy's nod was much curter.

Brick went through all the hand signals he might use, and the kids both nodded again in understanding.

We could hear the things below us moving off, certainly wanting a taste of tinned MARSOC that was in a freshly fueled MRAP. Yeah, I know, a lot of capital letters right there.

We gave it a half hour and made a phone call, "Rogue Two, Rogue One, how copy?"

"One this is Two, five by five. Towing hostiles from your location now. Pied fuk'n Piper. ETA back to you, one hour at most. Recommend you exfil immediately upon next comm. Triple squelch, over."

"Confirmed triple squelch. Rogue Two copies all, good luck, out," Ray said and threw up. He shook as he passed his radio to Brick. "Just in case." It was hot in that attic, but Ray was sweating a different kind of bullets. He didn't have too much longer before it would be difficult to walk.

A few minutes later, Brick and I removed the plywood and looked down into an empty hallway. Well, empty except for the shit the dead leave in their wake; nasty fluids, chunks of themselves, bits of clothing, you've seen it. Brick snapped his fingers three times and we waited. He looked at his watch and did it again in one minute. One minute after that, he pulled his telescoping mirror from his tac-webbing and checked the hallway.

He nodded in the negative, and I had no friggin' idea what that meant. No hostiles or not clear? I mean I'm kind of new to this whole military thing. I'm learning but come on.

I motioned that I didn't know what he meant, and he looked at me like I took the short bus to school. He pointed down and gave a thumbs up. *Way* better than nodding no.

What seemed like an eternity later, the radio squelched three times. Brick squelched back and turned off the radio

He looked at the kids, put his finger to his lips in a *shhh* motion, and dropped into the corridor. He scanned both directions, looked up at me and nodded, motioning for me to drop him the kids. I passed the boy down first, then his sister. I looked at Ray. He was sitting on the Home Depot bucket, elbows on his knees, looking down.

"Ray, we're moving out. Ray?"

He looked up at me. His right eye was blood red. A single tear of the red fluid rolled down the crease between his nose and cheek, seeming to halt for moment on the crest of his upper lip before dropping to the floor. I watched as the corpuscles in the white of his other eye positively exploded, turning it into a crimson orb almost instantly.

"Might stay here for a bit," he said and looked down. "Good luck, and stay alive."

"Good luck to you too, pal. Want me to tell the guys anything?"

"Nope."

I nodded, not that he could see me, looking at the plywood floor as he was, and dropped down soundlessly with Brick and the kids, suppressed Sig at the ready. Brick stared at me and raised his eyebrows. I looked down and nodded in the negative. When I looked back up, this guy who had just lost one of his most trusted allies and friends was already moving off with the kids behind him, his suppressed handgun pointing forward.

The house was nasty with all the zombie detritus, and I finally noticed how equally filthy the kids were. Can you imagine being stuck in an attic for a year? Anne Frank kind of shit.

We came to a corner of the hall, and Brick did a quick recon looking in two directions. He immediately backed up and quick-pointed back the way we had come. All four of us spun and hurried to the room at the end of the hall, Brick rushing past and taking the lead again. The door on the left was the bathroom we had come in initially, the one on the right had a closed door. Straight ahead was open and inviting. It was a small bedroom and the door had a pink and white sign with *Chloe* printed on it in cursive. We moved under the open attic trap-door, and I was two steps past it when Hell came calling. A thump sounded close behind me and I spun quickly. Ray-Ban crouched there, shaking and heaving, flexing his fingers. The floor creaked behind me, Brick or one of the kids stepping on an unfriendly floorboard. Ray whipped his head up and glared at me.

It wasn't Ray, but it wasn't dead.

The thing gave this growling hiss, then launched from its crouch. It hit me all claws and teeth as I fired. My hesitation had slowed me just enough, and my shot went wide. The round penetrated the sheetrock, and it must have hit something particularly vulnerable in the room beyond because there was a small but exceptionally loud explosion of glass from the room.

I didn't have tons of time to spend worrying about what I had shot because the thing that had been my friend, and had saved my ass on several occasions, was now trying to see what my face tasted like as it threw haymakers. Then it started to scream. That awful, terrifying shriek that will make anybody shit them self, came from it as it tried chew on my pretty face

I fought it hard, but it was wicked fast and damn strong. He scratched my face and arms, the deep furrow on my left forearm dropping blood in my face. The thing made one fist with both hands and raised it above its head in what was going to be a cave-man thump.

Fucker was going to Jim Kirk me!

Never got the chance though as a flying hammer took it in the mouth, breaking teeth and snapping its head to the side. Two shots sounded from behind me, the MARSOC-Runner toppling backwards. I crab-scrambled in reverse, and Brick gave his former buddy one more tap to the dome sealing the deal.

The whole event had taken less than ten seconds, but in that time, the end of the hall had filled with the slower variety of infected. Brick helped me up, and we got in Chloe's room quickly, shutting the door. We pushed her bed against the entry, wedging it closed.

Thumps sounded on the other side of the door soon after. Lots of thumps. I guess these were the less industrious of the pus-bags, and hadn't been fast enough to chase down the MRAP.

Brick tore some remarkably beautiful curtains from a window and threw the sash up. He checked both directions, and slipped out into the yard. "Twenty seconds and we're screwed." He reached for the kids, and I helped them out. I heard firing outside as I looked back to see a panel in the cheap door splinter and a dead face stare at me. They were making short work of my barricade and I slid out the window.

Brick had gone to the rifle, and there was no doubt that every infected in Big Water was now moseying in our direction.

"Rogue Two! Exfil ASAP, east side of the development! We're on foot and moving fast, over!" We ran for it, listening to Remo tell us my truck was thirty seconds out.

Thirty seconds was twenty seconds to damn long.

TRAPPED.

There was no moving fast. There was no moving anywhere. The dead came from all directions. We were between two houses, maybe forty feet apart, and again I had to wonder why they had stacked these houses so close together when there was so much area to be had.

All I could think was that we should have left well enough alone. These two kids were going to get torn apart because we had brought them down from their sanctuary. I have no doubts that hunger would have forced them out in a few short days anyway, but still, I felt this was on me. I looked at the two of them as the dead closed. I knew for sure I had killed them.

Brick was selecting targets and popping domes on single shot, and I followed suit. He performed a tactical magazine switch, and I remembered our ammo situation. Three shots later and his rifle was hanging on its single-point sling, dangling while he pulled the suppressed Sig Sauer he had just put away. I did my best to imitate his re-loading technique, and pulled it off, but not as quickly. I had sixteen shots and I was out.

"Move forward but stick close!" Brick yelled, and I saw that the window we had just come through had dead arms sticking out of it reaching for us. I glanced behind and noted that the pus-bags were forty feet away, arranged twenty deep and spanning the width of the houses. The ones in front were twenty feet in front of us, but there were gaps in their line.

I clicked empty, and I thought the pride I felt for dropping a solid twenty of these dead fucks wasn't misplaced, even though I would be eviscerated in moments. The good thing: there were way too many of them for any of us to rise when they were through. There would be little left, and I considered that a consolation. Brick tried to holster his pistol, but he caught the suppressor on the leather and it dropped to the ground. He pulled his entrenching tool, and I drew the best weapon on planet earth, my SOG.

The MRAP pulled up in front of us, sixty feet from our position, and the back door exploded outward, spilling Remo and Tim. Remo had the EBR rifle and began dropping undead as he moved forward slowly. Tim shot a few as well, but it was too little too late.

Brick looked at me. "Get 'em out, shoot that gap!" He pointed his tool at a five foot break between the dead, then ran headlong into them, hacking. He had cleared another five feet for us, I grabbed Chloe's hand and we ran. We almost made it too. We were at the very end of the procession, most of the infected turning as we ran past. One shot its stinking paw out and latched on to the strap of Chloe's pack. She screamed, and before I could react, Richy put his left hand on the thing's wrist and used a right palm-heel strike to snap the creature's arm at the elbow. It was so rotten it came right off. His sister gave a side kick to the thing's mid-section, knocking it down and we were through.

We reached Remo and Tim, Tim was out of ammo too. "Mags in my pack," Remo said casually, "top's open."

"Tim, get them in the truck!" I reached into Remo's black back-pack and yanked out a mag for my HK416. Slapping it in, I glanced at Brick, who looked like a cross between a grave-digger and a samurai, slashing with his shovel, kicking, punching, then poking with the tool. The kids and Tim ran for the vehicle, but all the dead were far from them. They were damn close to me though, and Brick was hand-to-hand.

The bass *boom-boom* of the EBR was louder than my HK, and both Remo and I moved forward as we mowed the things down. I saw my partner charge his weapon, the mag switch had been so fast that I had missed it.

One of the things encircling Brick locked its mitt on the entrenching tool and that momentary lapse in speed was enough for the others to swarm my buddy. He went down swinging, disappearing beneath the throng. I started to run forward, but Remo put his hand on my chest. There were just too many, and he was fifty feet away from us. Several of the infected decided we were tasty looking and began their slow plod toward us.

Remo passed me the EBR, and I took it by the shoulder sling. He pulled something from his tac-webbing and it made a *ting!*

sound. "Frag out." He tossed a black baseball in an arc into the fray of them, right where Brick had gone down, and he pulled me back toward the truck. We made it all the way to the back door before the grenade detonated with a mighty *WHUMP!*, tossing infected like rag dolls and blowing in the unbroken windows of the houses. The blast knocked the ones stumbling after us over on their faces, but they immediately began to get up.

"Get in," he said, and I did. He followed me, and I looked at the kids, who were hugging each other, sitting on one of the benches and crying softly. The door slammed and Remo shouted for Kinga to go.

I sat down next to Chloe and Tim sat next to me. "Brick and Ray-Ban?"

I looked at my boots, nodding my head side-to-side slowly.

Tim put his head in his hands and sobbed. "All we wanted was gas." It occurred to me that this was the first time Tim had lost anyone he really cared about since this thing had started. Sure, everybody in Baldy was chow, and his family were undoubtedly gone, but this was the first time a comrade that he had spent time with, had bought it. The first time someone who he'd saved the life of and had been saved by, had been claimed by the dead. He hadn't even seen a zombie up close until a few weeks ago.

Remo sat down across from us and pulled something out of his shirt pocket, offering it to Tim. It was an individually wrapped tooth pick.

Tim took it.

BORING

Joint Base Jackson-Gray was not as deserted as Tim's Sentinel Satellite would have led us to believe. At least not now. Several corpses were shuffling towards us from an open hangar as we pulled in. Kinga took them out with the MRAP.

We got there just as the afternoon cool began to hit us. It had been hot during the day, but it was getting cold at night. I didn't know that the southwest could get chilly in the summertime until I had experienced it in the attic in Utah.

Here in Arizona it was friggin' hot in the day time but really nice in the late afternoon. The heat of the day must drive the zombies inside as well as the humans, because when we showed up at JBJG, there were no zombies (or strippers) waiting for us at the gate. There was no gate either; it had been smashed down from the inside. Whoever had left, had left in a hurry driving something enormous, as the tube steel gate was crushed and bent like a pretzel baked in the crazy factory.

This did not fill me with confidence, but we needed an aircraft. We had also decided to bag the idea of a helicopter in lieu of a large plane. The helicopter would need to be a flying gas tank in order for us to make it the fourteen hundred or so miles to Atlantis, and there was still no guarantee of making it. We would have to take too much fuel, and then our operational range would drop because of the weight of said fuel. Tim calculated a hundred and sixty miles per tank instead of the two hundred we thought we had if we took a gassed-up Chinook helicopter. He didn't know how big the fuel tank was, or the miles per gallon the bird averaged, he only knew the range of a full tank.

JBJG had a bunch of planes though, and while Tim could only fly a couple of them, he had been training in a C130J, which the base happened to have. It had two actually, but one was in pieces in an open hangar. The other one was very much not in pieces, and very much not in a hangar.

It had two very undead SOBs in the back of it when we got there though. They stumbled down the ramp when we pulled up next to it. Kinga backed over them with the MRAP, which was becoming one of our best zombie-dispatching tools. When we cleared the area from the safety of our truck, we got out and stretched.

"We're going in that?" Richy asked pointing into the back of the empty plane.

"Yeah," said Tim. "Yeah I hope so." He looked nervous.

"Cool!'

Kinga and Remo walked the perimeter of both our vehicle and the aircraft. They both went up the ramp and checked the rear area out too then Kinga came back out and told us to follow him. We came to the nose of the plane, and there were seven truly dead people and sporadic spent brass on the tarmac. The dead looked like they had been infected by the wounds on them. They also had holes in their heads. Somebody had shot them.

Kinga pointed to the plane. "Look." He nodded at an open window, hinged-out, on the top-side of the nose. "Somebody was in the cockpit and fired on these ones."

Chloe looked at the glass panels when she leaned toward Kinga. "What if he's still in there but, you know, less alive?"

"We'll have to check. We can't get in through the cargo hold, the bulkhead door is locked. We're going to have to go in through there." He motioned toward the window that everybody was now staring at. He cupped his chin, feeling his stubble. "How we getting up there?"

Richy actually raised his hand. "Drive your truck around," he said to Kinga, "climb up on the roof and look in."

"Uhh, yeah, it's *my* truck, but good idea." I took a swig of my water.

The kid thumbed at Kinga. "But he was driving."

I burped. "I let him."

We followed the kid's plan, and it worked out with a little finagling. There's a detachable ladder on the side of the MRAP, and we were able to get on the roof and use that to get up to the window. I held the ladder while Kinga climbed up and peeked in the window with his flashlight. Remo stayed with the kids.

Kinga banged on the fuselage three times and waited a moment. "Clear."

"So I guess the shooter made it?"

"He made it out of here at least. Hold the ladder tight, I'm going in. Check-check," he said into his mic.

"Green," was Remo's one-word answer. Guy had found his pithy switch again.

Kinga made it in, and called for us to come through the back to meet him. I passed the ladder to Remo, and climbed down using the non-detachable ladder on the rear. We made our way up the ramp and looked at Kinga as he waved us in. Tim sat in the chair on the right and began fiddling with stuff. "See if there's a manual in there, please." He pointed to a small locker. Inside was a plethora of shit, including several manuals, all of which I passed to Tim.

He began to read, and he didn't stop for six hours. In the interim, we backed the truck near the plane. Tim had figured out how to close the rear ramp, and we had two fortresses to spend the night in. The kids and Kinga in the MRAP, Tim, Remo, and I in the plane

I didn't think we needed a watch, but Remo woke me up at about three AM for mine. "Last watch is yours. Get us up at first light and we'll walk the runway."

I had no idea what *walk the runway* meant, but I was not about to tell Remo that. Actually, now that he's reading these journals, he'll find out, so sorry, Remo.

I moved up front to the cockpit. Tim was asleep in the pilot's seat with a manual in his lap. He woke up and smiled groggily when he saw me.

"You'll be able to fly this, yeah?"

"I've already flown one. I've taken off with an instructor, and sort-of landed." I looked at him hard, and he let out a sigh. "I wouldn't worry about landing. We're going to have to bail."

"Uhh what?"

"Do you think I'm going to able to set this thing," he spread his arms wide, "down on an oil rig?"

"Wait, you mean like jump out of the plane? Skydive?"

"I don't think the MARSOC guys will call it that, but yeah."

I swallowed hard.

"What about the kids?"

"Both certified skydivers, I already spoke to them. They have over one hundred jumps. I was thinking we jump at about forty thousand feet."

He looked at my nervousness and laughed out loud. "Relax, Mr. Airborne, I'm just kidding." He frowned. "I mean they *could* be certified, I don't know, but I didn't ask them." Bastard actually shrugged. "The plan is easy: We fly in at about forty feet above the water as slow as possible. Open the rear ramp, pop a chute, it catches the air, and we drop to the water safe and sound."

I visibly relaxed. "Good plan." I glanced out the window and saw a couple of things shuffling around on the runway in the moonlight. "If they let us leave."

Tim followed my gaze. "Afterthought. I don't want to hit them if possible, but I don't think they would do much to us if we're taking off. We'll just turn them into strawberry jam, as you're so fond of saying. We will have to check the runway for anything that could pop a tire before we take off."

That's what Remo meant!

Tim picked up a clipboard and passed it to me. "Someone, probably the guy who shot the dead on the runway, already completed a pre-flight check. It's dated about four months ago. At least I think so, I'm kind of unsure of the present date. The plane is good to go and already fueled. There are a couple of things I want to look at, but I think we're good. I'm a little uneasy at why the clipboard is here as is the aircraft, but the pilot didn't take off."

"Yeah, me too, *now*. Thanks for that. Get some sleep then, tomorrow should be interesting."

He stood, cracked his neck, and strode to the fold-down bench-style troop seats in the cargo area of the plane opposite Remo, who was on the deck of the plane. Tim looked at the lawn-chair type seats and also opted for the deck. Stretching out, he gave me thumbs up, rolled over and went to sleep.

When I was alone, I thought about Ship. I thought about Kat. I thought about all my other friends on Atlantis, and how I desperately wanted to get back there. I hoped they were all OK. I couldn't wait to call them on the radio when we were in range. I really couldn't wait to see them. I wanted to introduce my new friends to my old ones, and tell everybody what the country looks like a year into this mess. I wanted to fix stuff again. I wanted to feel safe.

I heard a thump outside and looked to see if it was one of the dead ones. It was. There were a bunch of them out there now. Eight or ten, and they were just milling about. I couldn't see what they looked like, just shadows really. I could see a brightening in the east and knew it was almost time to rock and roll.

I thought about the folks we had lost. I wondered if my family and friends went fast, or if they were still alive and fighting the dead. The sun peeked over the horizon and hit me right in the face. It was pretty, and I felt its warmth immediately. I sighed and went to wake Remo. He was sitting on his bench rubbing his neck.

"We've got company," I told him.

"How many?"

"Just a few that I can see."

"Rogue One, this is Two," he said into his mic, "how copy?"

Kinga's tired voice replied instantly, "Two, One, five by five, over."

These guys could carry on a conversation using nothing but numbers apparently.

Remo said something unexpected right then, and it was hard for me not to smile. "How're the kids, over?"

Let's pretend, Reader, you understand that every communication these guys, or any military guys, have via a radio ends with either *over*, or *out* when they are done speaking. I'm tired of writing it every five seconds, and if you haven't caught on by now, you're dumb. For a great demonstration of this, see the nineteen fifties movie *Them* if you can find it and have power. Great flick about giant ants in the New Mexico desert.

"Up and rearing to go. We've had some hostiles knocking for about an hour. Nothing to worry about yet."

"Copy that One, we see and hear them." Actually, I could hear them now. "We'll reveille and get on mission. Call you back in ten."

I woke Tim, not knowing what the hell *reveille* was. He sat up immediately, rubbing his arm where the lion had tried to relieve him of it. (I must admit, I never thought I would write a sentence like that.) Tim looked rested, even though he had only gotten a few hours of sleep on a floor.

We prepped the inside of the plane as best we could, but that was just trying to clean up the shit the zombies had left behind. I didn't want the kids sitting in any of that crap, or having it get on any of us. There was a push broom stuck between two metal braces and I used that. It was still a bit messy.

I was sitting down on one of the fold-outs, finally noticing that the plane had a bit of a death odor to it, when Remo tapped me on the shoulder.

"Time to make the donuts."

WTF? Did he just say that? The guy had made a joke? Right then, the weirdest thing happening was not that there were dead people trying to eat us.

I nodded, and began to check over my gear. I had one full mag in my rifle, one full mag in reserve, and a mag with four rounds in it. I had a total of seven rounds for my sidearm. Shit was getting bleak, but hey, my knife was beautiful.

I told Remo I was ready, and he called Kinga. "Rogue One this is Rogue Two, we are ready for Operation Tow Truck."

TWO jokes! The time/space continuum was broken! Rips in the fabric of reality and shit.

"Rogue One copies. Commencing drag-away. Call you back when we're far enough away."

Huh. Decidedly un-military talk, but hey, what do I know?

He called back in ten minutes and told us we were clear. Tim lowered the ramp, and we walked the runway, side-by-side until the pus bags decided to come back. There were nine of them, Kinga had run over another few. We dispatched them quickly, one of them getting almost close enough to grab me before Remo shot it. After we dragged the bodies off of the runway, we met Kinga and the kids at the plane.

It took fifteen minutes to load everything from the MRAP into our new ride including the kids. I drove my beauty to the open hangar and parked it about fifty feet away from the maw, not wanting to go in there for hell or high water. I had previously written a note and put it in a plastic baggy, which I attached to the door handle with a zip-tie:

To whoever finds this vehicle: It's yours now. Don't be a dick and use it to hurt people. This thing is completely zombie proof, but it isn't a tank. Medium arms fire can penetrate the glass. You'll never get a flat tire, and it runs on diesel. I wish you the best of luck, but if you've made it this far, luck has been on your side. Hope it doesn't run out.

I was a hundred yards away from the aircraft when it started up. It's a fat plane when you're standing behind it, and I liked looking at its butt. The C-130 has four props, and they started quickly. I could feel the wash from this far out. They were loud, but the area was clear and I was enjoying my stroll. I saw Remo dart out of the plane and look around for a sec before he saw me. He waved his right arm frantically, pointing at me. I assumed he wanted me to hurry now that the vehicle had started up, so I started jogging toward him. I was perplexed when he raised Kinga's EBR, aiming it at me. Even more so when he pulled the trigger.

L.A.P.E.S

I'm unsure if anywhere in these journals I've ever written *I felt the bullet go right past my head.* You probably know by now, if you've put in the time to read all off this stuff, that I've actually been shot in the head. *Grazed* is the word, as it didn't penetrate my skull, but did leave a significant scar. I was shot at pretty much on a daily basis for a while, and I've returned fire too. Being shot at sucks. Being shot is worse.

Hopefully you are reading this while both of us are sitting someplace safe, where the infected can't get to us. You're probably also thinking to yourself that these journals are bullshit, and I'm playing myself up to look cool. I'm not. Wait. No, I *am* cool, I'm just not amping up the story. Everything I've written has really happened. More than likely you have just shot me in my zombie dome and are reading this, but I really do hope it's the first option.

Regardless, take your hand, make a flat palm, and move it quickly past your ear. Don't hit yourself or it stings, I know this because I just did it. Do it a few times and you're bound to hear the sound of your mitt whipping past you. Take that sound, add a whining *sssssssssoooo* to it, and that's the sound of a .308 round almost drilling you in the melon. Now add a half pound of shit to your drawers, drop to the ground, and the experience is complete.

Now, as previously discussed above, I am cool. I do not cower, or faint, or plead. At least I haven't yet. Not that any of these things make one cool. It's how you act during the times when those actions are *not* being performed but *should* that makes you fashionably attractive.

So Remo shoots at me, I drop to the ground fumbling for my weapon, and he shoots again. This second time I feel more than hear a bit of a thump behind me. Keep in mind that about two hundred and fifty feet in front of me is a freshly started C-130J

Hercules aircraft, and it's loud. I glance at the thump and see two infected, one about fifteen feet away, on its back sort of rolling around. The other is also on the ground, on its front, just touching my boot. It has a hole in its right shoulder that if wasn't spewing infected fluids, I would be able to put a broomstick through. It is a Runner, and it is exceptionally messed up.

Now these damn things, Runners, really don't give a shit about pain. However, where their dead cousins are not bound to the same results of trauma and injury other than to the brain, these speedy sons-of-bitches will drop or fall over or in some other way go down when shot. At least usually. What they will also do is expend their very last energies in an attempt to rip into any living thing in close proximity until death comes. Actually, proximity has nothing to do with it. They'll bleed out trying to get to you if you're a half a mile away. Also, once they expire, they tell death to take a hike, get up, and come for you. Slower, but significantly more durable.

The point is, this horrid thing that had its nasty paw on my Altama Desert boot had no intentions of doing anything other than playing jump rope with my lower intestine. Having a deep rooted love for, and burning desire *not* to share any or all of my innards, and not wanting to supply the equipment for a game of rope jumping, I hastily withdrew my size thirteen from its vile grasp. It attempted to stand and the top portion of its noggin popped straight up in the air, the creature stiffening and collapsing on to the exact spot I had just scuttled away from. I looked behind it and noticed a few of its undead counterparts making their way toward me from the hangar I refused to enter prior. The other Runner was still lying on its back coughing blood, Remo's shot having taken it center mass.

It was time to vacate the premises. I got to my feet and ran to the plane while Remo covered me. The rest of the infected were of the slower variety, so I made it with no issue. Kinga was on the ramp with his rifle and a frown when I got there, and he shook his head in disgust, turning his back on me and entering the aircraft. Remo jogged up the ramp as it was closing, taking a seat next to Richy and Chloe on the fold-out bench seats, checking their seatbelts.

"Buckle up," he yelled to me over the prop noise.

Kinga returned to us from up forward, carrying four sets of headphones and wearing one. He passed them out to each of us, the kids too. Then he lit into me.

He pointed at me after he showed us how to switch on the headsets. "Next time you run off by yourself and the infected have you, I'm just going to watch. And for Christ's sake, don't turn off your fucking radio. Ever." He strode down the cargo bay to the cockpit. I could feel his boots on the aluminum.

It was at that point, chastised by the MARSOC guy in front of the kids, that I realized I had royally screwed up. Guess I'm not as cool as I thought. Remo wouldn't even look at me. Damn, what a douche. Me not him. I had wanted to leave a message with the MRAP, and had almost become a banquet. I should have taken one of the boys with me, or better yet, just left the truck where it was.

Cool to fool in under ten seconds.

We felt the plane lurch forward a little, then it began moving slowly. The nose turned to face a different direction, then we all heard the engines speed up.

I heard Tim's tinny voice over the radio: "There are a few newcomers on the runway in front of us, and we seem to have gathered a bit of a crowd behind. We're taking off in thirty seconds, so make sure your seatbacks and tray tables are in their upright positions."

True to his word, the plane shot forward, jerking us a bit. It sped down the runway, and suddenly there was a small *thump!* followed by two more, then one more. In no time, we felt the ground disappear beneath us and we were airborne. The angle on this takeoff was like nothing I had ever experienced. It was crazy steep after such a quick departure, and I was a bit nervous after Tim had just told me the day before he was a newbie with this aircraft. The steepness continued for a solid two minutes, then Tim leveled us out. Kinga came back to speak with Remo, and I shamefacedly moved to the cockpit to talk with Tim.

I sat down in the right side seat. "Well, you got us in the air, buddy."

"I did, yeah." He sounded distant.

"Aren't you happy? You're flying this giant plane," I looked around, "which we're going to jump out of."

He looked at me. "You're a dumbass! We get this far and you go and try to get yourself killed."

"You're right." I totally disarmed him. He had been expecting a fight. Knowing Tim, he had probably gone over fifty different conversations in his head, but he hadn't accounted for instant acquiescence of dumbassery from me.

"Uh…yeah, so, quit being dumb and stay alive. We need you."

"Aww shucks, buddy." I punched him lightly in the arm. It was the lion-arm and he gave me death eyes while he rubbed his boo-boo. "Sorry."

"Jackass."

I smiled. "Jerk. At least it wasn't my idea to jump out of a perfectly good airplane."

He took in a huge breath of air and turned to face me again. "Yeah, about that. Remo says it's a bad idea. He says the landing will be much harder than I thought, even in the water. He changed the plan."

I was quizzical-nervous and he picked up on it. "So what's the plan now, Captain Tim?"

"A water landing."

"A water landing. You mean like, we land in the water?"

"Yes."

"Dude! What the fuck? Your plan was great! What do those jarheads know anyway?"

He put his finger to his lips. Like they could hear me over the noise of the plane. "Remo said that a rapes? Tapes? extraction could kill us."

"LAPES," Kinga said over the radio. "Low Altitude Parachute Extraction System. LAPES. And we can hear everything you say. You're on the radio, dickhead."

"But I like LAPES!" I yelled into the radio. "LAPES sounds good. In fact, LAPES is now my favorite. Do you know why it's my favorite? Because it doesn't involve crashing a god damn airplane THAT I AM ON into the ocean!"

Tim coughed. "A crash would indicate the pilot isn't in control. I will be performing a water landing."

"Water landing," Kinga repeated. "It's our best option. We exfil through the top hatch and pop the rafts."

It was my turn to repeat. "Pop the rafts. Pop the rafts! Do you have any idea how dumb that sounds? Pop the rafts?"

"Technical term. You don't like it, stay in the plane."

Holy shit, they were serious.

I stood up and looked back at Kinga with my hands out as if to ask WTF?

Kinga looked at the twins. "You kids OK with a water landing?"

Both kids gave a thumbs up.

Kinga looked at me. "Pussy."

Chloe giggled and Richy smiled as they looked at me too.

Remo was asleep.

SPLASH

"Our economy speed is about three hundred forty knots," Tim told me.

"Yeah, like I know what a damn knot is. Gimme that in miles per hour, Homie."

"Just under four hundred. Three ninety I think."

I blinked. "But if we were about twelve hundred miles away, and we're going four hundred miles per hour…"

"Yeah," Tim looked at me, "I know. We've been in the air a little more than two hours. We'll be there in under an hour."

I was both excited and terrified. Excited to see my friends, terrified to be an integral part of a plane crash. Hey, if I had survived all the shit I had survived, a plane crash would be cake, right? Besides, it was going to be a *water landing*, remember?

When we were sixty miles out, I made a phone call. OK, so it was a radio, but you get it.

"Atlantis, this is Hercules, come in?"

They came back immediately, and I almost cried. "Read you Hercules, this is Atlantis. What can we do for you?"

"Ted? Ted is that you?"

"Yeah," the voice said, "who's this?"

"I've been known by many names, Teddy. Last year you bastards on board all of those floating asylums were calling me Captain."

"Cap? Holy shit! We thought you were…wait…what's your best friend's name?"

"You mean that friggin Sasquatch I call Ship? His name is Douche. Capital D if you please. I've got some new friends I want you to meet as well."

Tim smiled from ear to ear, mirroring me.

I heard the tail end of Ted yelling for everybody to come into the radio room. "Got some people here that want to talk to you, buddy!"

The next guy to come on was Austin. "Afternoon, young fella. Heard you've been away."

"Screw you, old man! You know you've missed me!"

I heard a young girl in the background yelling for *you assholes to get out of the fukn way* and for the second time in two minutes, I almost burst into tears.

"You!" she yelled into the mic. "You dick! We all thought you were being experimented on in some damn government lab." She was crying, I could tell.

"Uhh…yeah, we'll talk about that when I get there, kid. You OK?"

We continued talking for a while, and then I asked for Ship. Kat said he was OK, but unavailable. I had to admit, at least to my own dumb self, that I didn't like the sound of that.

We got the MARSOC boys up front with us, and discussed the best way to crash a plane into the Gulf. It was decided that we would set her down three miles to the northwest, as there were no boats in the vicinity, and the sinking plane wouldn't hit any of the suspension cables on any of the rigs from that far a distance out. Atlantis would have two rescue vessels and a full crew of scuba divers just in case.

In another ten minutes, I saw my home. It looked small. We circled once, and I saw a shit load of folks waving and yelling at us from the deck of the rig. It was heaven. I couldn't stop smiling. Until Tim said it was time to buckle up. "We'll be touching down in two minutes," he said over the radio, "assume crash positions."

Kinga had taken my place up front, and I was sitting on one of the folding lawn-chair style benches across from Remo and the kids. Remo took the toothpick out of his mouth and looked at it. "Last one." He put it in one of the pockets on his load-bearing vest, and relaxed.

"Both vessels are in position, beginning our descent."

I swallowed hard. I was really hoping there wouldn't be a handful of zombies in a sunken plane at the bottom of the Gulf of Mexico in a half hour. You know how when you're on a plane and they tell you to put your head between your knees? There was none of that on this plane. We all had these X-style harnesses as seatbelts that came over our shoulders and met in the middle with a round buckle. Remo tightened it so much I could barely breathe.

The plane began to get lower and we slowed down. We could all feel it just like a jet liner. Unlike a jet liner, there wasn't one friggin window to look out.

"Ten seconds! Nine...eight..."

We hit the water at two. To this day, I don't know if Tim did that on purpose or if he just miscalculated his altitude. The ass of the plane hit, and the nose jolted down. Then there was a tremendous splash and our nose spun to the right a bit. I felt like I was going to tear in half for a couple of seconds and it was over. I looked at the kids and they were both smiling. Remo was already out of his harness and opening a small compartment near the exterior door by the cockpit. He pulled out a small, orange cylinder. "Let's go."

Let's go? That's all he had to say? The cockpit bulkhead door opened, and Kinga came out followed by Tim. Kinga was bleeding over his right eye.

I was still nervous, but I asked in the most uncaring way possible, "How long do we have before this thing sinks?"

Kinga wiped his eye with his forearm. "Three hours maybe?" He looked at Tim, who shrugged.

The sun streamed in when Remo opened the door. We all jostled for a glimpse, and it was beautiful outside. Winds looked light and variable with almost no chop to the water. I heard before I saw the first rigid inflatable boat come zipping around the nose of the plane. Two more showed up shortly after, and I looked down into the face of my friend Greg, who had a grin so wide on his face, he must have just eaten a fecal sandwich.

"Yup, you're still ugly."

His smile got so wide I thought his face would rip. "I lost the pool on you by a damn month," he yelled. I realized I was mimicking his face-splitter.

"Pool?"

"Yeah, get in the damn boat and we'll talk about it."

Remo tossed our gear to a guy in BDU's that I didn't recognize, but he was with Greg, so he must have been a newbie. Our gear almost filled one of the boats, and it backed off when we were done with our assembly line. The kids went next and then the four of us.

A most manly hug from Greg ensued.

"I knew you were gay." It was Tim! Tim had made a funny. I introduced him to Greg, also telling him I didn't know the other guy, who was the boat driver. Sailor? Whatever.

He stuck his paw out and told us he was Ensign Caliber. Remo and Kinga were in a different boat, shaking hands with different guys I didn't know.

"Where's Ship?" I demanded, looking around. The motor on the inflatable roared its tiny roar, and we were heading back to the bigger boats. The Ensign wouldn't look at me and Greg's smile disappeared.

"You'll have to talk to Austin or Captain Schumitz about him."

Now I've got to tell you, I didn't like that at all. No sir, not one bit.

"Greg, I'm asking you: Where the hell is my buddy?"

"I'm not supposed to—"

"Greg, I don't give a fuck about *supposed to*! Is he alive? Is Ship alive?"

He looked me in the face and sighed. "I don't know."

REUNION. WELL, ALMOST.

We arrived at the bigger of the two boats, the *Iago*, in just a few minutes. We unloaded our gear and our people, and we were all checked out by Doctor Dan. Nice guy. We were cleared of infection, but still escorted everywhere by armed folks. Greg stayed with us, and we were allowed to keep our weapons, even during the bite exam.

I was anxious to get back to Atlantis so I could ask Austin what all the secrecy surrounding Ship was. I was thinking (and saying quite loudly,) that he had better have a damn good reason why he wouldn't allow anybody to talk about Ship. As it turns out, he did.

In forty five minutes, I was hugging Kat on the lower dock of the Atlantis. I asked her about Alvarez, and she said *we should talk upstairs*. She looked sad, and that scared the shit out of me. I was a little hurt that Austin and Donna, my lady friend, weren't there to greet me on the dock, but when I got up on the main deck, it was busy up there.

All of us, the kids too, were escorted to Austin's office, and I got a good look at the leader of Atlantis for the first time in a year. He looked rough. Haggard is the word. He was standing with a man I didn't recognize. Average height and indeterminate age. Austin smiled at me from across the room and came almost running to me. He gave me a great bear hug that reminded me of everybody's favorite hillbilly; Dallas. But where Dallas resembled a grizzly bear, Austin was thin, albeit tall.

"It's really good to see you."

"You too, buddy. Where's Ship?"

Smile vanished. Look of sadness mixed with a little anger. Oh shit.

"Ship is on the Majestik Maersk with two squads of my men."

While I tried to process that statement, I turned to look at the other guy in the room, who had spoken, my eyes, quite literally bugging out of my head. "What the fuck did you just say?" I stabbed a finger at him, but spoke to Austin, "What did he fukn say to me?" I was boiling with anger. *Pissed.* Livid, and if I had a damn thesaurus right now I would use every single word for *mad* that damn book would provide.

Austin raised his hands in supplication. "Hang on! We can explain."

"Who's he?" Again, I pointed at the new guy.

"I'm—"

"I wasn't asking you!" I must admit, my voice had a hint of a scream to it, but I had my reasons, and I was about to lose my shit. Kat put her hand on my shoulder.

"This is Captain Schumitz of the USS Destroyer Stockdale," Austin told me. "He's a friend."

"A friend who put *my friend* on board a floating fucking death trap, which, incidentally, should have been rammed right up Mexico's ass by now." I looked back at Austin. "Explain."

"Ship volunteered!" Austin revealed quickly. "Survivors on the Majestik radioed a distress call. One of them made it to a radio, but he was bitten. There are a few people alive on the Majestik. Ship went to go assist in their rescue. He's well-protected."

"Austin, you weren't on that tub. Trust me, there's no such thing as well-protected. Where's Alvarez?" I demanded looking around. "He shouldn't have allowed this." I looked at Kat and knew before Austin told me.

"He led the team."

I shook my head. "Course he did. And I bet you needed an extra medic too, which is why my girl isn't here." I put my bag down and started to go through it, tossing some items I didn't think I would need right on Austin's office floor.

"Austin, Captain Schumitz, this is Tim, Kinga, Remo, Richy, and Chloe. Tim is a hero, Remo and Kinga are MARSOC, and the other two are the toughest kids on planet earth." I looked at the kids and they were beaming. I glanced at Tim and he was too. "Find them rooms, or stick them in mine, assuming you haven't given it away."

"Listen, son," began the captain.

"Nope. You listen shithead, I'm not your son, your soldier, or your friend. I just crossed the US of fuk'n A to get back to my family, and I find out that three of the four of them are now in the worst place possible. You're going to stand there and tell me it was to save some survivors, and I'm going to agree to disagree. I bet Bob did find some people, but I also know that they're your second priority. There's another objective that you didn't tell half your team about, and that's what's going to get them killed."

The captain looked at Austin, who was smiling. "Told you."

Schumitz sighed. "There's something on that boat we need."

"Me too, and you sent them there." I shouldered my pack, and noticed that Remo and Kinga were sorting through their packs as well. "Captain, I need six magazines for my HK, and another hundred rounds loose. I'll also need four mags for my Sig." I looked at Tim and the kids. "You're staying here." Remo and Kinga looked ready. "Captain, get these boys what they need. Their needs will be considerable."

"Where the hell do you think you're going?" Kat demanded. She already knew.

"I'm going to that ship to get...well... Ship."

"Son, I'm sure they're fine. Probably just a communications problem."

"Yeah, the problem is that their communications are in the rotting stomachs of a bunch of zombies, just like most of your men. If you're lucky, very, *very* lucky, then my friends are not. Please don't call me son again. I *liked* my father. Are you going to give me the shit I asked for? Oh I will also need their position and a boat."

"Boat won't get there soon enough—"

I cut him off. "Then I'll fucking swim."

"—but we have a helicopter."

"Even better. These two Jarheads have some info for you, Captain. As soon as it's been transferred, I want to go."

"You can have a team of—"

"Don't want 'em. You already sent two teams. Them," I pointed at my MARSOC buddies, "and me. That's it. Oh, and a pilot. *That's* it. What is it you sent your men to die for?"

Schumitz honestly didn't know what to make of me. I could see it on his face. "May we have the room gentlemen? Austin, please remain."

Everyone but the captain, Remo, Kinga, Austin and I left. Kat was *pissed*. Tim looked hurt, but he had been through enough.

Captain Schumitz put his hands on the desk and looked up at us. "There's data on that boat that I need. A colonel from USAMRIID had some journals that I want, but more than that she has one of these." He pulled a little red key from around his neck. It was shaped oddly, with ridges and depressions.

"You mean a doctor colonel named Callus? She's dead."

Schumitz blinked. "How—"

"Been on the Majestik, captain. Remember? I read the ship's log. Captain by the name of Pederson. He wrote how you assholes took over his ship, carted throngs of infected on there for study, and how they, shockingly, got loose and killed everybody."

The MARSOC boys looked pissed. "They put infected on a ship to study them?" asked Kinga.

"They did," the captain returned. "Anything else?"

I saw Kinga back down almost immediately. I couldn't believe it. This guy could kill everybody in the room except probably Remo, and he backed down in an instant. He was still mad, but he wasn't going to question this Navy captain again.

"I've got something else," I said. "It seems that you military assholes," I looked at Remo and Kinga, "sorry. You military assholes aren't so bright, because you did exactly the same thing inside a secure facility in Montana. Brought in a bunch of infected, they got loose, and they killed everybody."

It was the captain's turn to get angry. I'm guessing he wasn't accustomed to being called names and having his authority questioned.

"Frankly, I don't give a shit about your problems. I'm a naval officer and I follow orders. That having been said, neither I nor anyone under my command, had anything to do with what happened on the Majestik Maersk. I'm *allowing* you on this mission because you can help me. That's it. Get the data, the key, and the survivors, and we will take it from there."

"Take it from there. Right. And how long until you're *ordered* to fill Atlantis with a hundred infected to study?"

That took him aback. Literally, he stepped back.

"I...that wouldn't—"

"Wouldn't what?" I snapped. "Happen? Occur? Give me a break. Let me ask you a question, Captain: would you follow orders if you were ordered to bring infected here?"

Remo put his hand on my shoulder and I glanced in his direction.

"Easy," was all he said.

I turned and looked at him. "Easy? Remo, he's going to do the same thing they've done to me twice. They won't be satisfied until everybody's dead."

"They won't."

"Clearly this man isn't military," the captain thought out loud in reference to yours truly. Bastard shook his head like he was better than me.

"Neither am I," Remo followed, and I almost shit myself.

I looked at him expectantly, *WTF!?* all over my face.

"Two years retired. I was on base dealing with some insurance crap when the shit hit the fan. Hooked up with these boys," he thumbed at Kinga, "and now I'm here."

Schumitz looked at me. "I have no plans on bringing infected to Atlantis, son."

"But you would if ordered. Forget it, let's just go. You and I can talk when I get back."

Remo and Kinga stayed behind while I went in search of Kat.

END

It took almost an hour to get to Kat. Everybody wanted to know how I was and what was done to me and how I escaped and everything else. My friends, and folks I didn't even know, stopped me to ask me those questions. They asked others too, like how were the roads, and did I pass through—insert state and town here—and how many infected had I seen and killed.

I answered patiently, even when one of the roughnecks, Bear, grabbed me around the middle and hoisted me in the air like a sock-puppet, telling me how good it was to have me back.

I got to my room and Kat was waiting with Tim and the kids.

"You're not really leaving are you?" asked Chloe, a bit scared.

"I have to help my friend. Actually, he's more like my brother, and if Richy was in trouble, wouldn't you want to go help him?"

She looked down and nodded. Kat had already packed a bag and was checking her shotgun.

"Kat." She didn't look at me.

"Kat!"

She looked up. "Don't! I'm coming."

"Kat, I need you and Tim to watch out for the kids while I'm gone. I don't trust that Schumitz guy as far as I can throw him."

"But I—"

"No, Kat. No, I need you here." I grabbed her hands in mine. She was still holding the shotgun, so it was weird. "This isn't me trying to keep you safe, it's me trying to keep everybody safe. You're a badass, and that's what I need right now. I've already spoken to Greg, and he and a few of the boys we came in here with are going to keep an eye the sailors from that destroyer, especially its captain. This guy," I nodded at Tim, "is also a badass, and he will do whatever is necessary. I not only trust him with my life, but with yours."

Her eyes welled up and a single tear rolled down her cheek.

"You just got back."

"You'll be saying that again tomorrow. Maybe even tonight."

She threw her arms around me, crushing me with an embrace. If I wasn't so friggin' tough, I might have followed suit on the tear thing.

I heard a sound behind me, and Austin was there with Kinga.

Kinga nodded. "It's time."

I nodded back and held Kat at arm's length. "I want striped bass, grilled with garlic, salt, and pepper when I get back. You be safe, watch the kids, and bring Tim up to speed on this place. If anybody tries to bring a shipping container on this rig, you shoot them."

"I will."

I hugged her, the kids, and Tim. "Watch your ass out there, hero," he said to me.

"Remo will be with me."

"Then I pity those zombies." He smiled.

I looked at the people in my shack once more and followed Kinga out into the sun. It smelled like metal, grease, and sweat on the deck. I took a deep breath.

I love that smell.

ACKNOWLEDGEMENTS

Sometimes it's easier to write a book than it is to recognize everyone who helped in its creation. Seriously, if I were to make an attempt to individually express gratitude to all those wonderful folks who pitched in to make this story what it is, the tome would be twice as long. But I'm going to try anyway. Thanks to my family; Mom n Pops, Lovely Wife, and Brats X3, whose patience with me only exists because they are family. To those friends seen by me each day for the same reason. For those specific friends, like the excellent and admirable James Schannep, who has not only written his own fantastic series of books, but the foreword for this one, I thank you. To Sara, J.R., and FF, Zombie Fiends and friends; this book would be sitting on a hard drive in my basement without your feedback. To the Wardroom (wdrmmta.wordpress.com) without whose input this tale would suck even more than it does. To you, Dear Reader, who was either smart enough or dumb enough to beg, borrow, buy, or steal this work; you have my utmost thanks as you have generated enough revenue for me that I might just be able to purchase some Cheetos with my next sandwich. Thank you all.

CHECK OUT OTHER GREAT ZOMBIE NOVELS

DEAD ASCENT
by Jason McPhearson

The dead have risen and they are hungry...

Grizzled war veteran turned game warden, Brayden James and a small group of survivors, fight their way through the rugged wilderness of southern Appalachia to an isolated cabin in the hope of finding sanctuary. Every terrifying step they make they are stalked by a growing mass of staggering corpses, and a raging forest fire, set by the government in hopes of containing the virus.

As all logical routes off the mountain are cut off from them, they seek the higher ground, but they soon realize there is little hope of escape when the dead walk and the world burns.

CHAOS THEORY
by Rich Restucci

The world has fallen to a relentless enemy beyond reason or mercy. With no remorse they rend the planet with tooth and nail.

One man stands against the scourge of death that consumes all.

Teamed with a genius survivalist and a teenage girl, he must flee the teeming dead, the evils of humans left unchecked, and those that would seek to use him. His best weapon to stave off the horrors of this new world? His wit.

CHECK OUT OTHER GREAT ZOMBIE NOVELS

RUN
by Rich Restucci

The dead have risen, and they are hungry.

Slow and plodding, they are Legion. The undead hunt the living. Stop and they will catch you. Hide and they will find you. If you have a heartbeat you do the only thing you can: You run.

Survivors escape to an island stronghold: A cop and his daughter, a computer nerd, a garbage man with a piece of rebar, and an escapee from a mental hospital with a life-saving secret. After reaching Alcatraz, the ever expanding group of survivors realize that the infected are not the only threat.

Caught between the viciousness of the undead, and the heartlessness of the living, what choice is there? Run.

THE DEAD WALK THE EARTH
by Luke Duffy

As the flames of war threaten to engulf the globe, a new threat emerges.

A 'deadly flu', the like of which no one has ever seen or imagined, relentlessly spreads, gripping the world by the throat and slowly squeezing the life from humanity.

Eight soldiers, accustomed to operating below the radar, carrying out the dirty work of a modern democracy, become trapped within the carnage of a new and terrifying world.

Deniable and completely expendable. That is how their government considers them, and as the dead begin to walk, Stan and his men must fight to survive.

CHECK OUT OTHER GREAT ZOMBIE NOVELS

DEAD PULSE RISING
by K. Michael Gibson

Slavering hordes of the walking dead rule the streets of Baltimore, their decaying forms shambling across the ruined city, voracious and unstoppable. The remaining survivors hide desperately, for all hope seems lost... until an armored fortress on wheels plows through the ghouls, crushing bones and decayed flesh. The vehicle stops and two men emerge from its doors, armed to the teeth and ready to cancel the apocalypse.

TOWER OF THE DEAD
by J.V. Roberts

Markus is a hardworking man that just wants a better life for his family. But when a virus sweeps through the halls of his high-rise apartment complex, those plans are put on hold. Trapped on the sixteenth floor with no hope of rescue, Markus must fight his way down to safety with his wife and young daughter in tow.

Floor by bloody floor they must battle through hordes of the hungry dead on a terrifying mission to survive the TOWER OF THE DEAD.

CHECK OUT OTHER GREAT ZOMBIE NOVELS

Z BURBIA
by Jake Bible

Whispering Pines is a classic, quiet, private American subdivision on the edge of Asheville, NC, set in the pristine Blue Ridge Mountains. Which is good since the zombie apocalypse has come to Western North Carolina and really put suburban living to the test!

Surrounded by a sea of the undead, the residents of Whispering Pines have adapted their bucolic life of block parties to scavenging parties, common area groundskeeping to immediate area warfare, neighborhood beautification to neighborhood fortification.

But, even in the best of times, suburban living has its ups and downs what with nosy neighbors, a strict Home Owners' Association, and a property management company that believes the words "strict interpretation" are holy words when applied to the HOA covenants. Now with the zombie apocalypse upon them even those innocuous, daily irritations quickly become dramatic struggles for personal identity, family security, and straight up survival.

ZOMBIE RULES
by David Achord

Zach Gunderson's life sucked and then the zombie apocalypse began.

Rick, an aging Vietnam veteran, alcoholic, and prepper, convinces Zach that the apocalypse is on the horizon. The two of them take refuge at a remote farm. As the zombie plague rages, they face a terrifying fight for survival.

They soon learn however that the walking dead are not the only monsters.

 SEVERED**PRESS**

 facebook.com/severedpress

 twitter.com/severedpress

CHECK OUT OTHER GREAT ZOMBIE NOVELS

900 MILES
by S. Johnathan Davis

John is a killer, but that wasn't his day job before the Apocalypse.

In a harrowing 900 mile race against time to get to his wife just as the dead begin to rise, John, a business man trapped in New York, soon learns that the zombies are the least of his worries, as he sees first-hand the horror of what man is capable of with no rules, no consequences and death at every turn.

Teaming up with an ex-army pilot named Kyle, they escape New York only to stumble across a man who says that he has the key to a rumored underground stronghold called Avalon..... Will they find safety? Will they make it to Johns wife before it's too late?

Get ready to follow John and Kyle in this fast paced thriller that mixes zombie horror with gladiator style arena action!

WHITE FLAG OF THE DEAD
by Joseph Talluto

Millions died when the Enillo Virus swept the earth. Millions more were lost when the victims of the plague refused to stay dead, instead rising to slaughter and feed on those left alive. For survivors like John Talon and his son Jake, they are faced with a choice: Do they submit to the dead, raising the white flag of surrender? Or do they find the will to fight, to try and hang on to the last shreds or humanity?

CHECK OUT OTHER GREAT ZOMBIE NOVELS

VACCINATION
by **Phillip Tomasso**

What if the H7N9 vaccination wasn't just a preventative mea-sure against swine flu?

It seemed like the flu came out of nowhere and yet, in no time at all the government manufactured a vaccination. Were lab workers diligent, or could the virus itself have been man-made? Chase McKinney works as a dispatcher at 9-1-1. Taking emergen-cy calls, it becomes immediately obvious that the entire city is infected with the walking dead. His first goal is to reach and save his two children.

Could the walls built by the U.S.A. to keep out illegal aliens, and the fact the Mexican government could not afford to vaccinate their citizens against the flu, make the southern border the only plausible destination for safety?

ZOMBIE, INC
by **Chris Dougherty**

"WELCOME! To Zombie, Inc. The United Five State Republic's leading manufacturer of zombie defense systems! In business since 2027, Zombie, Inc. puts YOU first. YOUR safety is our MAIN GOAL! Our many home defense options - from Ze Fence® to Ze Popper® to Ze Shed® - fit every need and every budget. Use Scan Code "TELL ME MORE!" for your FREE, in-home*, no obligation consultation! *Schedule your appointment with the confidence that you will NEVER HAVE TO LEAVE YOUR HOME! It isn't safe out there and we know it better than most! Our sales staff is FULLY TRAINED to handle any and all adversarial encounters with the living and the undead". Twenty-five years after the deadly plague, the United Five State Republic's most successful company, Zombie, Inc., is in trouble. Will a simple case of dwindling supply and lessen-ing demand be the end of them or will Zombie, Inc. find a way, however unpalatable, to survive?